"Anything you'd li[ke] look at?"

"I, uh..." Her pulse whipped into double time.

His brow lifted.

"I, um..." Her gaze slid involuntarily from his sensual lips to his neck and along the narrow band of naked, bronze flesh running down the entire side of his body to his moccasins. Trying in vain to ignore the thundering of her heart, she bit her lip.

In a fluid movement he rose.

He moved behind her and, putting his arms around her, grasped the pad of paper in one hand and with the other guided the pencil in her shaking fingers to correct the mistake in her drawing. "You just tell me what you'd like a closer look at, and I'll see what I can do."

"I think I—"

"Don't think, Fire Eyes." He caught her hand and brought it down to her side. "Just feel. If it stops feeling good, tell me no."

Dear Reader,

This is officially "Get Caught Reading" month, so why not get caught reading one—or all!—of this month's Intimate Moments books? We've got six you won't be able to resist.

In *Whitelaw's Wedding,* Beverly Barton continues her popular miniseries THE PROTECTORS. Where does the Dundee Security Agency come up with such great guys—and where can I find one in real life? A YEAR OF LOVING DANGEROUSLY is almost over, but not before you read about *Cinderella's Secret Agent,* from Ingrid Weaver. Then come back next month, when Sharon Sala wraps things up in her signature compelling style.

Carla Cassidy offers a *Man on a Mission,* part of THE DELANEY HEIRS, her newest miniseries. Candace Irvin once again demonstrates her deft way with a military romance with *In Close Quarters,* while Claire King returns with a *Renegade with a Badge* who you won't be able to pass up. Finally, join Nina Bruhns for *Warrior's Bride,* a romance with a distinctly Native American feel.

And, of course, come back next month as the excitement continues in Intimate Moments, home of your favorite authors and the best in romantic reading.

Leslie J. Wainger
Executive Senior Editor

Please address questions and book requests to:
Silhouette Reader Service
U.S.: 3010 Walden Ave., P.O. Box 1325, Buffalo, NY 14269
Canadian: P.O. Box 609, Fort Erie, Ont. L2A 5X3

Warrior's Bride
NINA BRUHNS

Silhouette®

INTIMATE MOMENTS™

Published by Silhouette Books

America's Publisher of Contemporary Romance

SILHOUETTE BOOKS

ISBN 0-373-27150-6

WARRIOR'S BRIDE

Copyright © 2001 by Nina Bruhns

This edition published by arrangement with Harlequin Books S.A.

Visit Silhouette at www.eHarlequin.com

Printed in U.S.A.

Books by Nina Bruhns

Silhouette Intimate Moments

Catch Me If You Can #990
Warrior's Bride #1080

NINA BRUHNS

credits her gypsy great-grandfather for her great love of adventure. She has lived and traveled all over the world, including a six-year stint in Sweden. She has been on scientific expeditions from California to Spain to Egypt and the Sudan, and has two graduate degrees in archaeology (with a specialty in Egyptology). She speaks four languages and writes a mean hieroglyphics!

But Nina's first love has always been writing. For her, writing for Silhouette Books is the ultimate adventure! Her many experiences give her stories a colorful dimension and allow her to create settings and characters that are out of the ordinary. Two of her books, including this one, won the prestigious Romance Writers of America Golden Heart Award for writing excellence.

A native of Canada, Nina grew up in California and currently resides in Charleston, South Carolina, with her husband and three children.

She loves to hear from readers, and can be reached at P.O. Box 746, Ladson, SC 29456-0746 or by e-mail via the Harlequin Web site at http://www.eHarlequin.com.

This book is dedicated to all the lost birds who are trying to find their way home. I hope you find it. And to the whole Wiesnet clan, for being the family I never had. Thank you.

Chapter 1

May

Santa Susana Hills, California

Suddenly, Katarina Herelius was completely surrounded by Indian warriors. Big ones. With fierce expressions on their painted faces and feathered headdresses flying in the wind. It was as if she had somehow dropped back in time.

Her carefree mood slipped precariously.

With a gnarled hand, the Indians' ancient leader lowered the tall staff he carried and pointed it right at her. A tingle of panic skittered up Katarina's spine.

She edged backward, out of the gang of wild-looking men, but her back bumped firmly up against a solid wall. Then the wall moved. It reached out and grasped her bare arms with warm, strong hands.

Letting out a gasp, she spun around, and was greeted by the sight of a porcupine-quill chest plate covering a male torso so broad it nearly blocked out the hot California sun. The man it belonged to was tall and lean, his ample muscles oiled and rippling under his sparse clothing. All the man wore was the chest plate, a long fringed breechclout, moccasins and a few bells.

Oh, Lord.

She shivered, tore her eyes away from the warrior's body and looked up into his face. His obsidian hair hung long, shiny and loose, braided on one side with beads and leather thongs, and topped with a small headdress bearing two upright feathers. A pipe-beaded choker graced the man's powerful neck below his Adam's apple. Black stripes and dots adorned his high cheekbones and square chin. Deep, brooding eyes peered back at her from behind a solid black painted mask.

The stranger was just about the most intriguing, sensual man Katarina had ever seen in her life. He had the body of a dangerous warrior, but, oh, those eyes—he had the dark, fathomless eyes of a passionate lover.

Not that Katarina'd know anything about lovers, passionate or not. But this man—he stirred something deep and hidden in her. Something she'd never felt before, something almost elemental. Senses whirling, she held on to her hat and took a calming breath.

"Hey, bro, no terrorizing the tourists," an amused voice called out from behind her.

Her warrior's somber face split into a saucy grin that did the oddest things to her pulse. He looked her up and down, as if considering whether or not to fling her over his shoulder and carry her off to an uncertain fate. Nervously, she took a step back.

He glanced past her and, in a voice too gravelly to suit his finely chiseled features, he inquired, "No scalping or flaming arrows?"

The solemn answer came from behind her. "Nope."

"No tying them to anthills?"

"Sorry, bro."

The warrior folded his arms over his chest and slid a leisurely, flutter-inducing gaze down her body, all the way to the tips of her sandaled toes, and then slowly back up again. "No doing unspeakable things to their womenfolk?"

Her eyes widened and a small sound escaped her throat. The short, puffed sleeve of her calico dress slid off her shoulder. Swallowing, she tugged it up.

"*Especially* not that."

The warrior let out a sigh. "Hell, things are getting way too civilized these days."

Just then a loudspeaker directly overhead blared out the announcement that the grand procession was about to begin from the east side of the dance ring. Katarina clapped her hand over her mouth as she realized she was standing right in the middle of the queued-up dancers. *Oh, brother.* How did she always manage to do these things? She sidled past the warrior toward the crowd of tourists behind him.

A gust of wind lifted her straw hat, and before it could fall to the ground he snagged it and returned it to her. "Well, darlin', looks like I'll have to spare you this time." Then he winked.

Her body tingled as a thousand tiny fireworks went off in her bloodstream. She bit her bottom lip to give herself a much-needed jolt back to reality.

What was with her? Here she was, barely weeks out of the ego-numbing relationship with her ex-fiancé, David, and already she was practically swooning at another man's feet! It was totally unlike her. Katarina did not swoon over strange men. Katarina did not swoon over men at all. At least not these days.

"Go on," the warrior urged, smiling. "Your boyfriend will be looking for you."

Her gaze flew up, narrowed, and she frowned. "No." Thoughts of swooning vanished, and she shook her head determinedly. "No boyfriend."

A question played in his eyes. "Husband, then?"

Inexplicably, her vision blurred. She shook her head again, turned and fled into the crowd. She didn't stop running until she passed the booth farthest from the dance circle, then leaned against a wooden fence post. She gulped down several steadying breaths. The beat of drums kicked up over the loudspeaker, the nasal wail of the singers joining in. Exhaling slowly, she forced her heart to resume its normal cadence.

She swiped at her eyes. *Damn that warrior, anyway.* She did not want to think about David now. Not today.

Today was a celebration! She had come to the Cardinal Ranch Powwow to lose herself in the bright colors, the haunting music and the beautiful dancing. In the wonderful diversity the world had to offer. To revel in life. A life that was finally her own.

She was free!

Running unsteady fingers along the brim of her hat, she repeated the word firmly to herself, hardly able to believe it. *Free.* Liberated, after two long years of trying to be someone she couldn't—wouldn't—ever be. Free to follow her dreams and rebuild the fragile self-esteem that had been so soundly shattered.

Lord, how could she have stayed so long with a man who obviously didn't love her anymore? A man who had taken every opportunity to belittle her opinions and crush her hopes? A man who cheated on her, because he claimed she wasn't woman enough for him?

How naive she had been! To think she'd honestly believed David would change, that her love could transform him from the cold, domineering womanizer he'd become, back to the person she'd thought he was in the beginning—a person worthy of her devotion.

But she'd finally realized that had been an impossible dream. One she had no intention of repeating in this lifetime. She was so grateful for the courage she had somehow managed to scrape together to leave him.

To start over. And this time, to do it right.

Now she would do with her life what she had dreamed of for as long as she could remember—finishing the course work for her nursing degree. She would slowly put her life and her self-esteem back together. And most importantly, she would make her own choices. Choices neither David nor her mother would ever again be able to mock.

Closing her eyes, she let out a long breath that ended in a smile. No, she wouldn't let David ruin today. She wouldn't allow him to ruin another day ever again.

No man, especially one who didn't love and respect her, she

promised herself, would ever ruin a single solitary day of her life.

Katarina lifted her gaze to the glittering heavens. It was truly a glorious morning. In more ways than one. Yesterday she had gotten a letter from UCLA confirming her reacceptance to the nursing program. And a few minutes ago, a sexy, intriguing man had actually flirted with her.

Life was good.

The weather matched her buoyant spirits. A sparkling bright sun shone in a brilliant blue, cloudless sky. A breeze whispered through the fragrant wildflowers on the rolling Santa Susana hilltop where the powwow grounds were located, stirring the canopied booths that were filled with silver and turquoise jewelry, antique reproductions, souvenirs and T-shirts sporting political and decorative logos.

She pushed off the fence post, fueled by her happiness at finally being in control of her own fate.

Laughing, she swung around in a circle, the full skirt of her summer dress billowing about her like a bell. She felt light-headed and happy. For the first time in years she felt feminine and attractive.

This was crazy! She wanted to twirl up and down the hills until she fell over with giddiness! *She* was crazy.

For the first time in her life she wanted to *do* something crazy!

The sound of drums and bells and the thump of dancers' feet vibrated over the meadow. She felt a warm glow wash over her as she thought of one dancer in particular. *The warrior.*

Now *there* was a choice bit of craziness just waiting to happen.

Colton Lonetree spotted the woman at the Navajo taco stand. He'd been thinking about her ever since she'd dashed off so quickly after he'd put his foot in his mouth at the dance circle. And he'd thought he was being so subtle.

The woman was pretty as a picture in that little calico number, blond curls cascading from under her straw hat, all dressed up like a country girl on a picnic. He didn't usually go for the tourists. In fact, he never did. Ever. But this one... Well, this one just might be an exception. In any case, she was definitely worth a closer look.

He pushed through the crowd in front of the taco stand. Luckily, it was run by his pal, Ricky Lee. The throng of gawking tourists parted easily for an Indian in full regalia, until Cole stood just behind the woman, who was giving her order to Ricky. The intriguing scents of gardenias and fry bread mingled in his nostrils.

"Hey, good buddy," Ricky said, grinning over the blonde's head as he counted out her change.

Cole smiled at her as she turned to him in surprise. He reached around her and gave Ricky a good-natured thump on the arm, brushing hers as he did so. He heard her little intake of breath, and grinned inwardly.

Ricky ducked into the depths of the booth, and Cole glanced back at the woman. He had her effectively cornered between his body, the booth and the condiment table. This time she wouldn't get away so easily.

"Was it something I said?"

Her head came around. "Sorry?"

"When you ran away."

"Oh!" Her mouth parted slightly, and the tip of her tongue peeked out, moistening her upper lip. "No." She shrugged a shoulder, then tugged up the sleeve that slipped over it at the movement.

Hell. He really wished the damn thing would stop doing that. Her smooth, bare shoulder was driving him to distraction big time.

"I was a bit embarrassed at being where I wasn't supposed to be, that's all," she murmured.

"No need. We did sort of swoop down on you. The guys never could resist teasing a beautiful woman."

She lowered her lashes, blushing, and when she raised her sky-blue eyes again, fire danced in them like sparklers on the Fourth of July. Beautiful blue fire eyes.

"Thank you," she whispered.

Ricky returned and looked from Cole to the woman and back again. With lifted eyebrows, Ricky handed her a Navajo taco and a can of soda. "Condiments are over there," he said, pointing to the table behind her. "You eating, *amigo?*"

"Better not. I'm dancing hoops in half an hour." Cole waved and followed Fire Eyes to the napkin dispenser. She juggled her plate in one hand, the plastic fork and a root beer in the other, so he obligingly peeled out a few napkins for her. He paused, searching her hands for somewhere to put them, then pursed his lips and examined her dress for a possibility. He didn't get much farther than the curvy bodice with about a million tiny buttons running down the front. *Ho boy.*

"Don't suppose you've got a pocket anywhere?"

She shook her head. As his gaze fastened on her scoop neckline, her eyes widened in alarm. "Don't you dare!" She tried to step back, but the table blocked her path. Her sleeve slid off her shoulder.

He swallowed hard.

Prying two of her fingers away from the soda can, he inserted the napkins, then moved his hand and gingerly pulled up her sleeve. His fingers lingered on the silky-looking cotton fabric, close enough to her skin to feel the warmth emanating from it.

He looked into her fire eyes. "Watch me dance later?"

Slowly, she nodded.

He smiled then, and forced himself to turn and walk away before he made a complete idiot of himself—as there was no doubt in his mind he would. Those fire eyes did things to him no other woman had managed to do in more years than he cared to count.

And made him completely forget about women and how they always, *always* left.

Katarina eased herself through the crowd of people lining the dance circle. The master of ceremonies had just announced the hoop dance demonstration. She didn't catch the dancer's name. A buzz in the public address system prevented her from hearing anything more than that he hailed from the Luiseño nation, but she knew it would be her warrior.

She'd just found an empty space up front when the singers started the drumbeat. The warrior walked into the circle, bells

jangling and hoops clacking. His bearing was straight and dig-
nified; every movement conveyed pride in what he was doing.
Katarina caught her breath at the pure, feral virility of the man.

The breeze lifted the ends of his midnight hair, which
skimmed over the lustrous bronze of his broad shoulders. When
he turned to walk to the other side of the ring, her gaze feasted
on the undulating muscles in his back and biceps—her gaze and
that of every other female in the audience. Until, that is, it found
more interesting territory below his tapered waist.

Leather cording held up his breechclout along with an elaborately embroidered and fringed bustle that hung from his waist
to the back of his knees. But unlike most of the other male
dancers, he did not wear modern gym pants or sweats under
them. The tantalizing bit of bare hip showing between the edges
of the breechclout and the bustle was enough to make her mouth
go completely dry.

Lord above. She fanned herself with her straw hat and
watched, mesmerized, as his hoops started to fly.

It was amazing the things he could do with those hoops. And
with his body. Graceful and athletic, his moves took her breath
away. When the dance was over, all she could do was murmur,
"Wow."

"Not bad for an old man!" the master of ceremonies quipped
over the loudspeaker. "There'll be an encore at four o'clock this
afternoon, folks."

Drums started again; suddenly Katarina's warrior was swept
away in a wave of backslapping friends and fellow dancers and
returned to the ring for an intertribal dance. She craned her neck
to see him, but he was hidden from view in the throng.

She pushed out a sigh. Just as well. There were a hundred
booths to explore, weaving to watch, music to listen to. She
didn't have time to stand here and gawk at some man just because he had called her beautiful.

Which was why she just didn't understand how she came to
be in exactly the same spot at the dance circle at four o'clock,
nervously fidgeting with her hat.

Sure, she had spotted him several times during the course of
the afternoon, and he'd always smiled at her. A luscious, inviting

kind of smile that made her dizzy just looking at it. The same kind of smile he was giving her now as he entered the ring and pinned her with his dark, seeking eyes. Her pulse zinged in response, echoed by the resounding drumbeats that kicked up from the center of the circle.

The warrior lifted his hoops and started to dance. His moccasined feet bounced off the dusty ground in a quick heartbeat rhythm as he swooped and twirled the wooden hoops in intricate patterns around his body, increasing the number of hoops and moving them in ever more complicated arrangements. The crowd applauded at each additional hoop he worked into the design, and cheered as the drums beat ever faster.

He slowly traversed the circle, adding hoops as he went, until he danced right in front of Katarina. His skin glistened with sweat, the bells tied above his calves jingled madly as the tempo surged to a fevered pitch. Muscles bulging, his face etched in concentration, he snapped up the final nine-hoop figure, and the crowd went wild. Katarina stood transfixed as he executed one last deep-knee spin and collapsed the hoops in a quick motion to a single orderly bunch in his hand. He lifted the hoops high over his head, and with the last pounding beat of the drums he swooped down on her and slipped them over her head and shoulders, capturing her in a final, unexpected move.

The audience roared and clapped and the public address system blared, but all Katarina could hear was his low declaration, barely audible above the din as he reeled her in. "I've got you now, Fire Eyes."

Her body thrummed, tightening in places she'd forgotten she had. *This is crazy,* she thought as her blood got lazier and lazier. How could a man she just met do this to her?

He gave her a slow smile and raised the hoops, saluting the audience, waving the wooden rings in the air.

Again he was swept away by the crowd of dancers, although this time she was treated to several curious glances from his friends.

Face blazing, she turned and hurried from the dance ring.

Despite her intense reaction to the man—or, if she were really honest, because of it—Katarina was grateful for the reprieve.

She was in an absurdly reckless mood, and heaven knew what she might get herself into if she weren't careful. Just look at what had happened the last time she'd let herself be charmed.

Plopping her hat decisively onto her head, she lost herself in the mass of tourists heading for the conglomeration of tables and benches where the barbecue dinner was being served. After picking at her food, she remembered a promise she'd given her nephew to help with a school project, and made her way to a secluded pasture behind the last row of booths, looking for tepees.

The green meadow was filled with exotic grasses and wildflowers, fragrant and glowing in the pink-and-yellow rays of the setting sun. Rippling gently in the warm breeze stood a dozen or so tepees in varying sizes, made with everything from aluminum poles and canvas to lodgepole saplings and deer hide. It was a gorgeous sight, and for a moment she just stood, taking it all in.

Then, humming in delight, she pulled a small sketch pad from her shoulder bag and threaded her way slowly among the tepees, sketching her impressions, stopping to admire the unique designs painted on the outside of each one.

There was one in particular she liked, and she spent a long time capturing it in a detailed drawing, thinking of her nephew. It was lovely, in natural-colored canvas that glowed red in the crimson sunset, with a buckskin door and accents. When she was finished drawing the outside, she wondered what the inside might look like. She fingered the flap. But she didn't feel right lifting it without permission.

Suddenly, she heard footsteps, and the accompanying loud jangle of bells stopped right behind her. Katarina turned and looked up in surprise.

The warrior!

She jumped back and guiltily hugged her pad of paper. "I'm sorry. I was just drawing the tepee. I hope you don't mind."

He was watching her carefully, taking in her pad and thick pencil.

"Lodge," he said.

She blinked. "What? Oh, right. Lodge." She'd heard Native

Americans preferred that term, but somehow it always made her think of moose and men in funny hats. She cleared her throat. "Well, I didn't mean to intrude. I'll be going—"

"No," he said, and took a step closer. "Come in."

Chapter 2

"Really, I..." Katarina retreated, emotions warring.

"Don't you want to draw the inside?" he casually asked, shifting the flap to one side.

"I, um..." *Crazy.* "Okay. That would be great."

She felt just a little uneasy when he lifted the flap and she stepped inside. *What was she thinking?* The tepee was empty except for a folding lawn chair, a rolled-up Indian rug and a small radio. Letting the buckskin flap fall behind them, the warrior walked to the rear of the tepee, tossing the gym bag he carried onto the floor.

He gave her a reassuring smile, gesturing to her pad. "Go ahead. Just pretend I'm not here."

Yeah, right.

There was barely enough light filtering in through the smoke hole to allow her to see. Putting pencil to the paper, she tried desperately to remember what she was doing there in a dimly lit tepee with a complete stranger.

A sexy stranger who made her body yearn to feel things she'd never felt before.

"I didn't think the Luiseño tribe used tepees," she said, hoping to distract herself as she drew the details of the canvas floor.

He chuckled. "Not historically. But a field full of modern multicolored nylon camping tents wouldn't exactly impress the tourists."

She smiled. "No, I s'pose not."

She glanced up, catching him standing with his arms folded over his broad chest, studying her. Her face heated at his intense scrutiny. *Draw.* She had to remember to draw. Dragging her gaze away, she turned to a fresh page and started outlining the door opening.

While she worked, the warrior removed his headdress and placed it carefully on the lawn chair, followed by his embroidered bustle. She forced her attention to her task and started filling in the details of the bone fasteners used to secure the door. Behind her she heard him untie the bells around his legs, unzip his bag and toss them in. A click sounded, and the radio started playing soft country music. There was a loud snap as he shook out his rug, and a quiet rustle as it drifted to the floor. He must be making his bed.

Katarina squeezed her eyes shut. *She had to stop thinking like this.*

Suddenly, she felt warm breath in her hair. She started, eyes flying open. He stood right behind her.

"May I?" His fingers brushed hers when he reached around and eased the pad from her hand, sending a shower of awareness over her. She nodded, not daring to move, fearing she would accidentally touch him again.

She couldn't understand this outrageous attraction. The sudden heat flowing through her body must be an overreaction to being out of David's chilly embrace. The delicious thrill of being so close to this warrior, surely, a primal response to the knowledge that the only barriers between them were those she herself placed there. It was a heady feeling.

He came around to stand next to her, flipping through her tepee drawings. "These are very good. But why mine?"

She met his searching look. "It's so pretty. And I promised Kenny lots of details."

A thundercloud seemed to pass through the warrior's black eyes. He lifted a brow. "Kenny?"

She glanced down at her pencil. "My nine-year-old nephew." When the corner of his mouth twitched, she added, "School project."

He nodded and turned to the page she'd been working on. After a moment he pointed. "You've got these fasteners wrong."

She frowned and took the pad from him. "Let me see." She compared the drawing to the door and saw he was right. She pushed a damp lock off her forehead. Mercy, it was getting awfully warm in here.

He strolled to the door, pulled the flaps together and began lacing two long leather strips around the bone fasteners sewn along the edges. He shot her a sultry glance. "The view might be better when the door's properly closed."

Her heart skipped a beat.

In a few seconds it was laced up as tight as a sneaker before a marathon. "See how it works? Now it's impossible to get in from the outside."

He sat on his haunches and slowly looped the ends of the ties through two holes in the doorsill, and pulled them tight. He regarded her from behind his painted mask. "Anything you'd like a closer look at?"

"I, uh…" *Oh, lord.* Her pulse whipped into double-time.

His brow lifted.

"I, um…" Her gaze slid involuntarily from his sensual lips to his neck and along the narrow band of naked, bronze flesh running down the entire side of his body to his moccasins. Trying in vain to ignore the thundering of her heart, she bit her lip.

In a fluid movement he rose.

She was backing herself into a corner, and she knew it. But for the life of her, she suddenly couldn't think of a single reason why she should deflect what was happening between them. She was still raw from David's rejection of her as a woman. It felt good to flirt with this man, to reconfirm that she was pretty and desirable. And if it went a little further than flirting, well, she was a big girl. She knew how to say no if she had to.

It was her choice.

He moved behind her and, circling his arms around her, grasped the pad of paper in one hand and with the other guided the pencil in her shaking fingers to correct her mistake. "You just tell me what you'd like a closer look at, and I'll see what I can do."

Her head spun and her bones turned to liquid in her body. "I've—" she cleared her throat again "—I've never done anything like this before," she murmured, half believing he was still talking about drawing tepees. Her sleeve slipped off her shoulder and she reached to pull it up. "I think I—"

"Don't think, Fire Eyes." He caught her hand and brought it down to her side, leaving the sleeve where it was. "Just feel. If it stops feeling good, tell me no."

She swallowed, forgetting all about tepees, lodges and everything else except the provocative man who was making her come dangerously unglued. She could feel the erotic hardness of his body. His quill chest plate pressed against her spine, his solid thighs caressed her bottom. His growing arousal nestled provocatively at the small of her back. She closed her eyes. It felt good.

Lord above, it felt good all over.

"All right," she whispered, knowing she shouldn't.

He slipped the paper and pencil from her fingers and softly kissed her temple. "Are we done drawing pictures?"

She just couldn't resist. She tilted her face, raising her cheek up, rubbing lightly over his lips with her skin. He felt so very good. Her sketch pad hit the floor with a dull thud and his hands were on her arms, pulling her back into him. His mouth traced over her cheekbone and up the rim of her eye to her eyebrow, giving her small kisses, licking her with the tip of his tongue. She felt her other sleeve drop, then his hands were on her bare shoulders, massaging, caressing.

She reached back, grasping for purchase, and found his bare thighs. A small whimper escaped her throat. His erection flared, and he gave an answering groan. His fingers slid down her arms, splayed over her waist, and his thumbs began climbing up her ribs with lazy strokes until they grazed her breasts. His breath was quick and hot in her ear.

"Still feeling good?"

She dug her fingers into his thighs. "Yes." Her voice was breathy and deep, as unrecognizable as her behavior. *What was she doing?*

His hands cupped her breasts and squeezed. A shock of sensation hit her like a wall of fire. His fingers rubbed circles around the quickening tips, and a blazing trail of desire streaked straight through to her center. His mouth caressed her with hot kisses, working around her ear, biting the sensitive lobe as he pinched the tight buds of her breasts through her dress. She gasped out loud at the erotic sting.

He froze. "Shall I stop?"

Katarina closed her eyes and allowed her head to fall back against the warrior's shoulder. She couldn't ever remember feeling this good, this aroused, this vibrant. She knew she should tell this tempting stranger to stop, to unlace the door, and then she should run like hell. It wasn't her, this wanton woman in his arms. But she couldn't make herself do it. Not for anything. She wanted this. She wanted to experience these wonderful sensations she had been denied for a lifetime. To feel emotions that, for so long, she had thought herself incapable of feeling.

Bringing her hands up, she placed them over his where they lay on her breasts.

Cole swallowed, feeling the cords of his neck contract against his Fire Eyes' temple. For a moment he just stood there, listening to the sounds of his pounding heart and the rapid breathing of the beautiful woman in his embrace. Then she hesitantly moved her fingers and unbuttoned the top button of her dress.

He couldn't believe the delightful, innocent way this woman was inviting him to touch her. Where before he had been eager enough to drag her to the floor by the hair and ravish her, he now wanted to woo her senses, to introduce her body to delights she'd never experienced before. To bind her to him with lovemaking so unforgettable she'd never want to leave him. He'd never reacted to a woman like this before. It scared him and aroused him all at the same time. He slowly unfastened two more buttons.

Turning her in his arms, he looked into her eyes, surprised to see fear and uncertainty as she looked back at him. "It's all right, darlin'," he said quietly. "I won't hurt you, I swear. Tell me to stop anytime."

Lowering his mouth to hers, he pulled her close and kissed her tenderly. Her arms went around his neck and she sighed against his lips. He slipped his hand behind her head and held her, pressing his mouth over hers, teasing it with his tongue. When she opened to him, he groaned, sinking into her moist, velvety depths, losing himself in the taste of her. She was wonderful. Sweet and innocent, and everything he hadn't known he'd been looking for all his life. His heart stuttered at the thought, then raced at the unexpected rightness of how she felt in his arms.

He kissed her long and deep, holding her tight, until he felt her body tremble against his. He felt his way to her buttons and unfastened a half dozen more, then slipped his hand inside, cradling her bare breast in his palm. She arched into him, firing his desire. Quickly, he found her other breast, and she moaned in pleasure at his touch.

Her skin was like hot silk beneath his questing hands. He let them prowl her body, exploring every dark, warm place he could reach, making her writhe against him, fanning the flames of her passion. Her passion for him.

Impatient for more, he opened buttons to her waist and slid her dress down her arms, letting it fall to the floor in a pool at her feet. He tightened his embrace and covered her mouth, his tongue plundering, stroking deep and hard. Oh, how he wanted her! Wanted to feel her under him, surrounding him, hot and eager. Wanted to claim this woman for himself.

Suddenly he felt her push at his chest, withdrawing from his kiss, whispering urgently, "Wait. Please stop."

Immediately, he broke away, grabbing for the self-control that had vanished, consumed by flames of need.

God, what had he done? He had never lost it like that with a woman before. Never!

Cole jammed his fingers through his hair in frustration and consternation. "I'm sorry," he said, sucking down a ragged breath. "Okay, I've stopped." He tried for a properly apologetic grin. "But you're killing me, you know."

She looked at him in surprise, then her gaze turned soft. She reached up and sweetly stroked his jaw. "Is that why you're wearing the armor? In case I try to kill you?"

His brows drew together, his brain still lodged somewhere below the leather strap holding up his breechclout. "Armor?"

She traced a finger down the front of his chest plate. "If I promise not to kill you, would you take this thing off?"

He groaned, comprehension dawning. "Oh, honey, that must have hurt like hell." His eyes sought her breasts, which, sure enough, were covered with thin red marks.

"Oh, baby, I'm so sorry." He pulled her to him, then let her go. "Aw, hell." Quickly he undid the ties that held his chest plate, and laid it over the back of the chair. He stretched out a hand to her. "Come here."

She came into his arms, all warm, bare flesh, and he had to restrain himself from laying her down and taking her right then and there. He didn't understand how she had tied him up in knots as she had in the space of a few short hours.

He was never tied in knots. He was a lawyer. His job required him to be in control at all times. And up to a few moments ago, he always had been. Always.

But he had to admit he kind of liked being all tied in knots over his Fire Eyes. For once in his measured, carefully planned existence, he was enjoying being over the edge and irrational. Not knowing what came next. Letting this incredible woman take him on an erotic journey he suddenly hoped would last for months, years, or maybe even a lifetime.

Strange. For some reason, he felt safe with her. He'd never thought much about love at first sight—having long avoided anything to do with the emotion that until now had only brought him pain. But if love at first sight existed, this must be it.

Cole smoothed his hand over the red marks on her breasts, and murmured in her ear, "I'm a thoughtless idiot. Here, let me kiss them and make them better."

Katarina blushed furiously at the warrior's whispered suggestion, and buried her face in the crook of his neck.

He obviously felt guilty, but truth be told, she hadn't even noticed the chest plate until she was accidentally pinched between two quills. He'd obviously had a bad moment when she'd asked him to stop his lovemaking, thinking she'd meant to stop him for good. But the really unbelievable thing was he'd actually stopped, and hadn't whined about it.

If this masked stranger hadn't already stolen her heart well before that, she would have given it to him willingly at that moment.

Almost imperceptibly, she nodded.

"Oh, honey." He swept her up in his powerful arms and carried her to the rug he'd unrolled earlier. When he set her on her feet, he held her and smoothed the stray hairs from her face. "Are you sure about this? Really sure?"

She melted a little more at his concerned words, fell even further under his spell, held him closer. How could she tell him how much it meant to her that he asked?

"Because once I lay you down, I won't stop until I'm deep inside you."

She traced her lips along his jaw, ignoring the voice in her mind that told her it was wrong, that she would regret being so impulsive.

She needed this. Needed the affirmation of her feminine worth before she could move on from the destructive relationship she'd recently ended. In her heart she knew this man would not hurt her. He was sensitive, caring and passionate. Everything David was not.

This was the first choice in two years she had no doubts about at all. "I'm sure," she whispered.

"Thank God," he murmured, and before she could even think to protest, he slid her panties over her hips.

Her body thrilled and shivered to be naked in his arms. She felt wanton and reckless, desirable and sexy, and everything she hadn't felt for as long as she could remember.

She drew a finger along the edge of his breechclout, wanting him as naked as she was. As if reading her mind, he quickly disposed of the garment and his moccasins, then reached for the knot of his choker.

Without thinking, she laid a hand over his. "No. Leave it." She smiled shyly and flushed at his inquiring look. "It goes with the war paint."

He chuckled. "I keep forgetting I've got that on. Does it bother you? I have remover in my gym bag."

Wanting to make love to a nameless, faceless stranger was about as far away from her usual prim behavior as it got. But somehow she felt as though she had known him forever. She didn't need to see his face to know he was everything she wanted. Needed.

Winding her fingers through his long hair, she shook her head. "No. I know there's an honorable man under there, and that's what counts."

Cole lowered Fire Eyes to the rug and lay down beside her, gathering her tightly in his arms. He felt awed and honored by her trust.

"What did I do to deserve you?" he whispered into her hair, silently vowing to do everything he could to be worthy of that trust and this sweet, special woman.

He bent over her and kissed her until they were both breathless and he could feel her shudder with desire. His hands explored her, and hers him, taking turns raising goose bumps and drawing forth sighs and gasps of pleasure. Over and over they rolled, their bodies moving apart and together in perfect harmony.

Incredibly aroused, he tucked her under him, gazing at her body, heatedly murmuring what he would do to each lovely bit—the endlessly long legs, her smooth, pale stomach and round, full breasts. Already taut, her nipples hardened to tight points at his lustful words and hungry gaze. He wanted to consume them, her, every damned part of her, and keep her like this forever.

She looked up as he touched her again, kissed her. The pure bliss etched on her face raised a lump in his throat.

"Fire Eyes," he murmured. "You are so beautiful." She gazed mistily into his eyes, lips slightly parted. Her scent washed over him, sweet and sensual, smelling of woman, gardenias and desire.

"I want you so much," she whispered, pulling him down by a strand of hair. She made love to his mouth with hers—erotically, thoroughly.

He moaned, gritting his teeth, battling back from the edge, grasping for control. "Just ask, darlin'. I'll give you anything you want," he promised, and, unbelievably, meant it. "Everything I have to give is yours. Everything."

Katarina was ready to pass out from the sheer, blinding pleasure her warrior's hands and mouth brought her. Surely it was molasses flowing sweet and thick through her veins, since all her blood had pooled between her legs, throbbing furiously with every stroke of his fingers and tongue.

He drove her wild. He drove her to be wild.

He loved her breasts and shoulders and neck and stomach until she gasped for breath, begging for mercy. When he slid his fingers between her legs, dipping into the honeyed folds, caressing her until she writhed and moaned beneath him, she knew what it was to die and go to heaven.

"Make love to me," she pleaded, unable to wait any longer. "Please."

In a single lithe movement, he moved between her legs and drove his hard length into her. Then she truly went to heaven, stars and all, flying apart in his arms, shattering in a million, pleasure-laden pieces, her cries of joy captured in his loving mouth.

When she finally stopped shuddering, she looked up at him in contrition. "I'm sorry. I just couldn't stop myself—"

He grinned down at her, stroking her cheek with his thumb. "Don't be sorry. Do you have any idea what it does to a man's ego to have a woman come apart for him like that? Just from slipping into her?"

Could it be true? Relief mingled with embarrassment. "You mean it's not distracting?"

"Distracting?" His brows lifted, then his eyes softened. "Honey, it's the sweetest gift a woman can give a man. Anyone who tells you different needs his head examined."

He kissed her tenderly and started to move inside her. Filling her, stretching her, coaxing her once again toward oblivion. With a restraint she'd never experienced, he played her body with his, making them both hum and purr and finally sing in a hot, rhythmic lovers' duet that made all other music pale by comparison. When she crescendoed, he followed quickly.

Afterward, they lay panting, limbs tangled, warm contentment stealing over her like a blanket of stars.

And she slept.

The next morning Katarina awoke to find herself wrapped in the arms of her lover. What on earth had gotten into David? He *never*— She froze, suddenly recalling the night and the man she was with. And it *wasn't* David! Mortification rolled through her at what she'd done. Slowly, carefully, she tried to extricate herself from the warrior's embrace.

"At last you're awake," he whispered, and before she could even respond, he slipped between her legs and thrust into her. She sucked in a breath, daring a look at his face, darkly silhouetted against the sunlit canvas of the tepee.

He smiled. A tender, male smile. "'Mornin', darlin'."

"Good morning," she managed to answer, her face aflame.

He began to move inside her. An involuntary shiver rippled through her whole body at the delicious sensation. Secretly thrilled that he should still want to make love to her, she once again gave herself up to the untold pleasures of the warrior's touch.

He was wonderful. Generous and strong and all male. As the sun rose higher in the sky and the birds chirped a joyful melody, he loved her long and slowly, bringing them both to a shuddering climax almost an hour later.

"Oh, baby." He rolled on his back and pulled her to his side, guiding her head to his shoulder. "I could definitely get used to this."

Katarina hummed in boneless assent. "But surely it's not like this every time?" It just wasn't possible!

"No? How would it be?"

"I don't know." She shrugged and lowered her eyes, thinking of how it had always been with David. "Not as good?"

He looked down at her and frowned. "Honey, whoever he was, you're well rid of him."

She couldn't resist a smile of agreement. This man, on the other hand, would treat her right. Her smile faltered. But then, who said he even wanted to see her again?

And what did *she* want? True, she had never felt such warmth and contentment as she had in the short time she had spent in this man's arms. But no way was she ready for another relationship so soon after David.

What if she were hurt again? What if this remarkable warrior turned out to be just as faithless and cold as her ex-fiancé? What if he was able to undermine her fragile new self-esteem and bring back the doubts and inadequacies that David had drilled into her for two long years? Could she risk losing herself again after fighting so hard to find herself?

He leaned over her and ran his thumb along her bottom lip. "Honey? You still here?"

She smiled up at him, and he kissed her, gently, lovingly.

Oh, yes. She'd risk it. For this man, she'd risk it all.

Suddenly, a hand slapped a tattoo on the door flap. "Hey, bro! You in there? Time to dance. Wake up!"

"I really hate leaving you like this." There was too much to find out. Cole's hand hesitated on the door laces as he was about to leave for the dance circle.

Fire Eyes stood and slipped her arms around him. "I'll be okay. Go on, you'll be late." She licked a finger and rubbed a spot on his face. "Your paint is smudged."

He held her tight and kissed her, not wanting to let go. "You will come to the dance circle, won't you?"

"Try and keep me away."

"Promise?"

She kissed him back. "I promise."

He shook aside the uneasy feeling that had descended on him—the feeling that she would abandon him and he'd never see her again.

He was just being paranoid. When he got that feeling as he worked on a case, it was based on empirical evidence. Facts that didn't add up. Body language that was all wrong. But Fire Eyes was saying and doing all the right things, in the right way.

Paranoid.

"Lace up after I'm gone, okay?" He gave her a final kiss and stooped to unfasten the door.

"Finally woke from the dead, eh?" His half brother, Billy, punched him in the arm from outside.

Cole took a last look at Fire Eyes and put his finger to his lips. "Yeah, bro. In more ways than one."

Half an hour later, Katarina peeked around the tepee door and then slipped out. She adjusted her shoulder bag and walked dreamily through the wildflower meadow toward the dance circle.

Her sister, Alex, was not going to believe this. How could she? Katarina herself didn't believe it. After all, who would be foolish enough to believe it was possible to fall in love in the space of a single night in a tepee? With a man whose name she didn't know, whose face she couldn't see? She was so happy she practically walked on air.

She had to be out of her mind.

She approached the circle just as his hoop dance was ending. She slid between the spectators and stood, drinking in the sight of him, her warrior.

And as she watched, the world dropped out from under her feet.

Chapter 3

December, six months later

Heaving out a sigh, Katarina punched the elevator button for the fifth floor of the Pasadena building where the adoption attorney's office was located. The realization of what she was going to talk to him about suddenly hit her. Hard.

Turning, she looked at her swollen abdomen, reflected back at her in triplicate from the mirrored walls, and she sighed again. When she'd left her ex-fiancé nearly a year ago, she'd been so sure what she wanted out of life. To go back to school and finish her degree in nursing, work a few years here in L.A., then find a nice, small clinic or hospital somewhere in the country, buy a dog and a truck. Settle down.

Her wry smile held no trace of humor. She'd been so determined to take control of her life, make her own choices. So happy she finally could.

Katarina moved awkwardly to the back of the empty elevator. Things were not working out at all as she'd planned.

She had to accept that the warrior from the powwow wasn't

going to ride up on a paint horse, marry her and sweep her away
to live in his tepee. She swallowed tightly. Not that she would
want him to, of course. He was one mistake she'd just as soon
forget.

Her vision clouded to a watery blur as she thought of that
long-ago night. Then, stubbornly, she pressed her lips together,
furious with herself for succumbing once again to pointless sen-
timentality. Lord, you'd think she would have learned her lesson
by now.

The man was a natural born skirt-chaser, no better than David.
The one right choice she'd made at that powwow was to leave
him far behind.

She squeezed her eyes shut for a moment to compose herself,
then brought her thoughts back to her present predicament. She
would not give her baby up for adoption. There was no way.
"There are other choices," she murmured into the dull silence.
"There must be."

She gazed at her own pathetic reflection, eyes smarting from
lack of sleep and too much crying. She had never considered
terminating her pregnancy. That wasn't ever an option. But how
could she afford to keep her baby? "I can't even afford to keep
myself," she lamented.

Out of sympathy for her plight, her sister, Alex, and her
brother-in-law, Brad, were letting her stay temporarily in the
apartment over their garage. But that couldn't last forever. They
needed the income from the rental, and she couldn't afford to
pay. Not without a job. And unless she finished her nursing
degree, she couldn't land a job that paid well enough to cover
both rent and day care. But how could she finish her degree with
a newborn baby?

It was Alex who had suggested adoption. Alex and her husband had been trying to adopt for several years. They had their
son, Kenny, by Brad's first marriage, but wanted a bigger family.
Katarina knew her sister secretly hoped she would allow Alex
to adopt her baby.

It was true they could give her baby everything she couldn't—
a stable, secure home, the best education, every opportunity for
a happy, carefree life. And they wanted her child with an inten-

sity only those who have gone through the heartache of not conceiving were capable of. It just wasn't right—Alex trying in vain to get pregnant for so long, and Katarina succeeding after one solitary, foolish indiscretion. It was all so maddening. So unfair.

All she herself had to offer her baby was love. It was the ultimate act of selfishness to keep this child. But how could she ever give up her own flesh and blood? She couldn't.

Although she knew in her heart she would never give up her baby, she had agreed to talk to someone, just to gather information. Alex had helped her look through the yellow pages to find an attorney. There had been pages of them, but only one had listed Native American adoptions as a specialty. With a twisted sense of irony, Katarina had chosen that one.

Steeling herself, she made the long walk down the hall and opened the door to the attorney's office.

Colton Lonetree strode into Linder, Adams and Henderson, bypassed the receptionist and made a beeline for the administrative assistant at the back of the room. "Hi, Janey. Have a good Thanksgiving?"

Janey looked up and a flirtatious smile dashed across her face. "Cole! You bet. Stuffed myself silly. But you're early. Henderson's not done with his two o'clock yet."

Cole leaned against the mahogany desk and cocked his head at her. "I guess you'll just have to entertain me."

She giggled. "Want some coffee?"

"Sure." He rested a hip on her desk and looked around, noticing that he was being observed by the girl at the tall, semicircular reception desk in the middle of the room. "Hi, Pam."

"Hi." The girl paused, then said, "Are you going to keep your hair like that?"

He raised his eyebrows in surprise. He'd gotten a lot of comments when he'd come back after his summer "retreat" with a short, businesslike haircut instead of his trademark renegade ponytail. But most people had quickly adjusted to his new no-nonsense image and forgotten he'd ever had long hair. "Yeah," he answered Pam. "For a while, at least."

"Why'd you cut it?"

He shrugged. Why indeed? "Time for a change."

He caught his reflection in the window overlooking the busy street below and grimaced. Cutting his hair was just the tip of the iceberg. He'd been a changed man ever since the episode with that woman at the powwow.

He clamped his jaw tightly, fighting the anger and frustration that gripped him whenever he thought of the woman.

Fire Eyes.

Silently, he cursed the unbidden pictures that flooded his mind. Memories of her pretty smile, her soft, white skin and those lovely eyes gazing up at him with such adoration. Her silky body tucked under his, hot and responsive. A body any man would worship.

And he had.

Oh, yeah. He'd fallen hard, all right. Been caught in the trap he'd been running fast to avoid all his life—the fatal lure of love and the hope that somewhere there must be a woman he could trust with his heart.

Cole watched the young woman at the desk recross her legs and pick up the phone that was ringing in front of her. Before she hit the flashing button, she shot him a look. "I liked your hair better long."

His mouth curled in a humorless smile. "Yeah, me, too."

"Here you are, handsome." Janey returned and handed him a steaming mug of coffee. "You here to pick up those papers on the Chisko case?"

He nodded. "Yep."

She indicated a solid wooden door on the opposite side of the room. "Looks like Henderson is done."

Bringing his coffee to his lips, Cole glanced over at the door, which was opening. He froze in midswallow.

Hair the color of corn silk cascaded over a woman's slender shoulders. Lips as full as a harvest moon were turned down in a sad smile under eyes that blazed like the wildest desert opals.

It was her.

Shock nearly sent him sliding off the desk. He couldn't believe it. Right there, shaking hands with Bob Henderson, was the woman he had tried like hell for six and a half months to forget.

"I'm sure you'll come to the right decision, Rini," he overheard Henderson say to her.

Rini. So, that was her name. Cole swallowed the mouthful of scalding coffee, barely noticing the searing pain in his tongue and throat as it went down. *Rini Fire Eyes.*

You'll meet me at the dance circle, won't you?

Try and keep me away.

At first when Fire Eyes had disappeared from the powwow, he'd been upset and depressed. He had really thought she was different from all the others. Weeks passed in anger, then he'd gradually come to accept that she wasn't going to turn up on his doorstep. How could she? They didn't even know each other's names!

But the woman was always there with him, haunting his subconscious. She was there on the streets, in elevators, driving by in Mustangs. Once he'd actually run up and grabbed a woman in a grocery store, only to spin her around and find a terrified girl who couldn't have been out of college yet. That was when he'd taken a month's leave and gone back to his family on Rincon Reservation to put himself back together.

It wasn't Fire Eyes herself, he'd eventually decided, as much as that she had exposed his life for the hollow, solitary existence it was. The fact was, he was now thirty-six and felt the need for something more meaningful in life than work and an endless series of shallow, short-term relationships.

Paralyzed with shock, not knowing what to do next, Cole watched Bob Henderson and Fire Eyes walk toward the reception desk. His muscles screamed to go to her, but his renewed cynicism held him back. Would she recognize him without his war paint? Would she even want to? Or would she be embarrassed to acknowledge her sweet, savage little interlude? Should he blow his reputation and risk making a scene?

Before he could decide, she sidestepped around the desk, her hand at the small of her back as if in pain. Then she turned, and what he saw hit him like a hammer in the gut.

She was pregnant!

The mug slipped from his hand and landed with a muffled slosh on the carpet. Fire Eyes glanced up at him briefly, a glazed expression on her face, no sign that she even saw him, let alone recognized him.

"Pam, will you make an appointment for Miss Herelius for next week sometime?"

Miss Herelius. Miss Rini Herelius. What was she doing here, alone and pregnant? Cole's mind moved like lightning.

A nasty taste suddenly came into his mouth. One of Bob Henderson's biggest money makers was arranging private adoptions. Bob specialized in Indian children, and Cole often worked with him on cases involving the tribal councils. Could Rini be thinking of giving up her child for adoption?

Suddenly, his heart was squeezed by a pain so fierce he clutched at his chest.

No!

Feverishly, he counted back the months to May. He knew how many it was, even without going through the litany in his head. He looked more closely at her stomach. *It could be.*

It was just possible. After they made love, he'd realized they hadn't used protection. He'd soundly reprimanded himself, but it had never occurred to him that she wasn't protected against pregnancy, since she had never indicated any concern about it.

He gritted his teeth. *His baby!* It was *his* baby she was giving away!

"Cole, are you all right? You don't look so hot." Janey appeared at his side with a towel and dabbed at his pants. He had to pull himself together. There was information he needed.

Swallowing the bile in his throat, he tried to look as if his world wasn't shattering in a million pieces around him.

"Yeah, I'm fine. Sorry about the carpet." He leaned over and sponged up the coffee as best he could, surreptitiously watching Fire Eyes walk slowly out the door.

When he rose, Cole put on his bravest smile to cover his burgeoning anger. For six and a half months, he'd cursed the one woman he'd allowed to turn his world upside down, who had then run away without so much as a backward glance.

And now, here she was in the living, breathing, six-and-a-half-month-pregnant flesh. Carrying his baby.

His baby! He was going to be a father! Joy surged through him before it was mowed down by anger and outrage. It looked very much like she planned to rid herself of the unwanted burden of his child by giving it up for adoption. Wiping her hands of all responsibility. Abandoning it to strangers.

Just as his own mother had done to him.

He couldn't let it happen. No way. Not to *his* child.

He took the Chisko file, tucked it under his arm and forced a tight smile. "Thanks, Janey."

As Cole marched to the cobblestone lot behind the law offices, fury simmered in his blood. Shaking his head to clear it, he stabbed his key at the lock of his new ragtop Camaro Z28. On the third try he finally succeeded and wrenched open the door. Gunning the engine like a demon, he squealed out of the lot and onto Colorado Boulevard.

It was his baby she was giving away. He was all but certain. The question was, what was he going to do about it?

Katarina was more than surprised when Bob Henderson summoned her back to his office less than a week later. True, she had been avoiding his phone calls, knowing he'd pressure her to reconsider her decision not to go through with any adoption. But his last message said she must appear because she was being served with some kind of papers. She couldn't imagine what it was all about.

When she arrived at his office, she shook hands with Henderson, who introduced her to another woman. The woman was petite and slim, with long black hair falling to her waist.

"Rini, this is Tanya Proudhomme. She's from the Southern California Native American Center."

Katarina felt the first prick of uneasiness. She brushed off the feeling. What could the woman's heritage possibly mean? Nothing, of course. She looked at her again, more closely. Had she seen her somewhere before? Katarina's uneasiness settled in a roiling ball in the pit of her stomach. *At the powwow?*

Henderson brought her back with a jolt. "Have a seat, Rini."

Casting a furtive glance at Ms. Proudhomme, she sat. Suddenly, Katarina noticed a man on the other side of the room, standing with his back toward them, silhouetted against the window. Her heart nearly came to a screeching halt. *It couldn't be!* No, her imagination was working overtime. The man looked nothing like her warrior.

Besides, what would he possibly want with her, when he had so many other women to amuse himself with?

Moistening the bow of her lip, she forced her attention back to her lawyer. "What is this all about, Mr. Henderson?"

Henderson cleared his throat. "Ms. Proudhomme would like to ask you a couple of questions concerning your baby. I've told her you haven't made up your mind about the adoption yet, and in any case it couldn't possibly have anything to do with the Indian Child Welfare Act, but she prefers to ask you yourself."

Katarina's heartbeat kicked up a notch. "Indian Child Welfare Act?" She looked from Henderson to Ms. Proudhomme. "I don't understand."

Henderson shrugged elaborately, then gave a little laugh. "She's gotten the crazy notion somewhere that your baby might be—"

"Miss Herelius." The pretty woman with the serious face stepped forward, cutting him off, then sat down across from her.

Out of the corner of her eye, Katarina could see the black-haired man at the window. His posture was ramrod straight, his hands clasped behind his broad back. She blinked, her gaze lingering on the long, brown fingers.

"Miss Herelius, I really have only one question."

The man at the window took a deep breath. Katarina turned and tried to concentrate on the woman, but something about the dark man captured her attention. Something about his hands, and his bearing—straight and proud. Something familiar. She shook herself mentally and pried her attention away from him.

"Your baby, Miss Herelius, can you tell me…is the father Native American?"

Katarina was too stunned to answer. How did the woman know? Could the warrior be trying to contact her? Why?

She scanned the man at the window, her mind frantically comparing him to the warrior. The hair was all wrong, as was his elegantly tailored suit. He didn't seem quite tall enough, either. Still...

It couldn't be him. She wanted to order him to strip off his coat and shirt, so she could see the man beneath. Test the hard muscles in his arms and run her hands over the smooth, bronze skin of his chest. She gripped the chair's armrests and wrenched her focus back to the two people in front of her.

"—said it was absolutely none of their business—"

"Yes. He is Native American," she said, her heart pounding a tattoo. Hoping it was him. *Praying it wasn't.*

Against all odds, she hoped this could be the answer to all the prayers she'd whispered in the dead of night. To all the tears she'd shed, hoping for a miracle so she could provide for her baby.

The man at the window let out his breath at her affirmation but otherwise didn't move. Ms. Proudhomme seemed surprised but recovered quickly. She sat up in her seat and clasped her hands on her knee. "Thank you, Miss Herelius, for your honesty. It's refreshing these days."

Henderson jumped up from his chair. "Rini, you don't know that for sure." He gave her a used-car-salesman smile. "Did you ask him? Maybe he had black hair and looked like he might be—"

With each moment that went by, Katarina's nerves pulled tighter and tighter. "He was. Why should I lie? But what does his ancestry have to do with anything? We're no longer—" she halted and looked at her knees "—together."

How could it be him? The warrior was a rogue of the first order. Why would he want to help her? He must have more interesting projects to pursue than supporting the bothersome consequences of his careless, if masterful, seductions. After all, he hadn't even waited till the blanket was cold from their love-making before he went looking for his next target.

Ms. Proudhomme shot a smug glance at Henderson before continuing. "Are you acquainted with the Indian Child Welfare Act, Miss Herelius?"

She shook her head. "No."

The lawyer sank down in his chair and closed his eyes, sighing.

"Basically, what it says is that where an enrolled Native American child is concerned, the child's nation, or tribe, may have jurisdiction over custody matters regarding that child, and that its own relatives have first preference when a child needs an adoptive home."

Katarina nodded, wondering where this was going. "I understand."

The woman rose and looked at her squarely. "At the center, our work with Indian children is based on one thing alone. What is best for the child." She took a few steps toward the man, then turned back to Katarina and grew serious. "Indian children who are brought up outside their culture often suffer emotionally and experience confusion about their identity later in life. They have the highest rate of suicide among all adopted children."

Katarina swallowed. Her blood hammered ominously in her ears. Where was this going? Maybe the tribe just wanted to be a part of the child's life, to teach it about its heritage. She could live with that. "I'm sorry, but I don't see what—"

"I'd like to introduce you to someone." Ms. Proudhomme looked at the man at the window. "Cole?"

As the man turned, Katarina sucked in a breath of panic. There wasn't a trace of warmth about him. The expression on his face was hard and cold, filled with resentment. An icy chill blew across the room and straight into her soul.

Time ground to a halt, and all she could see was his disapproval boring into her as he slowly—agonizingly slowly—covered the distance between them and came to a halt in front of her chair.

It can't be.

For the briefest second, something flared in his eyes as they fastened onto hers. A spark of heat, of desire, or maybe it was longing. She would never know, because just as soon as it appeared, it was gone. Replaced by armor as impenetrable as the chest plate she had once teased him into removing. She swallowed.

"Miss Herelius, my name is Colton Lonetree. I'm a lawyer."

Colton. Looking up, filled with turmoil and confusion, she saw the answering knowledge in his eyes. *Oh, God.* Could it really be?

"I'm also the—"

"Warrior!" she whispered tremulously.

Chapter 4

The silence in the room was palpable. Katarina could feel the others holding their breath.

Lonetree straightened, a vein pulsing in his temple, his expression held carefully neutral. But he couldn't hide the hint of raw vulnerability in his eyes. "Yes. It was me."

Without thinking, she pushed awkwardly to her feet, raising her hand to his face. With unsteady fingertips, she traced his jaw and up his cheek, stroking over his cheekbone. When she reached his brow, his eyelids drifted closed.

Suddenly, they jerked open. He took a step back and regarded her coolly, all the defenselessness that had been there a moment before gone.

Her fingers, suspended in midair, curled into her palm as hurt coiled in her breast. Her eyes narrowed. "Prove it."

Bob Henderson's head turned, revealing his astonished expression. Katarina crossed her arms and stuck her hands under them. She was in no mood to explain why she didn't know who the father of her own baby was.

"Please leave us," Lonetree quietly ordered, and before she

could take a breath the room had cleared, leaving them squared off, face-to-face.

She swallowed heavily, but stood her ground. "Well?"

"Prove it? I can do that. In a couple of different ways."

"Such as?"

"We could do a paternity test. Or I could give you a detailed account of what we did in that lodge—" he jammed his hands in his pockets "—starting with the 'armor' I had on."

She felt her gaze falter and a deep heat creep into her cheeks.

"And your charming suggestion about what to do—"

"Stop!" She buried her face in her hands. "Please. No more! I believe you." Her shoulders slumped.

"You never doubted it."

She lowered her hands. "No." She looked Cole in the eye. "What do you want?"

"My child."

The two words slammed into her solar plexus, nearly knocking the wind from her lungs. She stared at him in horror, struggling to gain purchase on a wisp of breath. "No!" The panic inside gripped her heart like a steel claw. "That's impossible! I'm not giving up my baby!"

Lonetree looked down his long, regal nose at her, his black eyes glittering with scorn. "But that's just what you are doing, Ms. Herelius. Giving away your baby. Otherwise what would you be doing here, in the office of an adoption attorney who specializes in Indian children?"

The yellow pages had come back to haunt her in ways she'd never dreamed. "You don't understand—"

"No, *you* don't understand. I'm hereby serving you with notice of intention to block the adoption and sue for custody of my child, after it is born, according to the statutes of the Indian Child Welfare Act." His stony gaze slid down her body until it lingered on her swollen belly. "You don't want it. I do. End of story."

The muscles in her womb contracted around the baby and her hands came up to rest protectively on top of it. "But I do want it! It was just…"

His narrow-eyed gaze drilled into her. "Just what? Bad timing? Inconvenient?"

"Oh, for crying out loud, you don't—"

"Or perhaps it's the wrong color?"

The man was a lunatic. "Don't be ridiculous." How could she convince him—

"I'm glad to hear that. But frankly, Ms. Herelius, I have a hard time imagining any reason good enough for abandoning your own child."

His words pierced her soul like a poisoned arrow. Wasn't that exactly what she had been telling herself all these long months, no thanks to him? With a strangled gasp she fell back into her chair. "You pompous jerk! I am *not* abandoning my child!"

Lonetree's condemning gaze fastened on her. "What would you call it then?"

What was wrong with this man? Why wouldn't he believe her? She had to make him see.... Katarina wiped her eyes and took a steadying breath. Falling apart would not help her or the baby. She mentally kneaded her despair into anger.

"I'll say it one more time. This is my baby, and I have no intention of giving it to you or anyone else. Now, if you'll excuse me…"

Katarina rose with as much dignity as she could muster. She couldn't stay in this room another second. If she did, she knew she'd either break down completely or kill somebody. And she was pretty sure it wouldn't be herself.

Lonetree stood rigid before her, fists clenched. She could feel his gaze burning holes in her as she brushed by him. "You're telling me you're keeping it?"

"I'm not telling you anything."

A peculiar look swept over his face, as if he'd just eaten something that didn't agree with him. "It's money, isn't it? I'm a successful lawyer so you figured you could—"

She nearly knocked him over when she spun on him. "Mr. Lonetree, *my baby's not for sale.*"

He scowled furiously. "You know that's not what I meant!"

"And if you'll recall, it was you who contacted me!" Fury

arced between them like lightning. "I'm leaving now. I have an anatomy test to study for."

"You can't just walk out. I have rights! I'm the baby's father."

"Are you sure?" she spat out.

Stalking out, she smacked the door closed before he had recovered the ability to speak. *Thank God.* Dragging a trembling hand over her eyes, she leaned against the reception desk to gather her wits.

Once again she was stunned by the unfairness of it all. She couldn't believe that control over her own decisions seemed about to be snatched away from her. Yet again. By a man who, in one thoughtless night, had changed the course of her whole life. A man who now came brazenly back into it, making outrageous demands about rights. Well, what about *her* rights?

She heaved a sigh. Was it something in her karma, or what? Lord, give her strength.

Speechless, Cole stared at the door through which Rini had disappeared. He quickly opened it and glanced at his cousin Tanya, who looked up from shuffling papers.

"What happened?"

"Hell if I know." He pulled in a breath and tried to ignore the odd feeling that had gathered in the pit of his stomach. He didn't like it one bit and fought it like hell, but there it was anyway, gnawing at his gut. *Was he wrong?*

He strode out of the office in time to see Katarina vanish through the front door. "Rini! Miss Herelius!" He ran after her and grabbed her arm when she showed no sign of slowing. "Please wait!"

She yanked away from his grip and brushed at the place his hand had touched. "What is it now? Haven't you done enough for one lifetime?"

"I'm sorry." He said it without thinking. No, he wasn't sorry. He had no reason to apologize for anything. This was all *her* doing, not his. He shouldn't feel sorry.

So why could he still feel that gnawing at his gut?

"I'm sorry I doubted your honor for a moment in there."

She turned on a toe and started for the elevator. "Forget it."

Cole hurried after her. "Miss Herelius, Rini, there are still some things we need to discuss."

She stabbed the down button and glared at him, eyes full of fire. "It's Miss Herelius to you, Counsellor. And I have no desire to discuss anything." She turned her back on him.

He grappled momentarily with a memory of her standing just that way, wearing a flowery sundress, breathlessly awaiting his next move. "Miss Herelius, I…"

He wanted so much to hate her. *Did* hate her. And yet…why, when she'd recognized him just now and reached out to touch his cheek, had he wanted to tug her hand to his lips, to pull her to him and bury his face in her hair? To tell her how hurt he'd been when she'd left him like that? Tell her she still haunted his dreams at night?

He was scared as hell of the answer.

"Miss Herelius, I'd like to know what I can do to help you with this."

She speared the elevator button again. "You can drop dead."

A smile played at the corners of his mouth. "Let's assume I'm not willing to go that far. Do you need money? For your medical expenses," he added quickly, "and what have you. Insurance can't be covering everything."

"I don't have insurance, but you can be damned sure I wouldn't accept one penny from you even if I had to have the baby by myself in a cave!"

The elevator doors swept open and she shot in, punching buttons frantically to make the door close before he could follow.

He stepped in after her. "No insurance? Are you getting prenatal care?"

He could see her jaw clench when she faced him. "Yes, I am," she said through gritted teeth. "Now please stop following me. I have nothing more to say to you."

"What about hospital expenses? Are you preregistered anywhere?"

Her eyes squeezed shut and she let out a breath before she answered. "Yes. At UCLA."

The elevator stopped at the ground floor and she flew out,

leaving him stroking his jaw contemplatively, grateful that she'd given him one small morsel of information. But he needed more. Much more. Maybe he'd just give UCLA a call.

"If I weren't the nonviolent type," Tanya said as she eased into the passenger seat of Cole's convertible after the meeting, "I'd try smacking some sense into that thick head of yours."

"Nice."

"What the hell did you think you were doing in there, anyway?" She snapped her seat belt on.

"I'm sure I don't know what you mean." Cole jammed the Z into gear and rolled out of the parking lot. "None of your business, anyhow."

"Anytime I bring the center into things, it is my business. What did you hope to accomplish by coming on like some kind of heartless monster?" He'd made the mistake of detailing what had happened after she'd left the room.

Horns blared when he whipped a left turn across traffic. "Couldn't help it. I took one look at her and my insides just tied themselves in knots. I am so angry with her for all this. For the way she disappeared. For what she might be doing to our baby." He raked a hand over his hair. Hell, for what she was doing to his sleep. "But I have to stay cool and professional."

"Cold and ruthless, I'd say."

"It's the only way I'll get through this, T."

"Well, I don't like it." Tanya huffed out a breath. "Though I guess I understand. But what if it's true that she's not giving up the baby? Couldn't you just talk things over? And why invoke the ICWA before you're sure she isn't?"

"I'd think that would be apparent. I don't trust her. Not for a minute."

Tanya met his gaze when he was forced to stop at a red light. "I'm questioning your motives, Cole. I see better solutions to this thing."

"Oh?" He couldn't wait to hear this. "My cousin Tanya, the relentless pursuer of Indian children's rights, suddenly has a change of philosophy?"

"No. But I'm wondering if this is about you wanting your baby, or if it's about that huge chip on your shoulder."

"Tanya…" He tried to warn her off with his tone. "You're treading on thin ice."

"Well, call me reckless, but I've got to say it. Cole, it's me, *nuyukssum*—my cousin. Remember? I was there when you first came out to Rincon Rez twenty years ago looking for your birth family. It hasn't escaped my attention that in all that time you've never attempted to speak to your real mother, even though she certainly wants to. I also happen to know that the line next to 'father' on your birth certificate is blank. But Cole, doing this won't make up for past hurts. You don't have to prove anything to anyone. There are other ways to handle this."

"Yeah. I could force my paternal rights, but I'm not," he reminded her contentiously. "By invoking the ICWA, I only gain custody if she gives up the baby for adoption."

"I suppose that's something."

"Read my lips, T. I want my baby. Not to prove anything. Not for revenge, or some misguided sense of obligation. But because I want to have my child with me. To love him or her, and be a family."

She tilted her head and tossed him a sly smile. "If that's true, why don't you try the obvious solution first?"

He sighed in resignation. The only thing obvious to him was that she wasn't going to shut up until she'd had her say. "And what would that be?"

"Marry the baby's mother."

The brakes squealed as he slammed the car to a halt in front of the center. "Excuse me? I think I must have heard you wrong."

Tanya jumped out of the Z. "From what I could see, that woman is not what you seem to think she is, Cole." She leaned in through the open window. "I remember you being ready to take a chance on her back at the powwow when you told me and the girls you'd fallen in love after one night with her."

"Temporary insanity. That was before she'd run off on me without a word and tried to give away my baby. I'd say those are both damned good reasons for not marrying the woman now.''

She shrugged. ''That may be true, but maybe not. Either way, don't let ancient history blind you to the possibilities. You think about that, *nuyukssum.* By the way, this new car of yours is too fancy by half. It'll ruin your harmony completely. What happened to the truck?''

''Sitting in the driveway with a For Sale sign in the window. And the only thing ruining my so-called harmony is your infernal meddling.'' Her and her damned Navajo philosopher boyfriends. Cole glared at her when she had the gall to wink, then beat a hasty retreat up the center steps.

Holy moly. The *chica* was on drugs. Marry Rini Herelius? Not on your life, *nuyukssum,* cousin mine.

It would never happen.

Not in a million years.

Katarina took a deep breath, opened the door to the swanky offices of Dr. Lynn Morris and went in. She glanced quickly around the waiting room and let out a breath of relief. Colton Lonetree was not there.

She couldn't believe she had agreed to this. It had been five days since the father of her baby had served his notice at Henderson's office, four since he'd somehow tracked down her address and three days since Alex had convinced her she had to make a few concessions. Compromises, in order to show her willingness to include him in the baby's life. Even if she didn't like it. In other words, she would have to let him pay for some fancy obstetrician in order to convince him that he would be welcome to take the kid to powwows whenever he liked. So he wouldn't sue her for custody.

Katarina gave her name to the receptionist and accepted a pile of forms to be filled out. She'd been worried Lonetree would show up for her appointment with the obstetrician, but apparently the hotshot lawyer had found a more lucrative way to spend an hour.

Alex's warning echoed in her mind. *You have to be nice to the man, Rini. Show your moral superiority.*

Be nice.

Right.

Katarina skipped over a few financial questions she didn't know how to answer. Maybe she'd get lucky and they wouldn't let her in. She felt perfectly comfortable going to the clinic at UCLA, along with fellow students and other poor people. She didn't want to be here in this posh office, accepting what amounted to charity. Lonetree claimed to be concerned that she got the best care possible, but Katarina knew better. It was conscience money.

When the outer door opened, every other woman in the room looked up. She'd be damned if she would. She sensed more than saw when he stood before her. "I wish you hadn't come," she muttered.

There was a pause before he answered. "Now, you don't mean that, Fire Eyes."

Fire Eyes? She scowled, shooting him a dagger look. "Oh, don't I?"

He smiled and motioned to the woman sitting in the chair next to her to move down one. She was more than happy to comply, Katarina noted with disgust. In fact, if the woman weren't at least eight months pregnant, Katarina would be convinced she was flirting with the man. Unbelievable.

Rini took a critical look at her one-time lover as he settled into the chair beside her. His well-tailored gray suit was impeccable, his tie a rich turquoise silk, his shoes undoubtedly Italian leather. His crisp white shirt looked fresh and starched and complimented his dusky complexion to perfection.

She frowned in reluctant admiration. Good grief, the man was even sexier than she remembered. She stared openly as he reached over to retrieve a magazine from a rack across from his chair. His thighs were muscular and his rear lean and tight under his trousers. *Mercy.*

He caught her staring.

His answering honeyed smile was designed to melt the heart of every female in the room. It was also so full of male smugness Katarina wanted to whisper in his ear that there was a rip in his pants, and then sit back and watch him squirm. Just the thought made her smirk. He looked down, quickly checking his clothing.

Be nice to the man, Rini.

She smiled sweetly and with a flourish deposited her sloppy pile of forms over his magazine. "I can't answer some of these questions."

He straightened the stack slowly and meticulously. "Okay, darlin', I'll take a look."

God, he was insufferable. "Oh, sugar, you are just so sweet to me." She batted her lashes.

She could see a muscle work in his jaw, but otherwise his face betrayed nothing. He went back to the paperwork, and she felt a small sense of victory. She didn't want to be here. It was his fault that she was. He would pay if he chose to play games with her.

A moment later, a nurse appeared. "Ms. Herelius?"

Before she could push herself off the chair, Lonetree rose and took her arm, helping her to her feet. "Darlin'."

She yanked her elbow from his hand and walked with chin high through the inner door, which he held open, and followed the nurse into the exam room. He sauntered in after her and leaned against the wall behind the exam table.

Katarina looked at him, shocked. "Surely you don't intend to stay?"

"You agreed." He flashed that smug smile again.

She'd throttle him. "A gentleman would never…"

His eyebrow quirked. "I'm sure that's not the word you would have used two minutes ago to describe me. I think I prefer the other."

"Bastard," she obliged.

Despite his answering grin, she saw a darkness pass through his eyes. "Since the day I was born." He fingered the paper gown lying on the table. "But I'll be a nice guy and turn my back if it starts getting embarrassing."

Consternation and panic fought in her stomach as she imagined sitting in that paper gown in front of the despicable rogue. Or worse.

"Embarrassing for me, that is," he added.

She gave him a withering look as the nurse sailed into the room. The stout woman looked Lonetree up and down with an imperious expressed and asked, "Will the father be staying?"

He winked at the nurse. "She keeps telling me I'm not the father, but I'm staying anyway."

"Harrumph." She swept the gown from the table. "You won't be needing this today, Ms. Herelius. The doctor will just be doing a tummy check and listening to the heart. She'll decide about a sonogram during the exam."

Katarina let out a whoosh of breath. There was a God.

When Dr. Morris came in, she flipped through the chart that had come from UCLA. Lonetree wandered over to the window. "I trust it won't be a problem if I stay."

Apparently he had spoken with her about the situation. "That depends on you, Mr. Lonetree. If you make Ms. Herelius uncomfortable, you're history."

He turned and assumed his most professional manner. "Contrary to popular opinion, Doctor, I'm not here to be obnoxious. My only purpose is to monitor the baby's progress. I've no intention of making Ms. Herelius uncomfortable."

Dr. Morris tilted her head at Katarina. "Ms. Herelius?"

She looked first at Lonetree, then the doctor, and sighed. "It's okay. As long as it's just a tummy check."

She swallowed her surprise when the exam began and he turned to face the window, talking to the doctor over his shoulder, interjecting questions about what was normal and how Rini was doing. He asked questions she had never thought to ask and, in the end, she learned things she would never have known if he hadn't been there.

"Well, everything looks good," Dr. Morris finally declared. "But your ankles are swollen. You haven't been getting enough rest, have you? I want you to promise to take it easy. Put your feet up several hours a day."

"I had finals at UCLA this past week. But classes are over until January. I promise to do my reading on the couch."

Hands in pockets, Lonetree leaned against the windowsill, listening. He finally came back to her side when Dr. Morris pulled out the Doppler monitor and amplified the baby's heartbeat.

Astonishment flashed across his face when they heard the first tiny beats. Katarina watched as astonishment was replaced by wonder, and then awe—his reaction much as her own had been the first time she'd heard her baby's heartbeat. Cole looked like a kid who'd just seen Santa Claus drop onto the fireplace grate.

His gaze met hers over the hand-held monitor and he smiled. If the Doppler had been monitoring her own heart just then, it surely would have registered several skipped beats during those seconds his eyes held hers.

"That's amazing," he said quietly.

"Well, Mr. Lonetree, if a simple heartbeat can send you into shock, hang on to your socks, because you ain't seen nothin' yet." Dr. Morris grinned at the two of them. "How about a sonogram, kids?"

Katarina laughed. "That would be great!"

Cole's smile faltered. "There's nothing wrong, is there?"

The doctor shook her head. "No, no. The clinic did one a few months ago, but I'd like to do another. Just to check things out in there."

He grasped his tie and rubbed it distractedly, giving a nervous laugh. "The wonders of modern science."

Dr. Morris wheeled a formidable looking array of equipment over to the foot of the exam table and squirted a huge dollop of goo on Katarina's bare stomach, spreading it around. As she pressed a palm-size scanner over the baby, the TV screen before them sprang to life. As usual, the image on the screen looked more like a space alien than a baby, but after a moment, the wiggling, disjointed shapes took on the familiar cherublike form. Katarina murmured, "Ooh," when she finally made out the baby. At that same second, Cole sat down on the examination table just below her shoulder, gazing raptly at the monitor.

"Unbelievable," he murmured over and over between the doctor's explanations and descriptions of what they were seeing.

"Okay, you want to know the sex?"

Katarina stared at the doctor, then glanced at Cole.

He said, "I do. But it's your call."

She swallowed. Was he actually giving her a choice? She was tempted to say no, just to be contrary. But the expression on his face was so oddly full of hope, so like a little boy pleading with his mother for the puppy in the pet shop window, that she couldn't make herself do it.

Besides, she wanted to know, too. She wanted to know everything she could about the precious life inside her. She gave him a tentative smile. "All right. Let's go for it."

He grinned and she nearly fell off the table when he grabbed her hand and turned back to the screen. "Okay, Doc, work your magic." When the appropriate portion of the baby's anatomy came into focus, they all giggled. "Holy moly."

"Looks like a very healthy little boy."

Everyone laughed. Katarina was ecstatic. "A boy! It's a boy!"

Cole looked at her, emotion evident in his expression. His face lit up from within, radiating profound joy. "A son."

Suddenly, he must have realized he was gripping her hand between both of his, for he dropped it and slid off the table. "Congratulations, Ms. Herelius."

"Thank you. Either one would have been fine, of course, but it's exciting to know which it is."

He nodded, fingered his tie again and moved to the window. "Yes."

All at once a thought occurred to her. "I don't suppose you were hoping for a girl?"

He turned to face her and took a deep breath, as if to bring himself back to the present after being lost in his own thoughts. "I'd like a son very much."

Dr. Morris stood and handed Katarina a form and the pictures from the sonogram. "I'll let you two continue this discussion on your own." She helped her up and gave her a towel. "Take it easy, now, and keep those feet up. See you next week." Then she was gone.

Katarina looked at the towel in her hand and then at her stomach. "Yuck." She wiped it off as well as she could, then set the towel aside. A shadow fell across her lap and she glanced up.

"You missed a spot." Cole took up the towel and reached out to her belly, but stopped just shy of touching skin.

His gaze locked with hers, and a jolt of response surged through her. She was suddenly acutely conscious of sitting with her entire midriff intimately exposed to his eyes. A coil of sexual awareness tightened around her body like a spring, squeezing to life parts that had lain dormant for almost seven months. And a lifetime, before that.

A whip of panic cut across her. This was the last way she wanted to be reacting to this man. "I can—"

Too late! He was already gently stroking the side of her belly with the towel. His hand, large and brown against the white towel and her pale skin, caressed her softly, slowly. As she watched, an elemental recognition coursed through every molecule of her body, making her agonizingly aware that this man had touched her before, more intimately than anyone in her whole life.

Suddenly it was difficult to breathe.

Chapter 5

Katarina looked up into Cole's eyes, her mind a whirlpool of emotion.

This was nuts. She didn't want this man. God help her, she *couldn't!* Not after... It was only...

The searing intensity of his scrutiny short-circuited her brain. Terrified of her own reaction, she watched his face come closer and closer—knowing she should under no circumstances let him kiss her.

Knowing she would anyway.

Helpless to resist, she saw her pride and common sense sacrificed on the altar of her reckless attraction to this man, and abandoned herself to the moment. She tilted her face up to his and let her lashes flutter to her cheeks. When their lips finally met, it was all she could do to keep from melting into a puddle at the tenderness with which his mouth caressed hers. He was everything she remembered, and more. Much more.

Against strict orders, her disobedient arms slid around his neck. A moan rumbled in his chest like the prelude to an earthquake. He furrowed his fingers in her hair and held her head captive. For a split second the pressure of his lips increased, then he tore away, burying his face in her hair.

"Why, honey?" he asked in a strangled voice. "Why did you leave me?"

She dug her nails into his shoulders. How could he ask such a question?

Torn and suddenly miserable, she found her mind replaying those last horrible minutes at the powwow when she had learned, to her everlasting shame and humiliation, that he was no different than David. To the moment he'd cruelly jerked her out of her infernal naiveté.

You'll meet me at the dance circle, won't you?

Try and keep me away.

When the warrior had left for his hoop dance demonstration, Katarina had followed a few minutes later. She'd approached the circle just as the dance was ending, and sank down on one of the hay bales to wait for him. As she watched, he was again besieged by well-wishers, as he had been the first time she'd seen him dance.

A young woman put her arms around him and gave him a hug. Katarina frowned. Well, maybe she was his sister, she reasoned, trying desperately not to be jealous when he bent his mouth to her ear and whispered something that made the woman squeal and give him another hug. As she watched their embrace, Katarina fought the devastating images that flooded her mind— images of the first time she had caught David in the arms of one of his lovers.

No, she'd prayed silently. *Please no.*

A whole group of young women surrounded the warrior, touching him, flirting with him and whispering things in his ear. Then another woman approached him. This one was a little older, about Katarina's own age, a little more sophisticated looking and a whole lot prettier. She draped her hands over his shoulders and gave him a long, nuzzling kiss. *Oh, God.*

The beautiful fantasy Katarina had woven about the warrior shattered and the blood drained from her face. Her heart sank to her feet as the pretty woman spoke intimately with her lover, arm looped around his waist. Anger and humiliation had swamped Katarina as the woman drew a finger along his smiling jaw.

Katarina jumped up from the hay bale. She refused to sit there and watch her own betrayal. She absolutely would *not* go through this again. She wouldn't risk losing her tenuous self-confidence again after fighting so hard to find it. How dumb would she have to be to stick around and be hurt by yet another man who didn't care enough for her to be faithful for even one day?

What a fool she'd been! What an utter, utter fool! How could she have been so taken in by the man? Spinning fancy hopes and dreams about this handsome stranger, when all he wanted was a few hours of pleasure.

Would she never learn? Tears streaming down her face, she'd run all the way to her car and driven away without speaking to him.

Katarina's eyes stung now as she remembered the deep shame she had felt on that fateful day seven months ago.

Cole's hands moved over her hair, snapping her back to the present with a start.

Lord, what was she doing, standing so close to him, his hands cradling her head, their baby nestled between them? Letting him kiss her? *Would she never learn?*

Desperately, she tried to take a step backward.

"Why did you run away?" he repeated quietly, holding her fast.

But this was all wrong. The hurt in his voice sounded genuine. The anguish in his face. How could that be? *She* was the one who had been humiliated that day, not him! And he'd do it again if she wasn't careful. She had to be strong. For her baby as well as for herself. With determined hands, she pushed him away just as the door opened.

Cole dropped his grip on Rini and stepped away from her, grateful for the timely interruption when the nurse bustled into the exam room and began tidying up.

What the hell had come over him?

Ruthlessly, he suppressed all trace of the kaleidoscope of emotions that had tipped him off-kilter for the past few minutes. He had to get a grip.

He still wanted an answer to his question. But maybe if he was in familiar territory he wouldn't be so susceptible to the lure of her. Pulling a business card from his inside jacket pocket, he pressed it into her hand.

"This isn't the place for this conversation. If you want to continue it, come by my office. Anytime." He strode to the door. "If not, I'll be in touch to find out when your next appointment is."

Cole hurried out and down the hallway, not stopping until he was safely ensconced in the Camaro with the motor revved and the windows rolled up tight. He heaved a sigh, leaning his head against the back of the seat. He felt gut shot.

Damn, what had he gone and done now? He wondered how she felt about their kiss. About him.

Not that he cared, he reminded himself.

But the woman must have some sort of uncanny power over him. How could a simple kiss nearly reduce his determination to dust? His face still tingled from the caress of her hair. He'd literally had to force himself to step back instead of keeping her in his arms and dragging her home with him.

He stifled a groan.

He was finding it difficult to ignore all the things that had won him over seven months earlier. Beauty, certainly. But it was more than that. She had a quiet strength—one he wasn't even sure she was aware of, veiled as it was by a cloak of incredible vulnerability. He couldn't help but notice how surprised and bewildered she'd been at every little kindness shown her, before she'd retreated behind her anger. Almost as if she didn't think she was worthy.

He shook his head, clearing it of his wayward thoughts. He couldn't let himself think like this or he'd be lost. She'd fooled him once, but he'd be damned if he'd let it happen again.

She'd left him for no reason, abandoned him after everything they'd shared that night. And deny it though she might, she had also thought about abandoning their baby. She must have, to have been there in Henderson's office at all. It didn't matter that she'd apparently changed her mind. How could a woman even consider doing something like that?

There was no way he could ever sympathize with a woman who would seriously think about giving away her child. And he certainly couldn't love someone like that. He sat up and ground the Z into gear. He would never, ever let his son grow up knowing he wasn't wanted by his own mother or father.

As he had.

Even if Rini didn't love or want their baby, he did. So she just may as well get used to the idea of him being around. He would not abandon his own child. Not as long as there was a single breath left in his body.

Katarina peered up at the number on the shabby brick building in Old Town Pasadena and shrugged. Hardly the office style she expected for Colton Lonetree, considering the suits he wore and the shiny new convertible he drove. But then again, maybe he only spent money on himself. He wouldn't be the first man she'd known who did that.

She pulled into an empty spot a block away and trudged back, then groaned at the discovery that there was no elevator to his third floor office. It figured.

Why she had come was beyond her. Obviously, it was some sort of pregnancy-induced feeblemindedness. But she had to find out what Colton Lonetree wanted from her. He'd served her with notice of intent to block the adoption he was certain she was pursuing, and had hinted about claiming his paternal rights. Then he'd shown up at Dr. Morris's office yesterday, checking up on her. Obviously he didn't believe she was keeping the baby. She'd have to convince him she was.

But then what? What would he want from her then?

This had to be about his heritage. If she promised he could see the child and teach him about Native American culture, maybe he'd be satisfied.

Unless it wasn't about his heritage.

But what else could it be?

Her sister, Alex, was convinced he wanted to sue for custody. He knew how poor Katarina was; he knew that she had no job and little hope of completing her degree when the baby arrived. He was a rich lawyer who wouldn't want his child growing up like that. She had no money to hire her own attorney. Lonetree would surely win and take her baby away from her.

Katarina gripped the railing, fighting the feeling of helplessness that threatened to envelop her. It had been impossible to imagine handing over her child to her own sister. How would it feel to be forced to give him to a virtual stranger?

No! It wouldn't happen. *It couldn't.*

Taking a deep breath, she remembered the expression of joy and wonder on Cole's face as he'd listened to the baby's heartbeat and watched the sonogram monitor. She thought of her own father and how much he'd loved his two girls.

She let out her breath slowly. Maybe Cole wasn't a heartless brute. Maybe he really loved and wanted the baby.

What would she do then?

Catching her breath on the second floor landing, she leaned back against the wall for a moment. But no matter what happened, she could not allow herself to succumb to the lure of Colton Lonetree. That would be inviting disaster.

She recalled with mortification her reaction to him when he'd kissed her yesterday. Making her yearn for more, longing to relive the soothing touch of his hands and the warm feel of his skin against hers.

Pregnancy must have scrambled her hormones as well as her brains. Being attracted to him was not an option. Even if he was the father of her child. And even if she had once lain down with him and shared such a profound experience that she'd come away ready to risk everything to be with him.

Until she'd found out exactly what kind of a man he was.

Apparently, she had a weakness for handsome, sweet-talking cheats who wanted to control her life. She'd spent her childhood trying to please a scornful, overbearing mother, and it seemed that when she grew up she unheedingly fell for men who would take her mother's place without missing a beat.

Well, never again. This time she'd truly learned her lesson. She didn't need or want another man like her mother. Katarina was making her own choices now, and she didn't have to please a blessed soul except herself and her baby.

She'd see Colton Lonetree, demand to know what he wanted and then march right out of there. Okay, waddle out, she conceded, and firmly squelched an unwanted spark of anticipation at seeing him again.

She puffed up the remaining flight and was greeted by a tidy room, painted a warm adobe hue, with hardwood floors polished to a lustrous shine. On the walls hung several groupings of black-and-white photos of Indian country. Behind a big old, scarred desk piled high with papers and computer equipment sat a young man.

He looked up impassively. "Can I help you?"

"I'm looking for Colton Lonetree."

"He doesn't want to be disturbed." The young man went back to his work, apparently unperturbed that she didn't move.

"Will he be free anytime soon?"

He shrugged. "Dunno."

Katarina tapped her foot in frustration, wondering if the man was being deliberately rude or was just an idiot.

"I'm Katarina Herelius. He said I should drop by his office. He said anytime. Could you tell him I'm here?"

"Doesn't want to be disturbed."

She was just about to bean him over the head with the phone and stalk into the inner office uninvited when the door opened and Cole stuck his head out.

"Charlie, could you please get me— Rini!"

She edged toward him. "I probably should have called first."

His expression traveled from shocked surprise to cool and professional in about two nanoseconds. "No problem. Come on in."

Smoothing his tie, he opened the door wide, and she barely resisted smirking at the man behind the desk as she walked past.

"Where did you get Mr. Personality?" she asked when Cole had closed the door.

He chuckled. "Camarillo." *Prison!* He shrugged at her gasp. "Assault with a deadly weapon."

She covered her eyes. "Terrific."

"Charlie's a great photographer and a passable receptionist. Just needed a little direction in life."

Oh, brother. The man had a hardened criminal for a secretary. Her already sagging optimism slipped a little more.

Katarina ventured farther into Lonetree's office. Light poured through two large fanlight windows, reflecting off the Berber carpeting, bathing the room in a pink glow. Comfortably worn sofas and chairs surrounded a low-slung, battered wooden table half the size of Nebraska. Bookshelves lined the walls, filled with a jumble of law books, paperbacks, magazines and stereo equipment.

"Jeez. You live here?"

"Seems like it sometimes." He walked to his ancient oak desk at the back of the room and closed some files, then went to the wet bar behind it. "Tea? I've got mint and chamomile."

"Mint would be great, thanks."

Lonetree's jacket was off and his long white sleeves were rolled up to just under his elbows. His silk tie hung loose around his neck and suede moccasins encased his feet. When he bent over to pull a ceramic teapot from beneath the wet bar, Katarina was assailed by a vision of his breechclout fluttering around his athletic thighs as he dipped and swooped in his hoop dance at the powwow.

This had to stop. She would not let herself be swayed by the man's flawlessly masculine body.

Turning abruptly, she tossed her purse on one of the sofas, then wandered over to a collection of Native American garments he had mounted on the long wall opposite the windows. "These are beautiful."

"Thanks," he answered, punching buttons on a microwave.

"Do you collect them?" Her attention was captured by a quill chest plate, identical to the one he had worn at the powwow. She stood very still in front of it, memories washing over her. Barely aware of what she was doing, she reached out slowly, as if by touching it some of the magic of that night would rub off. Magic she badly needed.

She'd forgotten she'd asked the question when his answer sounded quietly, right behind her.

"I make them."

She jerked her hand back and whirled to face him, her breath quick with surprise. "Oh! Really?"

The look in his eyes was wary, possessive, almost predatory. He watched her for several long seconds before breaking the charged silence. "Kind of a hobby of mine."

He was standing close. Much too close. Sexual awareness crackled through her body, completing her misery.

She shouldn't have come. She didn't want to think of Colton Lonetree as a man at all, but preferred to keep him firmly in the neutral role of attorney, or better yet, heartless brute. Slipping past him, she went to one of the couches and sat down.

She bit her lip, picking imaginary lint off her knee-length sweater. "Did you make the costume you wore that day?"

He crossed to the table and started pouring tea into earthenware mugs. "Regalia. Yes, I made them."

Picking up her mug, she said resignedly, "So I can blame all this on your hobby, then."

He looked up as he took a seat across from her. "My hobby?"

"It was that damned outfit—sorry, regalia." She smiled wryly. "Maybe if you hadn't looked quite so sexy, I wouldn't have been so easily seduced that day."

His eyebrow lifted in amusement. "Miss Herelius, I am shocked. You don't strike me as the type who would fall for just another pretty face."

"Oh, it wasn't your face I—" She snapped her mouth shut. Good Lord, what he must think. "I mean…"

The corners of his lips curved up as he watched her expectantly. He was obviously savoring every word.

"I mean I fell for the whole man, Mr. Lonetree. Hook, line and sinker—fool that I am. But I might never have noticed you if you hadn't been quite so…so…noticeable."

He took a sip of tea, his gaze heating her skin. "Because of my outfit."

She picked up a magazine from the table and fanned her face lightly, cursing herself for getting into this topic. Was it warm in here, or what? "More like because of your *lack* of an outfit."

He smiled, and his eyes crinkled up. She watched, fascinated, as the already handsome man became utterly devastating. Like the pirate he was, he stole the very breath from her lungs. The magazine fell to the table. It was all she could do to hang on to her tea mug.

"Miss Herelius, you certainly know how to inflate a man's ego. If I didn't know better, I'd say you were buttering me up for something."

She carefully put down her mug and straightened her spine, avoiding his eyes. "Certainly not. We're both adults. Anything we have to say, I assume we can say straight out."

He nodded through the steam rising from his tea. The smile disappeared. "I'm glad you decided to accept the offer to help financially. There is no reason this should be anything less than amicable."

Then why did the room feel suddenly cold?

"That's true."

"I'm the baby's father. I only want what's best for him. Nothing more."

Silence fell and moments ticked by as she gathered the courage to speak, watching her own fingers knit and unravel themselves in her lap. "Please, Cole, what is it you want from me? Exactly?" She held her breath.

He got to his feet and looked stonily down at her, then stalked to the window and surveyed the traffic below. "I want my child."

Katarina wrung her hands. Could Alex be right? "I promise you can be a part of his life. You can see him, teach him about his heritage. I'll even sign papers giving you that right." She rushed on. "I know you don't think—"

Lonetree rounded on her. His eyes narrowed to slits. "If you're so interested in sharing so much with me, why did you run off that day? Why did I have to find out about my child six months after the fact?"

She nearly gasped at the ferocity of his accusation. Old fears nearly sucked her into their suffocating embrace. She battled in her mind, defending what she had done, fighting like hell against the tears that threatened to burst forth. "You know damned well why I ran away."

Rising clumsily, she grabbed her purse. She had to get out of there before she made things worse. Before she made a fool of herself all over again.

He blocked her path to the door. "Let's say I don't." His gaze bored into her. "Enlighten me."

Katarina felt a tear spill over her lashes, and dashed at it angrily. She hated feeling like this. Guilty, powerless, confused, like every choice she made was wrong, wrong, wrong. She knew she was right, but Lord help her, the man wasn't going to give her an inch.

Lonetree reached out and grasped her arms. His grip was firm, his shuttered expression insistent. "Please."

Another warm tear sluiced down the trail left by the first. She lowered her eyes, feeling ashamed and somehow at fault. Defeated. "All those women," she whispered. Her voice caught. "I know you never promised me a thing. Lord knows I probably got what I deserved. But it still hurt. I couldn't watch you pick up your next conquest."

She glanced up in time to see shock lingering on Cole's face. His fingers tightened around her arms. She tried to shake him off, but he held firm, bald emotion racing across his features. His mouth opened and then closed again, nothing coming out.

"It wasn't right, Cole."

Those words apparently broke through to him. His eyes unglazed. "My God." His fingers loosened their grip. "Are you saying you thought I was…that I was chasing those women?"

She nodded morosely, pulling away and rubbing her arms.

His hands went to his temples. "How could you think that? After everything we—"

Turning away, she shook her head. "I've had lots of experience recognizing the maneuvers."

"Rini, I—"

She held up a hand. "Don't. I've heard them all, believe me."

Cole couldn't stand seeing anguish extinguish the fire in Rini's eyes.

"It's not true." He ached to hold her close and reassure her. "Not true." To take things back to what they might have been. Before…

Moving slowly toward her, he lifted his hand, wanting to touch her cheek. "The only woman I was thinking about that morning was you, Rini."

She edged backward toward the door, avoiding him, until he'd nearly backed her up against it. She stared at him, her fingers clutching at the fabric of her sweater. His heart sank. She must think he was some kind of monster.

But, surely, it's not like this every time?

No? How would it be?

Her eyes squeezed shut, and he could see her bottom lip tremble. His stomach grazed hers, large with his child, and her eyes flew open. For an endless moment their gazes locked. He took a deep breath and smelled a hint of gardenia, mingled with her sensual woman's scent—the scent that had haunted him for so many lonely months.

Need and regret slammed into him, filling his body with a longing he couldn't ever remember feeling before. He needed to taste her. To fill the aching void in his soul with the light she had given him that spring day seven months ago.

Her eyes said she still wanted him. He reached up and slid his hand behind her, gently pulling her toward him.

"Cole, no." Her lips stopped just short of meeting his.

He continued to coax her forward, but she resisted. "I can't do this."

He pressed close to her, his baby nestled snugly against his abdomen. He breathed in Rini's sweet, warm breath, and willed her to yield to his embrace. But he could see the doubt written in her expression, and had to steel himself against pressing his mouth hard to hers and claiming its moist, dusky depths with his tongue.

Honey, whoever he was, you're well rid of him.

Cole closed his eyes and struggled to compose himself. "Rini, those women have nothing to do with you and me. With us. They're—"

Suddenly, the baby gave a little kick against his stomach. He looked down, and his baby kicked him again.

Oh, God, his baby. The baby she had planned to abandon.

What in the devil's name was he doing?

As if burned, he snatched his hand from her and looked up. She was staring at him incredulously.

"You arrogant, conceited bastard! How dare you tell me those women have nothing to do with us!"

She shoved hard against his chest, forcing him to take a step back to keep his balance. "You men are all alike! Only thinking of your own selfish needs. Never thinking of the wreckage you leave when you've taken your fill and moved on!"

"Rini—" He reached out but was firmly slapped away.

"Don't even think about touching me! You want to live the merry bachelor life, that's your choice. But my choice is that I want no part of it. Or you! And neither does my baby."

"Your baby?"

The irritation and frustration he felt boiled into anger, his mind homing in on her clear intention to exclude him from his baby's life, despite her assurances to the contrary. *He'd known he couldn't trust her.*

His voice became dangerously quiet. "*Your* baby?"

Surging forward, he placed his hands on either side of her belly, feeling the solid warmth within. "It was *my* seed that gave him life. He is *my* son, *my* family. I'll be damned if I'll give him up to be raised by strangers."

She scowled. "I'm telling you I'm not giving him up! Not for adoption, not to you!"

"And I'm telling you I want my child!"

Rini stared at him wide-eyed. "Look, I know I can't give him the things you—"

"Things!" Cole spat out, cutting her off. Turning on a heel, he paced to his desk, unable to see reason, unable to stand still, he was so caught up in the nightmare of his own memories. "What good are *things* when you don't have the love of your own mother and father?"

He strode back and stood before her, fists clenched. "What about when he grows up and finds out he was an accident, that you didn't really want him? That I just stood by and gave him up without a fight?"

Rini swallowed, looking thoroughly crushed. "I do want him," she whispered.

Refusing to believe her, he leaned in close, missing her slight flinch at his movement. "Do you have any idea what that does to a kid's self-esteem?"

She shook her head, her eyes liquid pools of hurt. "No."

"Well *I do.* And it's not going to happen to my son."

She let out a long, unsteady breath, her hunted gaze darting to his face before stubbornly retreating to the floor. "I won't let you have him, Cole. I can't."

He leaned back on his heels, the determination in his soul solidifying to granite. "Then we're in for a fight, darlin', because there's no way in hell I'll give him up."

Chapter 6

A few days before Christmas, Cole walked into his mother's kitchen and gave her a hug. "Hi, Mom."

"Hey, Punkus!" Julia McCleary smiled, holding her flour-covered hands away from his clothes. She had a smudge of butter on her cheek.

"Mom, I'm thirty-six years old. You're going to have to stop calling me that." He wiped the butter from her cheek and then laid a kiss where it had been. "It's embarrassing."

"Sorry, Punkus. I'll try and do better." She attempted to look contrite, failing miserably.

Chuckling, Cole helped himself to a cup of coffee and tossed a smile to his dad, who sat at the kitchen table struggling with a pile of nuts and a pair of pliers. "Hi, Pop. Mom got you cracking macadamias again?"

His dad, Ted, heaved a dramatic sigh and gestured helplessly. "Thanks to your cousin."

"Tanya knows how much you love macadamia nuts in your Christmas cookies. I hear she had a bumper crop this year. The bag she gave you must be worth a small fortune on the open market."

"That woman's kindness will cripple me one of these years," he said, stretching his fingers.

Cole chuckled. "Here, let me take over."

"Ah, respite for my aching hands. Just in time for the game, too. Come on in when the slave driver here gives you a break."

Thoughtfully, Cole watched his dad retreat into the living room—the same room where Cole had spent much of his youth reading, playing cards and watching TV with the loving couple who had adopted him as a baby. When he caught his mom observing him curiously, he forced a smile, sat down at the table and began cracking nuts.

It had been a ritual for as long as he could remember—he and his mom baking Christmas cookies together. Even during the rebellious years when he'd lived on the rez with Tanya's family, he'd always managed to find some excuse to come back home on the Saturday before Christmas.

"You're quiet tonight, Cole. Anything wrong?"

He wriggled out from under the doubt and indecision that had been building in him since he'd gotten there. He loved his adoptive parents and knew they loved him like he was their own. If he was bitter over his childhood ordeals, it wasn't because of them.

Still, a kid belonged with his real mother and father, didn't he? Cole was doing the right thing by his son, fighting to be included in his life. In his heart he knew it. Even if he'd gone a bit too far in his anger with Rini the other day and overstated his case. He had no intention of taking the baby away from her. He just wanted to be there for him.

Slowly, he set down the pliers and looked over at her. "Mom, I'm going to have a baby."

"You? I'd like to see that." Julia grinned. But her amusement over his choice of words faded quickly when she caught sight of his face. "Oh, my gracious. You're serious!"

He nodded.

She dragged out a chair and sat down, her face suddenly ashen. "With who? Lindsay?"

He made a face. "Mom, Lindsay and I never even slept together when we were married. Why would we start now?"

She smiled weakly. "Who then?"

"Her name is Rini Herelius. It's a boy. He's due in February."

She looked dazed. "Why haven't I met her?"

"It's complicated."

"I see." Her hand trembled as she reached up and pushed her graying hair back from her face. "She doesn't want to marry you?"

He shook his head, preferring not to bring up the minor detail that he hadn't asked her. "We're barely speaking. I might have to take her to court to establish my rights."

"Is she Native American?" When he shook his head again, his mom lowered her hands to her lap and studied them, obviously torn. He had to strain to hear what she said next. "And you don't want him going through what you did."

He knew his mom still blamed herself for the difficult years they'd gone through back when he'd rediscovered his Luiseño roots. "It wasn't your fault, Mom. You know that."

"If it wasn't my fault, why did you have to run away to find out who you are?" She rose abruptly and went to check on the batch of cookies in the oven.

"You did what you thought was right." He followed and put his arms around her from behind. "It's not your fault that when you looked at me you saw the son you loved, but when everyone else looked at me they saw an Indian kid trying to be white."

"If only I'd known, if I'd been more sensitive… If I'd let you learn about your heritage…"

"Yeah, and if I weren't adopted things would be hunky-dory and the streets would be paved with gold." He turned her to face him. "I had the best parents a kid could have. Still do. I learned a lot of things during those years at Rincon, and that was one of them." He hugged her. "I'll admit I went through a private hell back then. But you're not the one I blame for it. Never."

She sighed and pulled away, wiping her eyes. "Cole, one of these days you'll have to talk to her. Your real mother."

"I think those cookies are burning, Mom. Better check them."

Her gaze rested on his face for a moment longer before she took the oven mitt and turned her attention to the stove.

He let out a breath, grateful she didn't go on. He didn't want to hear about how he ought to make things right between himself and his biological mother. He wasn't interested. She'd made her choice thirty-six years ago, and nothing was going to change what had happened to him because of it.

"So how do you like the idea of having a grandson?"

Pulling the cookie sheets from the oven, she beamed at him. "I like it a lot. But I'd like it even better if I got a daughter-in-law, too."

"Sorry. Not this time."

"Surely you must have loved her if you...well, if she got pregnant."

He wasn't quite able to hold his smile in place as he answered. "Things just didn't work out."

"Have you really given it a chance?"

His lips formed a thin line. Rini was the one who hadn't given it a chance. Now it was too late for both of them. "It's not an alternative right now, Mom."

"You still have feelings for her, don't you?"

He didn't answer. He couldn't. But later, when Cole was ready to go, as if able to divine his deepest secrets, his mother slipped a round tin into his hands.

"What's this?"

"Cookies."

He frowned.

"For her."

"Tanya?"

"Rini. The mother of your baby. I want you to bring them to her, from me."

"Mom—"

"You've got three days until it's Christmas. That's plenty of time." She kissed him on the cheek. "Humor me."

He sighed, knowing he couldn't refuse her annoying request. He'd do almost anything to make up for the years of heartache he'd caused her. Almost.

"All right. But it won't do any good, so don't get your hopes up."

Cole stared at the tin of cookies sitting in front of him on the desk, and silently cursed.

The last thing he wanted to do right now was stand nose-to-nose with Rini Herelius. After what had happened in his office the other day, she'd probably throw the tin in his face.

Not that he didn't deserve it. He was still disgusted with himself for his unforgivable behavior. Oh, not the fight—that was perfectly understandable given the volatile emotions they both had concerning the subject of their baby.

No, it was what he'd done before that. When he'd nearly kissed the woman. *Again!* He must be completely insane.

But it was four-thirty on Christmas Eve, and he'd promised his mom. That meant he had to deliver the damned cookies tonight or tomorrow face the sad, disappointed look she had down to a fine art. And the guilt.

Hell.

He slowly straightened his tie, slipped on his jacket and tucked the cookies under his arm.

When the doorbell rang, Rini cast a disgusted glance at the front door. Impeccable timing, as always.

She'd just sunk down in Alex's big, comfy armchair, which was so hard to get out of once settled into. She glanced hopefully toward the kitchen, where the family was preparing dinner, but no one else had heard the bell over the din of pots banging and knives chopping. Groaning, she eased herself out of the chair with the grace of a buffalo.

Less than two months to go, she told herself. And not a moment too soon.

Looking through the peephole in the door, she caught her breath. A tall, broad-shouldered figure was illuminated in the twilight by multicolored Christmas lights. *Cole!*

She hadn't heard from him since that awful day in his office.

What was he doing here on Christmas Eve? It couldn't be good news. Cautiously, she opened the door.

He fingered the perfect knot in his silk tie. "Good evening."

"Cole?"

He smoothed the silk nervously with his fingers. "I tried the garage apartment. No answer."

"I'm having dinner with…" Her words trailed off and she looked at him uncertainly.

"Yeah, thought you might be. I, uh, I'm here to deliver some cookies."

"Cookies?" *What on earth…?*

"Christmas cookies from my mom." He showed her the round tin in his hands. "She wanted me to give them to you."

Katarina was floored. "Your mother sent me cookies?"

He glanced dubiously at the lights surrounding the door. "For Christmas."

Her face must have reflected her disbelief.

"I told her about the baby." One shoulder lifted almost apologetically as he stroked his tie again. "She's an incurable romantic."

"I…that's very sweet. Um…" What should she do? Invite him in? Good grief, Alex would love that.

Katarina felt a little panicked, but she had to admit she was glad to see Cole standing at her door. She'd been thinking a lot about him since the other day. Thinking about the fight they'd had. About how she'd never really given him a chance to explain his side of what had happened at the powwow. About how he was right to want to be a part of his baby's life, even if they disagreed as to the extent.

About his lips lowering to hers…

She looked quickly into the empty living room, then back to him. "Would you like to come in?"

He shook his head. "No. I don't think—"

"Look, Cole, I'm sorry I blew up the other day. Are you sure you won't come in for just a moment?"

"Yeah, me, too. But it probably wouldn't be too smart to stay, considering…"

She looked down at her own foot playing with the bottom of the screen door. "Since when have we done what's smart?"

His gaze trailed down her body to the evidence of that statement's truth. "Not so far, that I can tell."

The shadow of a smile that played across his lips seemed genuine, if cautious. Looking at that sad smile, she knew she had to try and make things better between them. She desperately wanted him to believe she wouldn't shut him out of his child's life, if only he wouldn't take him from her.

A hint of challenge covered the tremor in her voice. "You feeling smart tonight, warrior?"

His expression turned wary. "Hell, if I had half the sense of a polecat I wouldn't be standing here right now." He cleared his throat. "But even a polecat knows when to turn tail and run." He extended the cookie tin toward her.

Rebuffed but good. She lowered her eyes and bit her lip, then raised her hand to take the tin.

Suddenly she stopped. *No.* She wouldn't let herself give in so easily. Just as she had her whole life.

If she let him go now, there might never be another chance to straighten out this situation. To talk him out of taking her baby.

She drew in a breath. "How about a deal? I'll take the cookies if you'll take a walk."

He looked suspicious. "Off the end of a plank?"

She smiled, relieved he had chosen humor instead of anger. "Don't give me any ideas, Counsellor. No, around the block, with me." She grabbed her coat and slipped it on.

After a short hesitation he relented. "I suppose that would be okay." He eyed her ample midsection under the gaping coat and frowned. "Are you sure about this?"

"Don't be medieval. Exercise is good for pregnant women."

"If you say so." He stepped closer, his tall frame towering over her. Once again she was struck by his sheer masculinity. She took a steadying breath and the faint scent of dusky cologne drifted across her senses. He reached out and pulled her coat collar together, buttoning the top button.

She smiled up at him, won over by the tender gesture.

Over the months, she had gotten so used to being alone that she found it a bit frightening to think this overwhelmingly virile stranger had touched her deep inside and done things to her no other person ever had.

And yet, when he smoothed down her lapels with his fingers and tentatively smiled back, she felt unexpectedly comforted and protected by his powerful presence. She wanted to slip into his strong arms and just lean on him for a day. A year.

A lifetime.

No! This was crazy! He was a hopeless rake and he didn't want her. He only wanted the baby—to take him from her. She had to concentrate on talking some sense into the man, not letting herself fall for him again.

Going down the steps, he offered her his arm. After a second's indecision, she took it. Oh, why did he have to be so darned considerate? It would be much easier if he really were a heartless brute. She sighed.

"You okay?"

"Yes. Just thinking what a mess this whole thing is."

They reached the end of the walkway. Before she could steer them one way or the other, he stopped and moved in front of her, looking earnestly into her eyes.

"Before we get any further, I just want to say one thing." He waited for her nod before going on. "I want to say thank you."

Her mouth dropped open.

"In the same situation, a lot of women would have made a different choice. Regardless of what happens between us, I want you to know how happy I am you chose to have my baby."

She didn't know what she'd been expecting, but this definitely wasn't it. He started walking again, and, in a daze, she allowed herself to be led down the sidewalk. *He was thanking her for her choice?*

They walked along in thoughtful silence for a few minutes before she got up her courage and said, "Cole, I need you to believe that I am keeping the baby. And that I'd never keep you from—"

"I do believe you," he interrupted. "Honestly. I don't know

what came over me the other day, but I swear I would never, ever try to take the baby away from you.''

The tight squeeze around her heart slowly loosened. She stared at him, hope blossoming. ''Is that true?''

''Yes, it's true. I just want…'' He raked a hand in his hair. ''Look, I know I brought it up, but please, let's not talk about this tonight. It's Christmas Eve and I don't particularly feel like fighting. Let's just be Cole and Rini taking a walk, okay?''

She let out a little breath of exasperation, frustrated in her need to completely settle things between them. She looked up and found him carefully watching her expression.

''We'll talk,'' he said gently. ''I promise. I'll even try to keep my temper.''

She gave him a tentative smile, knowing she shouldn't let the subject go, but not wanting to ruin the tentative truce he'd declared. ''All right.''

In a companionable hush, they continued to walk. Fingers of darkness reached out from the trees along the street as the last sliver of sun disappeared. When they rounded the corner, Cole asked, ''At the obstetrician's you mentioned classes. What are you studying?''

''Nursing. When I graduate in June I can take the exam to be a registered nurse.''

''Like it?''

''Very much. It's always been my dream to be a nurse. I'm determined to finish this time.''

''You've started before?''

She nodded, plucking some leaves from an overhanging tree. The air rustled through the branches, sighing softly. She tore up the leaves and tossed them in the gutter. ''My ex-fiancé made me quit.''

''This the same guy who didn't want you distracting him in bed?''

Her cheeks burned under his gaze. She couldn't believe he remembered she'd said that. Right after he'd plunged deep into her and she'd come apart in his arms. *Do you have any idea what it does to a man's ego—* She closed her eyes against the sensual vision, barely aware that they had stopped. Fiercely, she banished the memory. "He liked being in control."

"He liked being a jerk." Cole ran a hand over his face, then turned, and they continued walking. "Sorry. None of my business."

She stole a glance at him, her mind wandering over the disastrous end to that day in May, then to what he'd said in his office. Suddenly, she had the sinking feeling maybe she had misjudged him back at the powwow. She should...

A twinge of terror rushed through her body at the thought of lowering her defenses long enough to find out. She reached deep inside and exorcised the chiding of her mother and David, drawing on the memory of her father's love to give her strength.

"Is it true you weren't flirting with those women at the powwow? That they meant nothing to you?"

He stopped so abruptly she was forced to halt and turn around. "Those were my... I coach some students in Native American dancing." He rubbed his fingers over the front of his shirt, as if seeking something, and started walking again. "Sometimes they get a little carried away."

"Just a little?" she muttered, following along beside him and feeling strangely giddy. "What about the older one? The one you were kissing."

He gazed up at the moon and said quietly, "That was my ex-wife, Lindsay. And I wasn't kissing her."

It was Katarina's turn to stop dead. *"Wife?"*

"Ex-wife. It happened a long time ago, and it was over almost as fast as it started. She left me after less than a day of wedded bliss." He took Katarina's arm and led her on.

She looked up at him, a twinge of something niggling at her conscience. "That must have been rough."

"Lindsay graduated same year as my brother, Billy. Her father was a gen-u-ine bigot. Big man in the country club set. She rebelled by getting drunk and hanging around with the Indian kids from the local rez."

He kicked a pinecone and continued. "One night Lindsay and her dad had a big fight and she got back at him by running off to Vegas and marrying one of them—me. She vowed her everlasting love and I believed her. Of course, it was all just a big joke. Unfortunately, I didn't know that until it was too late. See, I was actually in love with her."

"Oh, Cole. That's awful." Katarina's stab of sympathy materialized as a small contraction. She put a hand lightly on the baby.

He shrugged. "I seem to be cursed with women running off on me."

His voice was light, but Katarina detected a wealth of emotion behind the words. She swallowed a huge wave of guilt. She'd had good reason to run off. At least she'd thought so at the time.

"Anyway, Lindsay's daddy had the divorce papers drawn up the next day." He looked grim as they went around another corner. "I see her now and then, mostly at the powwows. She was there the day you and I… Anyway, she gets a sort of perverse pleasure tormenting me with the kind of display you witnessed. It's annoying, but everyone knows she isn't serious."

"You didn't look particularly annoyed," Katarina observed testily. She rubbed her belly as the volley of contractions continued. Lord, she'd be glad when this pregnancy was over.

He smiled at her and winked. "For some reason, I was in a good mood."

She wanted to smile back but was hit by another cramp, sharper than the others. She took a deep breath and put both hands on her stomach as it continued to tighten.

Cole's smile faded, his brows drawing together. "Are you all right?"

"Yeah." She let out the breath. "Just a bout of Braxton Hicks."

"Huh?"

"Contractions." She laughed at his alarmed expression. "Just practice ones. Don't worry, I'm not going into labor. But I may have overdone this walk thing. Could we sit down for a minute?"

"Of course." His eyes searched around, the concern in them apparent.

She felt her heart do a little flip-flop. "The curb's fine. Really. You'll just have to help me up is all."

Cole held Rini's hands, easing her down onto the shallow curb. He hoped like hell she wasn't going to have the baby right there on the street. He might be looking forward to being a dad, but that would be pushing it a bit. "Jeez, Rini. Are you sure about this?"

"Not to worry. I'm almost a nurse, remember? Watch out for your suit!"

He sat down beside her. "Forget the suit. Is this normal?"

"Perfectly."

A nervous laugh escaped him. "Guess I need childbirth classes or something."

She shot him a sidelong glance. "You want to come to mine?"

He stared at her, not quite believing his ears.

"Alex will be tied up with some award presentation for Kenny next time." She shrugged. "But I can go alone."

"No! I mean yes. I mean, yes, I'd like to come."

"It's Friday night. You don't have a hot date?"

He grinned. "I do now." He watched her smile shyly, her cheeks glowing as rosy pink as her soft, full lips. Damn, there she went again, going all shy and sexy on him. It was all he could do to resist leaning over and crushing the velvet of those rose petal lips with his.

He clamped his teeth together. *No, this was too much.* He'd really have to get hold of himself. This made twice in a week he'd almost lost his head. Rini Herelius was not the kind of woman he should ever let into his life.

But what was it about her that reduced him to a sparking tangle of live wires ready to short-circuit his common sense?

He stood quickly, schooling his expression. "We should get back. Feel up to walking?"

She nodded and reached up. He grasped her hands and pulled her to her feet. She teetered against him, wincing.

"Rini?"

"It's okay. I just got up too fast." When he saw the thin film of sweat on her brow, fear coiled in his gut. "To hell with this." He swept her up into his arms and started down the sidewalk, carrying her.

"Cole!"

"Put your arms around my neck."

"This really isn't—"

He strode quickly down the street, ignoring her irritated glower. "Look, my mother would kill me if anything happened to you or the baby while I was delivering her blasted cookies. So stop squirming and enjoy the ride."

A wistful smile slid over Rini's face, and she relaxed a bit. "You love your mother very much."

"I do." *His mom and her damned cookies.*

"Do you look more like her or your dad?"

Cole turned up the walkway to her sister's house and adjusted her weight before mounting the steps. "Neither. I'm adopted." On the porch, he set her on her feet.

"Now I understand," she whispered, closing her eyes. One hand went to her temple as the other dug into his shoulder.

"Rini!" The door flew open and a woman shrieked as Rini slumped against him. The sister, Alex, he presumed. "What have you done to her?" she cried.

Cole hooked one arm around Rini's limp form and another under her knees, then scowled at the hysterical woman. "Where can I take her?"

Alex pointed frantically. "The sofa."

He laid Rini out on the couch, going down on his knees beside her. Her eyes opened and she struggled to sit up, but Cole put a hand on her shoulder. "No way. You stay put."

Alex pushed her way next to Rini and glared at him. "Just who the hell are you, anyway? Can't you see she's having a baby soon?"

"My name is Colton Lonetree."

"Cole..." Alex stared at him, eyes narrowed in fury. "You!" She turned to Rini, stroking her hair. "What has he done to you, honey? Did he threaten—"

Rini interrupted. "Alex, I'm all right. I'm having contractions and stood up too fast."

"You're not needed here, Mr. Lonetree," Alex snapped. "I'll thank you to leave my home."

Rini held out her hand to him. "No, wait!"

Rising, he looked at her hand. He shouldn't take it. It would just complicate things. He shouldn't even be here. She'd abandoned him. She was nothing but trouble. And all he wanted was to pull her into his arms and hold her tight. He was so scared. Scared something was wrong.

More scared something was very right.

He took her hand. "What?"

"Do you still want to go to class Friday, or have I scared you off?"

He cleared his throat. "Scared? Me? Not a chance. What time shall I be here?"

Chapter 7

Cole watched in the mirror over the bar as two mean-looking, leather-clad Mohawks parted the Christmas revelers like the Red Sea. He squinted over his tequila and lime, and the two Mohawks merged into one mean-looking Paiute with really bad hair. "Renegade," he greeted his friend.

"Hey, *compadre*. Merry Christmas."

Cole grunted. "Warrior." He tossed back the rest of his shot.

Renegade looked at him quizzically as he climbed onto the stool next to him and ordered a mulled wine.

"Not *compadre*. Warrior."

"Warrior, eh? Soundum like heap bad script to me."

Cole snorted. "This coming from a man who calls himself Renegade." Roman "Renegade" Santangelo was Cole's best friend, right after Tanya. The three of them, along with RaeAnne Sommarby, had been inseparable those years back at Rincon Rez.

The other man chuckled. "Hey, the name Renegade was your idea, remember?" He straightened his leather motorcycle jacket and flicked one of the chains dangling from it. "At least I look the part."

"I'm wearing the anthropologically correct garb for an urban warrior."

"Anthrop—" Renegade squinted at the empty glass in front of Cole. "Jeez, Cole, how many of those have you had?"

"Three. I'm celebrating."

His friend glanced around. "Alone?"

Cole motioned for the bartender to bring him another round. "It's Christmas Eve, I'm thirty-six, about to have a baby, and I'm completely and unequivocally alone." He propped his elbows on the bar and leaned his chin on one hand. "Pathetic, isn't it? How'd you find me?"

The bartender brought the drinks, and Renegade sipped his mulled wine appreciatively. "Called your office. Someone named Charlie said you'd had a run-in with a batch of your mom's cookies. He suggested I try the bars in the area."

"An excellent judge of character," Cole muttered.

"What's this about a baby?"

He sighed and told him the whole, wretched story.

"So let me see if I've got this straight. You fall for this *chica* at the powwow, but she runs away. When you finally find her, she doesn't want to know you, but you've still got it bad. Why does this story sound familiar?"

"We're not talking about you and RaeAnne, here."

Renegade took another sip. "You want the kid?"

"I'm ready for a family, Roman." He sighed. "You know, it's weird. You spend twenty years trying to prevent this from happening, but when it does, all you can think about is how terrific it'll be when you're a father. When you're holding your own kid on your knee. You've got no idea how incredible it is to look at a woman who is big with a child and know it's yours. Your blood. Your body. Your future."

"Whew. Heavy stuff, man. What about the woman?"

Cole squeezed lime into his untouched drink. "What about her?"

"You going to marry her?"

"Nope."

"Because she ran away?"

"Among other things."

"Thanks, pal."

"You had good reasons when you ran away."

Renegade spun his stool to face the crowded room. "So did Rini."

Cole blew out a breath, shaking his head. "So she claims."

"Hmm." Renegade swirled his wine, watching a pair of legs in a green spangled miniskirt saunter by. "This woman of yours, she pretty?"

Cole licked the lime off his fingers and smiled dreamily at his friend's reflection in the mirror. "As a picture. Her eyes are gorgeous—like brilliant blue opals. I call her Fire Eyes. You should have seen her that day at the powwow." He frowned. "On second thought, I'm glad you didn't. Women never could resist your nasty image."

Renegade grinned. "It's the hair. I'm convinced of it."

Surveying the unruly strands of raven black coursing down the man's back—long on top and cropped short on the sides except for a thin braid above one ear—Cole made a disgusted sound. Even at its longest, his own hair had never looked this disreputable.

"If you say so. Man, doesn't the Bureau have rules about weird hair?" Renegade might have looked like an extra for the Road Warrior movies, but he was actually a special agent for the FBI.

"Not as long as I get the job done. So, you don't want this pretty woman who's having your baby?"

Light sparkled like fire off his shot glass as Cole lifted it to his lips. "Oh, I want her, all right. Every damn time I look at her. But I'll deal with it."

Renegade raised an eyebrow. "She want you?"

He laughed. "She wants my head on a platter."

"Sounds like you're going to have yourself an interesting couple of months." He crossed his arms over his leather jacket. "Me, I'm hittin' the road tonight. Got a job up north."

"Why don't you stick around for a day? Have Christmas dinner at my folks' place tomorrow."

An indecipherable look crept into his friend's eyes. "Thanks, but I'd rather get moving. Give your mom a hug for me."

"Still looking for RaeAnne?"

Renegade threw back the rest of his wine and gave Cole a world-weary smile. "I'll find her sooner or later."

"I know you will, *compadre*."

Motorcycle boots hit the floor and Cole felt a warm hand press onto his shoulder. "I hope it works out with the baby and your woman. Do me a favor and give her a second chance. We all deserve one. I'll see you in a few months."

Cole swung his stool around and watched Renegade disappear through the crowd as quickly as he had appeared. The man was a specter, coming and going at the oddest times and places. He was also a romantic fool.

His woman. Ha! No way. Cole would not claim Rini Herelius as his woman. Sure, he might lust after Fire Eyes in a weak moment, but lust was where he drew the line. Clearly and unmistakably. And as for giving her a second chance, well, his friend would just have to understand. He couldn't do it.

He tossed a twenty on the bar and headed for the door.

She was not his woman, and she would not be getting a second chance. And going to some harmless childbirth class with her would not change that one bit.

No sir. Not one little bit.

"Are you out of your everlovin' mind?"

Katarina winced. Alex always did cut right to the chase.

"You're the one who wanted me to be nice to him."

After a call to Dr. Morris just to be sure her spell wasn't something to worry about, Katarina had gone upstairs for a nap. Afterward, she had managed to get through dinner and opening half the Christmas presents without Cole being mentioned. But now she and Alex were in the kitchen washing up, while the boys played with their new toys, and Katarina knew she was in for a grilling.

"Don't remind me. But after the way that despicable man treated you at his office I can't believe you would even speak to him, let alone take a walk with him. What were you thinking of?" Alex's angry tone demanded an explanation.

The familiar pain of wanting to please stabbed through Katarina's chest. She'd grown up with that feeling, always trying so hard to keep from doing or saying anything that would vex Mama. Never being a bother, always doing what would please her—so Mama would love her. The pain was so natural to her, she'd never even noticed when David had started making her feel the same way, always finding fault, never giving support. But, finally, she'd seen what was happening and had begun to heal herself by leaving David and breaking the pattern.

Composing herself, Katarina carefully shook a dash of nutmeg into a glass of eggnog. "He brought me cookies. And I picked the fight at his office, not him."

Alex huffed. "So what changed?"

"I thought it was best to patch things up."

"I see." Her sister slammed the dishwasher door shut and spun the dial. "What did you talk about?"

She stirred her eggnog absently, thinking about Cole. "Oh, this and that. What I'm studying. You know."

"No, I don't know." Alex stood, her arms crossed over her chest. "I don't like the idea of him sniffing around you, Rini. It's some sort of lawyer's trick. I swear—"

Katarina looked up when the words suddenly halted in midstream. The expression on Alex's face could only be described as scandalized. "My God! You think you're still in love with him, don't you?" Her sister's eyes widened. "You're hoping he'll—"

"Love? Don't be ridiculous," Katarina said crankily, staring into her glass to avoid her sister's suspicious gaze. "Besides, he doesn't want any part of me. Except this part." She put a hand on the baby. "Cole told me he was adopted. I imagine that's why he's so adamant about being part of the baby's life, regardless of his feelings for me."

"Oh, Rin." Alex dropped into a chair. "What are you going to do?"

Laughter echoed through the kitchen door from the living room, where Brad and Kenny were engaged in a rowdy new game on the computer. "I'm going to let him."

Her sister set her jaw stubbornly. "Then will you at least make him help you financially? So you can finish your degree?"

Katarina shook her head. "You know I can't ask him for money. Maybe that degree just wasn't meant to be."

"Honey, you've worked too hard to quit now. All those nights you spent studying till dawn, all those weekends in the library. Your dreams! There has to be a way!"

"The baby is what's most important."

"It's just not fair! That bastard." Alex jumped to her feet, banging her fist on the table. "I swear if I ever see him again, I'll kill the man for doing this to you."

Cole squinted at the huge black garbage bag by her door, then looked up at Rini. "Pillows?"

"Um-hmm. For the childbirth class."

Grabbing the bag, he shook his head. "If you say so."

He'd worked hard all week to regain his composure and mental distance from Rini. But in one fell swoop she had his imagination working overtime, trying to figure out just what they'd be doing that involved so damned many pillows. And him with such a healthy imagination.

Taking in her brightly colored leggings and long angora sweater, he decided she looked especially pretty tonight. He opened the Z's door for her and handed her in, then dumped the bag of pillows into the back on his way to the driver's side. "I thought these classes were just supposed to teach you that breathing stuff. You know, ha ha, he he, ho ho ho."

She rolled her eyes. "I think you're mixing them up with Santa Claus classes. Must be the season. So, how was the rest of your holiday?"

He flashed her a wry smile. "Good."

Except for a slight hangover Christmas morning. He couldn't remember the last time he'd drunk more than two beers at a sitting, and those straight tequilas had wreaked havoc on his stomach and head. "Had dinner with my parents. My mom sends her regards."

She smiled wistfully. "You're lucky."

He darted her a suspicious look. "How so?"

"My mother... Well, your mom sounds really nice."

"I take it you don't get along with yours."

She shook her head. "Between Alex and me, we talk to Mama three, maybe four times a year. I can just imagine what she'll have to say when I tell her I'm pregnant."

"You haven't told her?" He couldn't hide his surprise.

She sighed. "I can do without the lecture she's sure to give me. She doesn't think much of my ability to make choices, and this will just confirm what she's always told me."

"And what's that?"

Rini bit her lip and looked away. "Wouldn't want to bore you with the litany. Like I said, she doesn't think much of my abilities. And she's sure to resent the thought of being a grandmother. She's still in denial over having two daughters who've hit thirty."

Cole was shocked. He thought about having a mother like that—one who made her own daughter afraid to tell her she was having a baby in less than two months. He couldn't imagine it.

He glanced over. That might explain the shy, almost disbelieving pleasure Rini'd showed whenever he had complimented her. He had to remind himself to do it more often. Her mother must be blind. Certainly, what he'd experienced of Rini's abilities had warranted compliments, and more.

Especially the physical ones. Even now, he continued to be plagued by the memory of her silken body under his, moving expertly to the rhythm he'd played on it. What he wouldn't give to be able to experience those particular skills again.

But that would complicate things. And the situation was already much too complicated for his liking.

He brought his wayward thoughts back to the conversation. "Well, someday I'm sure your mother will realize what she's missing, and regret it."

Rini shrugged noncommittally. "Maybe. I'm just glad Alex and I have each other." She pointed to a large private home coming up on the left. "Here we are. This is the house."

When Cole followed Rini into the family room where the Bradley Method childbirth class would be held, silence fell around him like he was a prisoner taking his last walk down death row. The only sound was the cracking and popping of a fire burning in the corner fireplace. It sounded ominously like a firing squad.

Drawing in a deep breath, he ignored the guarded stares of the couples scattered around on the floor, and plastered what he hoped was a pleasant expression on his face.

Rini addressed the group. "Everyone, this is Cole, my baby's father."

Judging by their expressions, he was definitely a condemned man. "Hi." He glanced around. No change. The four men glared at him suspiciously and their women looked plain angry. One woman sitting by herself in front of the room—presumably the instructor—gave every indication she was about to go into cardiac arrest. Damn, this was going to be a fun evening.

Rini led him to the closet, where they hung up their coats. She motioned for him to remove his boots and put them next to her shoes.

"Sorry," she murmured. "The others might be a little hostile. Alex may have mentioned you once or twice. She tends to be a bit—" she lifted her gaze apologetically "—dramatic."

He turned a lopsided grin on her. "No problem. I'll just be my natural, sweet self and win 'em over in no time."

She actually snorted. He had the irrational urge to pinch her butt in retaliation as she turned to look for a space on the floor where they could sit. He jammed his thumbs into his jeans pockets. Jeez, he had to control these primitive impulses.

Baring his teeth in the smile he always used for judges about to ream him out for a courtroom transgression, he helped Rini to sit, then squatted down beside her.

She leaned over and whispered, "Relax, Lonetree. It's not a lynch mob."

"Tell them that." His cheek muscles already hurt from holding his smile in place.

"Pretend you like me. I know it's a stretch, but it could help your case."

He glanced over at her as he settled onto the floor Indian style. She was serious. He supposed he had been trying so hard to keep his distance that she might really think he didn't like her. *If only she knew.*

He slid a hand onto her thigh and winked. "All right."

Her eyes grew wide, fastening first on his hand, then his grin. A soft flush crept up her neck. He knew instantly the move had been a mistake. Her flesh was warm and firm under her thin leggings, and his hand was suddenly seized with a will of its own. In a barely discernible movement, his thumb began kneading the slight hollow just above her knee.

He watched her tongue peek out and moisten her upper lip, then retreat hastily.

A *big* mistake.

Aw, hell.

He suddenly realized the instructor was speaking to him. A few of the others chuckled knowingly. "Uh, sorry, what?"

"I'm Linda. We're glad you could make it, Cole. Have you been doing any of the reading?" Her blood pressure appeared to have come down considerably since his unexpected entrance.

He glanced at Rini. "Uh, no. Didn't realize—"

"That's okay. Just follow along as best you can. The method is fairly simple. The role of the father is mostly to encourage the mother and make her comfortable. We'll start out with a little theory and then move on to the relaxation exercises."

Linda went on to explain, with charts, exactly what happened during the three stages of labor. Cole was fascinated, and when the lecture was over he found himself thigh-to-thigh with Rini, his arm nestled familiarly between her leg and the baby. His other hand had crossed over his lap to continue rubbing her knee.

He closed his eyes, instincts warring with common sense. It was one thing to create an illusion for the benefit of the other couples, quite another to relax into the role. On the other hand, it wouldn't do to pull back now and spoil the effect. Not just because he was breaking out in a sweat.

"Remember, the very worst part of labor is that ten to twenty minute transition between getting your body ready to deliver and actually starting to push. If you can make it through those few minutes without any anesthesia, the pushing part will be much easier because you won't have all those drugs numbing your muscles."

Cole looked at Rini, not envying her the coming experience

one bit. Still, he'd really like to be there. He wondered if she would mind.

"And dads, be sure to check the time when transition starts, so you can help her through it. Okay, once more, when do you look at the clock?"

"When she starts swearing and calling us names," the men chanted in unison, snickering.

Linda grinned. "Right. Or she says she's changed her mind and doesn't want kids." She looked at her watch. "Okay, every-one, break time!"

The couples rose and stretched, then wandered over to a table that held a couple carafes of juice and some plates of healthy-looking snack squares. He grimaced. Not a cup of coffee in sight. Sighing, he filled two cups with pink stuff he was sure would prove lethal, and stepped over to where Rini stood con-versing with a couple of the women. He offered her one of the cups.

"Thanks. Cole, this is Valerie and Liz."

They exchanged greetings. Valerie looked vaguely intrigued, but Liz seemed resentful of his presence.

"So, are you two an item now?" Valerie tipped her head curiously.

Cole glanced at Rini. "Um, we're still working things through."

Liz sneered. "Just like a man. Refusing to take responsibil-ity."

Cole set his jaw. "I—"

Rini jumped in. "Not at all. He's being very helpful." She looked at him pleadingly.

He forced the corners of his mouth up. He didn't want to make trouble for Rini, so he said, "We both want what's best for the baby."

"I'll just bet." Liz rolled her eyes.

His temper flared. "What's—"

"Cole, I'm feeling a little hungry." Rini looped her arm around his elbow and tugged. "Let's check out those granola squares, okay? Excuse us." She pulled him forcibly toward the snack table. "Sorry about that," she muttered, snagging the first food item she laid a hand on.

"What was her problem?" he demanded around a piece of frosted carrot bar, which Rini stuffed into his mouth as soon as he opened it. He chewed, swallowed and, with his tongue, worked loose a walnut that had jammed between two teeth. "Attacking me like that—"

"I thought you Native Americans were supposed to be all stoic and harmonious." Scowling, she crammed another bite between his lips, but this time he caught her wrist in his hand and held it.

"Only after we've tied the person annoying us to an anthill and poured honey over her." He flicked his tongue out and licked a spot of frosting off Rini's forefinger before dropping her hand.

Then silently cursed himself. Hell, he was getting into dangerous territory again.

But there was just something about having a woman feed him that turned him on in the worst way. Resolutely, he slugged down the dregs of his pink stuff. He almost choked on it when Rini put the remainder of the carrot bar into her mouth, forefinger and all, and licked the remaining crumbs off the moisture he had left there with his own tongue.

His expression must have given him away, because she suddenly looked at her forefinger, blushed furiously, and snatched up a napkin from the table to finish the job.

Mercifully, she hurriedly excused herself to use the rest room, so he had a chance to regain his self-possession. Between the hostile natives and the guilelessly sensual mother of his child, if he made it through the evening without some kind of major screwup it would be a pure damned miracle.

It was when she climbed into his lap a few minutes later that he knew with dead certainty no miracle would be forthcoming anytime soon.

"Relaxation," Linda the instructor called it.

Torture was the term he'd use.

He was supposed to sit on the floor with Rini encircled by his legs, her knees resting against his, her back to him. Her body pressed up so close to his there wasn't even enough space between them for an illusion.

Linda had turned out all the lamps, so the only light came from the crackling fire and the moonlight pouring in from outside. She spoke softly. "Let's start out by feeling where the baby is. Rini, you'll have to show Cole how to do this."

He felt Rini draw in a breath, hesitating. Then she gently guided his hands to her stomach, and, whispering what he was feeling, traced over the baby with his fingers.

Her angora sweater was downy soft under his fingertips, the baby warm and round. Unbelievably, he could feel his son's head, and his bottom, and a plump arm and fist that shifted to keep up with his touch when Cole's hand would have moved on. His throat closed around a lump, and for a moment he was sure he would lose it completely.

Oh, God.

Rini let her head fall back against his shoulder, and relaxed against him while he fought the watermelon in his throat and stroked his son's arm.

He was barely aware of Linda's voice quietly telling the couples to visualize the baby beneath their hands, that they should remember this moment when things got rough during delivery. That this was why they were going through the whole birth ordeal—to be able to sit like this afterward, with their baby in their arms. Cole stared up at the firelight shadows flickering on the ceiling, wishing the moment would never end.

When it did, and Linda instructed the dads to get the pillows for the next exercise, he was able to meet the quiet smiles of acknowledgment from the other men. Affirmations of the emotional experience they had shared, of the love they were feeling. A love for the families they were all becoming.

As he dragged the bag of pillows over to her, Cole thought about Rini and where she fit into his equation of family. Would it be possible to be on the best of terms with her after he had made it clear he wouldn't, couldn't, include her in that equation on more than a superficial level?

Truth be told, right at the moment he didn't much feel like excluding her at all. His lap and chest were still warm from her body heat; his arms still carried the memory of her within their embrace. And he realized, to his sorrow if not exactly his surprise, that he liked her. He liked her a lot. He liked her quiet determination, her serenity in adversity, her little flares of temper, her affectionate nature.

He watched her arrange the pillows in a line on the floor and then lie down on her side next to them, bending her top arm and leg over their soft bulk. It was as close to being on her stomach as a more-than-seven-months-pregnant woman could manage. She turned her head and looked up at him, smiling. Her eyes sparkled in the dim light, and his heart almost broke.

This was his Fire Eyes. The woman he'd gladly lie down with and spend the rest of his life loving. How could this woman and that other woman—the one who'd heartlessly abandoned him and thought about doing the same to their child—be one and the same?

Sadly, he returned her smile, then followed Linda's instructions and took his place behind her. His head shot up at the teacher's next word.

Massage.

He was expected to give Rini a back rub. He felt his wits slip precariously. It had been bad enough running his hands over her stomach. But at least he'd had the baby to concentrate on. Now there would be nothing but Rini under his hands.

This was not at all what he'd expected from a childbirth class. He remembered countless TV sitcoms depicting the crazy antics of hyperventilating expectant couples.

Linda effectively quashed that image, firmly declaring that Bradley moms did not breathe, they relaxed. She next instructed everyone to visualize the cresting waves of a beautiful ocean and to imagine the waves as contractions. The moms were supposed to float over the pain on a visual cushion of conscious relaxation. *Yeah, right.* His own role in that process would be to watch for and alert Rini to signs of tension, to massage her aching muscles in between contractions and to whisper loving words of encouragement when she didn't think she could go on.

Sounded simple enough. Until he laid his hands on her and drew a long, shuddering sigh from deep inside her. *Aw, hell.*

How could a red-blooded man possibly resist a reaction like that to his touch? It brought to mind the time she'd had an even more potent reaction to him—the first time he'd thrust himself deep inside her. The memory of her sweet physical disintegration coursed through his blood and heated him as nothing else could have.

He gently brushed her hair over her shoulder and leaned into his sensual task. While Linda timed simulated contractions, Rini visualized relaxing through them. In between, Cole's hands found the sensitive muscles in her back and sides, and his mouth murmured words meant to soothe and reassure. Words that, in his present mood, quickly took on an erotic edge.

Her body warmed under his hands, and a light flush settled on her cheeks. Rather than slow, her heartbeat picked up, the pulse in her graceful neck throbbing erratically. He felt her body arch imperceptibly under his fingers, and a breathless sound came from her throat. Her eyes flew open for a second and she frowned, no doubt reminding herself to concentrate on the exercise.

He took it as a delicious challenge to break down her resolve not to surrender to the magic of his fingers. It didn't take long to melt her resistance into soft moans of pleasure.

God, he wanted her.

Chapter 8

Rini couldn't bring herself to look at Cole during the ride back home. Her body was on fire. Her mind was horrified. How could she have let this happen? Honest to God, she'd tried to resist him. She'd done everything possible to ignore his sensual caresses, to concentrate on imaginary contractions. But he'd seemed to know exactly where and how to touch her to make her completely forget it was just an exercise.

Every nerve ending still hummed. She glanced down at her breasts—their peaks tight knots of longing at the vivid memory of how good his hands felt on her—wishing those hands would touch her there. Her body shivered in frustration.

"Cold?" Cole glanced over at her from behind the wheel, his gaze guarded. "I can turn up the heat."

She nearly choked. *No argument there.* "No. I'm plenty warm enough, thanks." But she was just plain dreaming if she thought he had any interest in her beyond the physical. His carefully neutral expression spoke volumes. She sighed. It was just as well. Any attraction to Cole was undoubtedly just her heart grasping at a last, desperate straw—hoping there was some way she could have this baby without sacrificing both his and her own futures in the process. But her future wasn't going to be with Cole, and she knew it.

Even if she did believe his story about the women at the powwow, she still didn't want a man who didn't even pretend to love her holding her life in his hands. But right now she wasn't totally convinced she didn't want him holding her body in them.

Cole pulled into the driveway. She struggled out of the car, its low-slung lines reminiscent of the bottomless easy chair in Alex's living room. Gratefully, Rini accepted his helping hand when he came around.

"I'll bring in the pillows."

"Thanks." She put a hand to her back and stretched her spine. She had to admit, Cole's massage had felt heavenly even on a purely therapeutic level. Her muscles felt more relaxed now than they had in ages. "And thanks for the back rub. It was wonderful."

His grin was suddenly wicked. "My pleasure."

Fumbling for the keys in her purse, she felt her cheeks grow warm.

He hoisted the giant bag of pillows and followed her to the stairs leading to her garage apartment. "I'll take them up for you."

She hesitated, glancing up the stairs. She wasn't sure she wanted Cole up there, even for a moment. The image of him standing in her private space, perhaps wandering around, touching her personal things...well, it was just too intimate. Once that image was branded into her brain, it would be impossible to get rid of.

"Key?"

On the other hand, the thought of hauling the huge bag of pillows up those stairs didn't appeal to her, either. Reluctantly, she handed him her keys and trailed after him, hanging well back. She just wouldn't go in. That way she wouldn't see him in there. That would work.

When she made it to the open door at the top of the landing, she couldn't help herself. She peeked. He was inside the one-room apartment, leaning casually against her bedpost and looking hopelessly sexy in his simple white T-shirt, his thumbs stuck in the pockets of his snug jeans. His gaze sought out her hands as they unconsciously supported her lower back, kneading the muscles with her fingertips.

He jerked his chin at her. "You having back problems?"

Instinctively, she yanked her hands away from her back. "Um. Yeah. Just a little. Something to do with being pregnant, the doctor tells me." She smiled wryly.

His answering smile was warm. Almost sultry. He stretched out a hand to her. "Come here. I'll finish the massage. We hardly got started before it was time to go."

She took a step back, bumping into a baluster. "I don't think…" Immediately, she regretted her choice of words. She half expected him to murmur "Don't think. Just feel"—the fateful words that had started this whole thing nearly eight months ago. "That wouldn't be a very good idea."

He pushed off the bedpost and came toward her, then halted. His eyes darkened to black, reflecting some inner struggle. Suddenly, his expression changed, falling back into the studied neutral it had been in the car. "No. I don't suppose it would."

She bit back a stab of disappointment, telling herself this was the way she wanted it. The way it had to be. "Thank you for coming tonight."

He touched the front of his T-shirt in that seeking gesture he occasionally made. "I enjoyed the class," he said. "Not what I expected, that's for sure."

"I'm sorry about Valerie and Liz."

"Don't worry about it. I think I won them over by the end of class."

Looking away, she ran her hand along the railing. "They weren't the only ones," she said softly.

He narrowed his gaze on her, and she could feel the wariness in it, but he remained silent. His eyes fell to the baby in her belly. He stepped closer and reached a tentative hand toward her cheek, but pulled it back before he touched her. "I want to help you any way I can. I'll pay for—"

She shook her head. "No. I'll manage."

Sighing, he drew her into the room, into his arms. "I don't

want you to just manage.'' He tipped up her chin to look into her eyes. "I want to help. This is my baby, too, Rini.''

Their lips met before she realized he was going to kiss her. His mouth was soft and warm and gently persuasive. She found herself melting into his embrace, reveling in the strength and comfort she felt there. *If only she could let her guard down and allow herself to lean on him.*

He angled his mouth over hers, easing her head to his shoulder as he kissed her. His body snugged up to the side of her stomach, enveloping her in his heat.

Even as her traitorous body surrendered, her mind protested. *Why was he doing this?*

Could it be…perhaps he…? His hand moved over her breast and she shivered at his sensual touch.

No! This was madness. She had made this same mistake—letting herself be swept away by the sheer virility of this man—one too many times. Kissing him would solve nothing. As tempting as it was, getting physically involved with Colton Lonetree would just be inviting trouble.

She *couldn't* do this to herself again.

"Cole, stop,'' she whispered. She needed time to think!

"Oh, honey, I want you so much.'' He covered her mouth with his once again, murmuring, "Please don't tell me no.''

Suddenly, footsteps pounded to the top of the stairs and Alex's voice sang out, "Rini, do you want to…oops.''

In a haze of desire and confusion, Katarina sought the source of the disturbance and saw Alex halt in the doorway. She glanced uncertainly at Cole.

"I was just leaving,'' he mumbled, and before Katarina knew what was happening, he'd dropped her arms and moved stiffly past Alex onto the landing. He gave her a rueful look. "Rini, call me. We need to talk.''

Coming slowly to her senses, she shook her head. "No. I don't think so.''

He halted. "What are you saying?''

"It would be better if we didn't see each other again until after the baby's born.'' Better to have a clean break and be done with it. "I'll be pretty busy until then.''

He frowned, his expression stormy. "I don't agree, Rini," he said firmly. "I'm going to call."

With that he was down the stairs faster than she could catch her breath.

"Sorry, Rin."

A sigh caught in Katarina's throat. "Don't be. I think you just saved me from myself." Unconsciously, she lifted a finger to her lips and touched them. Realizing what she was doing, she jerked her hand away.

Unconditional love and understanding shone in her sister's eyes. "Forget him. You don't need him, Rini."

"I'm just so afraid." Afraid of what was happening to her life. More afraid of the tempestuous feelings surfacing in her for the man who was the cause of it all.

"I know, hon."

"I don't think I can do this."

"You can do it. You have me, Sis. And Brad and Kenny. You'll always have us."

Katarina went into her sister's arms, wishing like hell they were Cole's instead. Hating herself for wishing for the impossible.

"I love you, Al."

"I love you, too, Rin."

"So what are you going to do?"

Cole paced in front of Tanya, who sat in his living room armchair watching him wear tracks in his already threadbare rug. He clamped his teeth together, trying in vain not to drown in the deluge of guilt and frustration that flooded over him.

"I don't know, T. But she has no real way to support herself after she has the baby, and she can't finish school if she's taking care of him all day. What kind of a jerk would I be if I didn't help her out?"

"What brought all this on?"

"Guilt." He let out a humorless laugh. "I kissed her."

"Well, no wonder she's not speaking to you."

"Very funny, T." He stopped pacing and jammed his hands in his pockets. He looked plaintively at his cousin. "I want my son, Tanya. I don't want to lose him because I messed up and pushed myself on her.''

She put out her hand and grasped his arm. "I'm certain Rini won't keep you from seeing him once he's born."

"How can you be so damned sure?"

"Your parental rights."

"Yeah, okay. But I want to see her now."

Tanya's brow lifted. "Why?"

He scowled. "Hell if I know."

"Does this mean you're giving her another chance?"

"Another chance for what?" His stomach clenched involuntarily. "To run off and abandon me again?"

"She hardly abandoned you at the powwow, Cole. You'd barely met." His cousin sighed. "It always comes back to that same old fear, doesn't it?"

He tried to shake off the familiar, automatic physical reaction snaking its way around his guts. "Yes, it does," he said belligerently. "And for good reason."

"You know, not all women are like your ex-wife Lindsay and your biological mother. Maybe Rini's different."

He shook his head. "She's already proved she isn't."

"And probably regrets it. Give her a chance, Cole."

He let his worst fears percolate to the surface of his mind. "That's the whole point. If I give her another chance, how long will it take before she regrets taking it? A week? A month? A year?"

"Surely, she wouldn't. She knows the baby needs a father—"

He threw up his hands. "So, what if she decides she doesn't want *me* as the father? She could go back to that David character. After all, she was with him for ages. I was only worth a night—"

"Oh, for crying out loud, Cole—"

"What would happen to my parental rights then?"

Tanya let out an exasperated breath. "How the hell should I know? You're the lawyer!"

He frowned, playing out the scenario in his head. "Some rich white guy...even if he didn't have a leg to stand on, he could make it impossible for me to see my son."

"Oh, boy, you really are going off the deep end now. The woman has already acknowledged you're the baby's father! What more do you need?"

Crossing to the window, he looked out, leaning his hands on the cold, wooden frame. Outside, the bleak January sky threatened rain. His lawn needed some rain, he thought absently, and sighed. Too bad it wasn't as simple to figure out what Colton Lonetree needed.

First and foremost, he needed to know that access to his baby son was safe and secure. But what of his heart? What would he do with this need for a woman of whom he was so unsure? This burning, passionate need for one who had already shown herself capable of leaving him without a goodbye or second thought?

Tonight at the childbirth class they had felt so good together.... Were Tanya and Renegade both right? Did Rini deserve another chance? Was it possible they could...

So, why wouldn't she take his calls?

Lord spare him from women who were as fickle as the California winter.

Turning, he looked at his cousin, who watched his inner struggle from across the room. "What more do I need? I need to be sure, *nuyukssum.*"

"That's not always possible, my cousin."

He swallowed, making up his mind. He'd undoubtedly regret it—curse the day the idea ever came to him. "There's one way."

"And what would that be?"

"A prenuptial agreement."

Tanya snorted. "Don't be silly. A prenuptial agreement implies nuptials."

Cole straightened. "I guess it does."

Tanya jumped up. "Cole! Are you serious?" Letting out a whoop, she ran to him and grabbed his hands, swinging him around in a circle. "I knew it! I knew you were meant for each other! But what happened to Doubting Cole?" She held up both hands. "No, don't answer—I don't want to know. You won't regret this decision, you'll see."

He grinned reluctantly, her exuberance contagious. "I'm already regretting it."

But the truth was, for the first time in nearly eight months he looked forward to facing his future.

Now if he could just convince Rini to share it.

Cole stared morosely at the telephone on his desk. Marriage proposal by proxy was not exactly his idea of romance, but Rini didn't leave him much choice.

He'd phoned. He'd tried repeatedly to see her. But Alex and Brad had screened her calls and had seen to it that he never got past the front door.

Flowers hadn't worked, either. He'd sent a huge bouquet of yellow roses. He'd tried a single white bud the next day, and old damask and baby's breath the day after that. Each time, the card was left unopened in the empty box and sent back with the delivery person. Every day for over a week he'd sent flowers and a card with the simple inscription, "Marry me." She still hadn't opened one.

Well, at least she'd kept the flowers. That gave him some reason to hope. But how the hell was he supposed to propose to the damned woman if he could never get her attention? Scowling, he picked up the phone. After dialing Henderson's number, he heard Pam's voice announcing he'd reached the offices of Linder, Adams and Henderson.

Cole hung up. *No.* They'd already had a rocky start, and this would only make things worse. Surely there must be a way he could get her alone for two minutes to pop the question in person.

He'd have to catch her when she was away from the house. He thought for a moment, then picked up the phone again and dialed.

Taking a seat under the window, Cole patted his jacket pocket, checking the small square box for the hundredth time in less than an hour. In his fist he clutched the stem of a lone fragrant gardenia—a last-minute inspiration.

Willing himself to relax, he leaned his head back against the hard wall of Dr. Morris's examination room and ran his fingers

down the smooth silk of his tie, calming himself with its soothing texture. The next fifteen minutes were likely to test him as
no jury had ever done. He'd managed to gain the good doctor's
help in his scheme by confessing what he planned to do, and by
paying an extra hour's worth of her fee for uninterrupted use of
the room. Dr. Morris never claimed to be a romantic.

Last minute panic crawled up his spine as he sat contemplating what he was about to do. What the hell was he thinking of?
This was exactly what he had sought to avoid by trying to keep
Rini at arm's length throughout this whole ordeal. Now he was
as good as inviting her into his heart. Giving her free rein to fill
it with her sweet love and caresses and then abandon it when
she got tired of him.

No. That wouldn't happen this time. Couldn't. He'd be careful. Very careful. He'd treat this marriage as a business proposition, tucking his heart so far away she'd never be able to reach
it to break. Until he could be absolutely sure she wouldn't—if
ever.

Meanwhile, he'd have the prenuptial agreement to ensure his
place in his son's life. That's what was important here. To make
sure his family was safe. Not his heart, but his fragile new family.

The soft tread of footsteps sounded outside on the hall carpet,
halting at the door. His heart raced. He looked at his watch.
Hell. Leave it to Rini to be five minutes early.

The door opened and she walked in, catching sight of him
immediately. He shot to his feet. Her jaw dropped. The nurse
mumbled something about taking their time, and then backed
out.

Rini looked shaken. "How did you get in here?"

"It was a setup." He shrugged. "What can I say? I needed
to see you."

"I don't want to see you." She turned and reached for the
knob.

"Rini, wait!" He sprang in front of her and blockaded the
doorway. "Hear me out. Please. Then if you want me to leave,
I will."

She crossed her arms over her belly and gazed resignedly at the door behind him. "It appears I have little choice."

Nervously, he skimmed a hand down his tie. "Why don't you have a seat?"

She gave her head a little shake, looking as though she'd rather be anywhere but there.

Discovering the flower gripped between his fingers, he stared at it for a second, then remembered he was supposed to give it to her. "Uh, this is for you."

She let the blossom hang between them a moment before accepting it. "Thank you." A blush crept into her cheeks and she looked away. "Gardenias are my favorite."

He stepped closer. "I remembered your perfume. I was hoping…" He swallowed and realigned his tie, feeling the buttons of his starched white shirt scrape along the back of his knuckles. "Anyway, I have something else for you, too. If you'll accept it." Fishing the tiny box out of his pocket, he trailed a finger along the velvet nap, then stuck it out at her.

Her eyes lowered, then narrowed on the box. Her head made a slight waver, and she bit her lower lip. She looked up at him, disbelief in her expression, and shook her head.

"Take it. Please." His voice was raw, his tongue thick in his mouth.

Slowly, she held out a trembling hand and he placed the box in it. Wrestling for a moment with the spring-loaded top, she set aside the flower and was finally able to lift the lid. He watched her eyes fill before she dragged them away from the ring inside and met his.

"It's beautiful," she whispered.

"Marry me, Rini."

She stared at him, her soulful fire eyes shining from twin pools of sparkling tears. "I don't understand."

He took the ring from the box and held her hand in his, slipping the gold-and-diamond band onto her finger. "Marry me, Rini. I'd like you to be my wife."

She looked for a long time at the ring on her finger. Suddenly, he was afraid she didn't like it. He did, but the style was a little different. Maybe she liked something more traditional. Or bigger. Or—

"Why?"

He was snapped out of his anxiety over the ring by her timorous question. "What?"

"Why?" she repeated, her voice a shade less timid. Her eyes shone big as saucers when she looked up at him. A tear broke loose of its mooring on her lower lashes and trailed down her cheek. She brushed it aside. "Why would you like me to be your wife?"

"Why?" His stomach did a free fall. "Because…" She was going to turn him down! He couldn't believe it. He fought renewed panic. This was insane. "Because of the baby, of course. The baby needs a father. He needs two parents."

Cole let her hand go and paced a few steps back and forth. He had to convince her! "And you, you need someone to provide for you so you can look after him. Someone who can take care of him while you're in school." He raised his palms in an appeal, playing his trump card. "So you can get your nursing degree, like you've always dreamed of."

As he spoke, her gaze came to rest on the ring again. If anything, she looked sadder. *What was wrong with her?* Was the thought of marrying him that awful?

"Rini?"

"And what about you? What does Colton Lonetree get out of this?"

He gaped at her, not knowing what to say. "Me?" He had to tell her about the agreement he would insist on. But somehow he knew that was not what she wanted to hear right now. What could he say? The truth? He cleared his throat. "A family. I'd be getting a family."

She nodded slowly, her gaze seeming to penetrate his innermost thoughts. Unconsciously crushing the end of his tie, he prayed he didn't look as guilty as he felt.

"What else?" She tilted her head. "What is it you're not saying?"

He pushed out a breath. She could read him like a motion to

discover. "I'd like you to sign a prenup saying that if you leave me I get custody of the baby."

"I see." Her gaze shuttered. "But only if *I* leave?"

He nodded.

She closed her eyes and considered for a couple of moments. "What if you…mistreat me?"

"Rini! I'd—"

She held up a hand. "I know. I know. You'd never hurt me." She didn't sound completely convinced, though. "Joint custody if I leave," she said firmly. "And Henderson writes it up."

Cole approached her and took her hands in his. "Does this mean you accept?" Pulling her closer, he leaned in for a kiss.

She turned her head, so his lips brushed her cheek. "Would I be required to share your bed?"

He jerked away, stunned as if by a physical blow. He stood in disbelief, watching her twist the ring round and round on her finger. He cleared his throat again. "I believe it's customary these days for a husband and wife to share a bed."

She shot him a level look. "It's also customary these days for a husband to be in love with his bride."

He shoved a hand through his hair. So that's what all this was about. Why did that have to matter to her so much? "I'm willing to take care of you, to give you and our baby a home and my name, to respect you and be faithful to you. What more do you want from me?"

Her chin went up a notch.

Hurt and anger twisted in his gut. "You made love with me when you didn't even know my name! But you won't share my bed when we're man and wife? Does that make any sense?"

"So, it is a requirement."

"Hell, no!" He clamped down on his temper. "No, of course not. I'm just…just a little surprised, that's all, considering…"

She started to take off his ring. "I understand if you want to take back your offer—"

"No!" He laid his hand over hers, thinking furiously. "The offer stands. We can make this strictly a business arrangement if it's what you'd prefer. I can live with that."

He'd just been telling himself that very thing not half an hour ago, hadn't he?

This would work fine. Regardless of his wounded pride, the fact was it was probably the best thing that could have happened. It would keep him from getting too attached to her, so when she left...

She regarded him seriously. "Are you sure this is what you want?"

"I'm sure."

"Okay, Cole. You and Henderson draw up the papers." She walked to the window and looked out. "Have him call me."

"How soon can you be ready to move?"

She spun to face him, her surprise evident. "You mean right away?"

"You've only got a few weeks to go. I want you settled into my house well before the baby comes."

He saw the flash of consternation in her eyes before she was able to cover it with a carefully unconcerned expression. "I don't have much to pack. I can be ready anytime you say."

He made a show of consulting his pocket calendar, suddenly needing to show her just how little her sexual rejection meant to him. "It'll take a couple of days to get the license and such. I have a hearing on Thursday. How about Friday?"

She laid a hand casually on the exam table, but it trembled against the white sheet. She snatched it back and stuck it under her arm. "To get married or move?"

"Both. That way we'll have the whole weekend to get to know each other." He tossed her a challenging look and hid a smile when that chin came up again. Sure, he'd go along with this business arrangement. But he was, after all, a man.

"Fine by me. Friday it is."

Chapter 9

Cole grabbed the mail from the box by the driveway and bounded into the house, thinking about what he would wear to his wedding tomorrow. Tossing his briefcase on the floor by his easy chair, he went through the mail. Bills mostly, but one looked personal, judging by the hand-addressed envelope. Settling into his favorite chair, he opened it. Carefully printed in pencil on standard-issue lined paper ripped from a notebook, it read,

Dear Mr. Lonetree,
My name is Jeff and I'm fourteen. I'm adopted. The agency told me Lindsay Walker is my real mom, but she didn't write down who my father is. I looked up her records and saw you guys were married the year before I was born, but I called her and she said you are not my father. But I'm hoping you might know who he is. Specially since your Indian. They say I look like one too. I don't want to butt in or be a bother or nothin, but I kinda want to find out

where my roots are at, like what tribe and all. And my
father. If you care to tell me please call.

                                                                    Jeff

There was a phone number at the bottom.

Jeezus! Poor kid. Damn Lindsay's hide. Cole swiped a hand
over his face. He somehow wasn't the least bit surprised she'd
gotten pregnant and then abandoned the child. *As she had him.*

Looking at the letter in his hand, he thanked his lucky stars
he had been thwarted in his youthful desire for the little tease.
Things might be a bit complicated now if there were any chance
this boy was his. But there wasn't. There wasn't a single doubt
about that.

Between the long drive and the effects of the bottle of champagne after—and before and during—the ceremony in Vegas
sixteen years ago, he and his ex-wife, Lindsay, had never gotten
around to making love the night they were married. And after
they'd gotten home, well, her daddy made sure they didn't spend
even a second alone together.

Not that her father's objections would have stopped Lindsay
if she'd had her heart set on sleeping with Cole, but by the time
they had arrived home, she had lost interest in him, and they
were soon divorced.

He shook his head. He had transferred to a distant college
shortly after the fiasco and then hadn't seen Lindsay for several
years. He hadn't even known she'd had a baby. It figured she
hadn't kept her son. Cole's heart swelled in sympathy for this
lost bird seeking his way back to the nest, and resolved to do
what he could to make the journey a little easier for him.

Leaning back against his leather chair, he stacked his hands
under his head. He remembered all too well what it was like to
go through the agony of trying to find out who he really was.
Endless red tape at the adoption agency, then that first heart-
pounding contact when you were so vulnerable you thought
you'd curl up and die if they said they didn't want to know you.

He'd like to give Lindsay a piece of his mind. What was she
doing to help her child? Not much, apparently, since Jeff had

written to him. Couldn't she even spare a moment to tell the kid who his father was?

He refolded the letter and headed for the kitchen. He wasn't about to get in touch with Lindsay. Not with his wedding the next day. If Lindsay caught wind of it, there was no telling what she'd do. No. He'd call Jeff and offer to help and pray his ex-wife left him the hell alone.

Katarina's eyes sprang open and she stared straight up for a moment in abject panic. It was Friday.

Her wedding day.

"What have I done?" she whispered to the ceiling. "Marrying a man who doesn't love me? The one thing I swore I'd never do!"

Outside, the sky streamed with sunshine and the birds were making a joyful racket in the mulberry tree. What did they know, anyway?

Across the driveway, through Alex's open kitchen window, she could hear cupboards banging over the hum of an electric mixer. Katarina squeezed her eyes shut. Alex didn't approve of the marriage, but was determined that a feast be provided for the handful of witnesses to the civil ceremony later that afternoon.

Later that afternoon. Groaning, Katarina pulled the quilt over her head. She dreaded the whole thing—suffering through Alex's disapproving looks, putting on a dowdy maternity dress to stand in front of a sour-faced judge with a condemning attitude who would stare at her belly while reciting hollow words of love and honor. Meeting Cole's family, being forced to smile and make chitchat when all she'd be able to think of was the coming night...

A night that should be spent in the arms of her beloved, making memories that would last a lifetime. A night that she'd instead be spending alone, dreaming of the father of her baby. Her husband. The man who didn't love her.

The man she was afraid to admit she was falling in love with.

Taking a deep breath, she flung aside the quilt. This was getting her nowhere. There was nothing to do about it. She'd made her bed and now she must lie in it. Determinedly, she sat up. There were things to do. She'd deliberately left her packing until this morning, so she wouldn't have to think about the coming ordeal. And it was nearly nine. Alex had let her sleep away the whole morning.

Katarina showered and dressed, then packed her few belongings in a cardboard box and two suitcases she'd borrowed from her sister, leaving out the pastel flowered dress she'd wear to the ceremony. She chose it because it resembled the little calico sundress she'd worn to the powwow, a lifetime ago. Not that it would make a difference to Cole. Sundresses didn't inspire love.

Packing took all of half an hour. She eyed her bed dubiously. The one thing of substance she owned, it had accompanied her since childhood from her parents' home to college after her dad died, then to her apartment when she'd moved to L.A. from Philadelphia to be closer to Alex. It had been in a guest room after she'd moved in with David, and now she was destined to follow its lead—residing in a guest room in the home of her own husband.

It needed to be broken down for transport to Cole's house, but she wasn't sure she could manage it on her own. She fetched a socket wrench and screwdriver and spent the next fifteen minutes wrestling with the mattress and box springs before throwing in the towel and phoning Alex.

A few minutes later, her sister appeared in the doorway, arms crossed. She glanced around Katarina's room, taking in the suitcases and cardboard box. "So, you're really going through with this crazy scheme."

She sighed. "It's not crazy. It's what I want."

Alex's face fell. "For God's sake, he doesn't even love you!"

Katarina flinched. "Look, I know it's not ideal, but what in life is? I'd give anything to be marrying a man who is head over heels in love with me, but that's one dream that doesn't seem to be in my cards."

She motioned to Alex to help her move the mattress against the wall. "There are more important things to consider now than my own happiness. I have to think about the baby. About having a roof over his head and food in his mouth. Cole's even letting me finish school. He's being unbelievably generous, even if he doesn't love me."

Alex snorted with wordless eloquence.

"That means even if this marriage doesn't work out I can still provide a secure future for my child."

Ignoring Alex's gloomy scowl, she got the wrench and started unscrewing the bolts holding the bed together, thinking about her impending marriage. If the worst happened, really, joint custody wouldn't be so bad. She would still be his mother. That was what mattered most.

But the unbelievable thing was she really wanted the marriage to work. Cole was marrying her for all the wrong reasons— noble ones, to be sure, but all wrong nonetheless. Still, he was marrying her.

Maybe things would work out. Maybe...

She put down the wrench and gazed longingly at the beautiful ring on her finger. Golden flowers cascaded around the simple gold band, sprinkled with glistening drops of faceted diamonds. The swirling petals of the delicate center flower held a large single diamond captive in its middle. It was the most gorgeous ring she'd ever seen, and he'd bought it for her at a time when she refused to see him. When she wouldn't even read the cards that came with the flowers he'd sent. Her heart filled with an unbearable yearning.

She caught Alex watching her intently, and lowered her eyes. "David was never this unselfish, not even in the beginning when he still loved me. At least Cole's honest."

She felt a deep certainty that Cole was a better man than David ever thought of being. She herself had seen how kind, generous and thoughtful he was. And behind the strong, ultra-masculine exterior, she'd caught glimpses of the vulnerable little boy she'd so like to clasp to her heart and soothe away the hurts and fears she sensed he carried.

Much like the little girl inside herself.

Her sister shook her head forlornly. "I can't believe you're doing this."

"He's going to be a wonderful father. And maybe with time, he'll grow to love me, too."

Please, she prayed silently, *let him love me, too.*

Judge Jayne Aire's gaze swept over the wedding party, one eyebrow uplifted. If Katarina weren't completely numb from the toes up, she was sure she'd feel the heat of embarrassment burn in her whole body. *Oh, brother.* Why didn't the woman just get on with it? Jayne Aire. Ha! She checked the name tag of the security guard by the door, half expecting to see "Rochester" stamped boldly in black. *Smith.* Well, thank goodness for small favors.

She snapped to attention when Brad coughed loudly behind her. She shot a quick glance backward and saw his annoyed glare directed at the judge. Her nephew, Kenny, stood to one side of Brad, Alex on the other, gripping his arm and twisting his sleeve in her fingers, obviously trying to keep from bursting into tears. Katarina sent her a reassuring smile, which, despite having no conviction behind it, was rewarded when a corner of Alex's mouth came up bravely.

Cole's parents stood behind him, accompanied by his Luiseño half-brother, Billy, and cousin Tanya—the woman who had been at Henderson's during that first horrible meeting. Katarina thought briefly that Tanya must be at a different wedding than she was, the woman's smile was so full of joy and excitement. Well, it was nice someone was happy.

Cole's mom, Julia, looked worried beneath her pleasant expression as she watched the judge expectantly. She seemed a warm and loving person—she had given Katarina a long hug when they'd met earlier on the courthouse steps. She'd joked about cookies and babies, and steadfastly ignored her son's cool, businesslike demeanor. The father—Ted—had seemed nice, too, if a bit bewildered by the whole thing.

Katarina looked back when Judge Aire cleared her throat.

"Shotgun, eh, Cole?"

That's it, Katarina thought. *Total humiliation.* She wished she could disappear through the floor.

"Very funny, Jayne," Cole mumbled. The judge's apparent amusement was surpassed only by his obvious aggravation. "Could we just get on with this, please?"

The judge's brows rose. "Watch it, son, or I'll hold you in contempt. You're lucky I like you, or you'd be waiting in that line down the hall with the rest of the unwashed masses."

Cole glanced at Katarina, then contritely back at Judge Aire. "Don't think I'm not immensely grateful, your honor. I owe you big-time."

She harrumphed. "That's more like it." Her smile returned. "Well, Cole, I always thought you were much too wrapped up in your lawyering for outside interests. I'm glad to see I was wrong. A young man needs a little love in his life."

Katarina heard him take a deep breath and hold it. She lowered her eyes to the bouquet he'd presented her with when she'd arrived at the courthouse—white roses and gardenias, with a sprinkling of orange blossoms mixed in—and tried hard not to imagine what he was thinking at that moment.

After an awkward pause, Judge Aire said gamely, "Well, shall we begin?" Katarina looked up to see her staring pointedly at Cole. "Call me old-fashioned, but I like my brides and grooms to hold hands. This may be a civil ceremony, but a little ritual never hurts. You of all people should know that."

"Yes, ma'am." Cole hastily took Katarina's hand between his. His hands were warm, but his touch was chilly and reluctant.

She kept her gaze on the judge, who in turn searched her and Cole's faces. Katarina did her best to muster the proper expression for an eager bride.

"I assume we are all here of our own free will?"

Her heart sank. Was it that obvious? "Yes, your honor," she answered in unison with Cole.

The ceremony was mercifully short. Five minutes and it was over. She couldn't remember saying "I will." But she must have done, because before she knew it, she had slipped the ring Cole had sneaked her onto his finger, and her new husband was brushing a quick kiss on her cheek.

Katarina wanted to scream, "Stop!," wrap her arms around

Cole's neck and kiss him lingeringly and lovingly, the way a bride ought to—the way she so longed to do. This was her wedding! It might be a marriage of convenience, but it should still mean something to be pronounced husband and wife.

But instead, she was shaking the judge's hand, being enveloped by an openly weeping Alex, and accepting a hug from Brad and a shy peck from Kenny.

She turned to find Julia waiting for her. Her new mother-in-law extended her hands and grasped hers warmly. "Welcome to the family, Rini. I hope we can be good friends."

"Thank you. I hope so, too," she said, hugging her. She felt instinctively that she had an ally in the kindly woman.

"Congratulations," said Cole's brother, Billy, shaking her hand.

Ted gave her a squeeze. "Anytime we can help you keep this guy in line, just let us know."

She smiled and glanced at Cole. "Thanks. I may take you up on that sometime." His parents were being so nice. It couldn't be easy, having their son's sudden marriage sprung on them like this. And a baby and all. She could hardly believe they were speaking to her, much less being as sweet as could be. "Thank you all for being so wonderful. You don't know how much it means to me to have your good wishes."

"Good wishes—are you kidding?" Tanya laughed, tucking her arm through Katarina's and leading them all toward the main door. "They're grateful as hell! We all are! Cole's been a moody bastard for months, and we're just glad someone else has to put up with him now. Isn't that right, Billy?" She winked.

Billy chuckled, a deep rumbling sound so like Cole's. "A new wife and baby ought to keep him too busy to make much trouble."

Katarina's eyes sought her husband. He was shaking hands with Judge Aire, making some witty remark as the judge headed out the back door. Cole's face became determinedly impassive when he turned to rejoin the group, his smile carefully measured. Still, her heart skipped a beat.

He was so incredibly handsome. His tall, muscular frame carried his dark suit with an effortless grace. The fluorescent light reflected off the lean angles of his face, exotic and mysterious in their starkness. His short hair had grown out a bit over the past month, looking thick and sexy as it grazed the collar of his white shirt. She imagined what it might be like to bury her fingers once again in its rich depths, pulling his face close as he whispered loving words in her ear.

"What?" she murmured as Tanya tugged lightly on her elbow. The young woman's smile beamed at her, her eyes sparkling with understanding. Katarina dropped her lashes in embarrassment over being caught with her heart on her sleeve. Especially since that's where it was likely to stay.

Tanya gave her arm a squeeze. "It'll be fine, you'll see. He's a good man."

Katarina sighed wistfully. "I know. He'll be a terrific dad."

The blazing California sunshine continued to defy the winter chill, so when they got back to the house, Brad set up tables and chairs in the backyard. The small wedding party basked in the afternoon sun, eating the mounds of delicious hors d'oeuvres and chocolate wedding cake Alex had prepared that morning. Champagne flowed freely, compliments of Billy.

Katarina sat next to Cole, listening absently to the conversations going on around her as the afternoon wore on.

His voice broke quietly into her thoughts. "Tired?"

She smiled up at him. "A little. Not every day a girl gets married."

He nodded. "Where can I find your things? I brought the truck, so hopefully it won't take me too many trips."

She bit back a laugh and stood. "I'll show you." She led him to the suitcases and carton, which she'd placed at the base of the apartment stairs. "Voilà."

He stared incredulously at her tiny collection of belongings. "Where's the rest?"

"The bed is still upstairs." At his dubious look she quickly added, "We took it apart, though."

"The bed?"

She nodded, starting to become nervous. Maybe he didn't want her furniture cluttering up his house. But she couldn't leave it—it was all she had of her own.

"A bed, two suitcases and a cardboard box? That's it?"

She nodded again. "You don't mind, do you? The bed, I mean."

"Of course not. I just can't believe you don't have more stuff."

She shrugged, relief rolling over her. "I left nearly everything behind at David's." She led the way up the stairs and opened the door to her apartment. "Once I'd decided to leave I just walked away with the clothes on my back and what would fit in my purse, so I wouldn't have time to change my mind. Brad went back for my bed a few days later. I've had it since I was a kid."

Cole folded his arms over his chest and leaned against the wall just inside the door. "You had your own bed at David's?"

She looked away. "It was in a guest room there, too."

He laughed a humorless laugh. "You and I, we've had some strange marriages."

"I never married him." She felt her sleeve slide lazily off her shoulder, and she absently tugged it back up.

His eyes followed the movement, briefly filling with something hot and hungry. But the look had been squelched by the time his gaze again met hers.

Brad stuck his head around the door. "Need some help with that monstrosity, Cole?"

Cole pushed off the wall, giving her a last searching look. "Yeah, thanks, I'd appreciate it. Rini, why don't you go back down and relax. I'm sure I can talk Brad into coming along to the house and helping me put this thing back together. We shouldn't be gone more than a few minutes."

Brad clapped him on the shoulder. "Be happy to. Go on, Rini, before everyone thinks you two have sneaked off to be alone."

Sneaked off to be alone. Oh, Lord.

Katarina did her best to take part in the lively conversation at the tables outside, but her mind kept creeping back to the thought of being alone with Cole. At his house. In his territory.

What would she do if he didn't want to respect their agreement?

More to the point, what would she do if *she* didn't?

Oh, Lord.

Cole was straight as an arrow. If she said she wouldn't share his bed, she knew he'd honor her wishes. Wasn't he at that very moment putting her bed together so she could sleep safely out of his reach? She so wanted this marriage to work. But how could any man possibly love a wife who wouldn't even sleep with him?

Should she give in to her own desire? Show him just how far she had already fallen in love with him, and hope that someday he could return her love? Or stick to her resolve and wait until he was able to feel more for her than responsibility and maybe a little lust?

Once again the familiar panic of wanting to please squeezed her chest before she could tamp it firmly down. She never wanted to be that insecure person from her childhood again. Ever. But it was easy to slip into old habits. Too easy. She lifted the hair off the back of her neck and sighed.

"He'll be back soon," Tanya reassured her with a smile.

"That's what I'm afraid of," Katarina mumbled, but she managed a lopsided smile of her own at her new cousin-in-law. How much did Tanya know about their situation? It sure would be nice to have someone to confide in. "Do you live in Pasadena, too?"

Tanya nodded. "A few blocks from Cole."

"I hope you'll feel free to drop in anytime. I have the impression you and he are close. I wouldn't want you to feel I've come between you."

"Don't worry, you're just what that man needs." She toasted Katarina with her champagne glass. "I'm thrilled he's finally come to his senses."

"I assume," a deep voice rumbled behind them, "that it's me who's so sensible?"

"How'd you guess?" Tanya turned to slide an arm around Cole, who had returned with Brad.

Cole's gaze landed squarely on Katarina, and the bones seemed to melt right out of her body at his gentle look, leaving her helpless to move or even respond. Falling in love? Oh, yes.

"Ready to go home, Mrs. Lonetree?"

Everyone in the small gathering hushed at his words, grinning at the two of them as if they imagined she and Cole were a perfectly normal bride and groom seeking to escape to a perfectly romantic wedding night. Katarina glanced around. They were all wishing so hard for her happiness that she wanted to give them the romantic departure they expected. She didn't have the heart to disappoint them with the truth.

Pushing to her feet, she smiled and nodded. "Yes, Mr. Lonetree. Ready as ever."

Chapter 10

Cole frowned and squinted stubbornly at the depositions in his lap, trying to ignore the faint noises from the kitchen. Rini had been in there forever—practically since they'd arrived home after the wedding. What the hell was she doing? Rearranging the cupboards?

Avoiding him, more likely.

Not that it mattered.

He gave the papers in his hands a snap and returned his attention to them, leaning back in his easy chair and recrossing his ankles on the ottoman.

But the subtle sounds continued to distract him. Finally he flung aside the papers and yanked his feet off the stool. Suddenly his nostrils filled with the heavenly scent of spices and brown sugar.

Baking. The woman was baking.

He settled back, blinking at the kitchen door. Well, hell. Grinning, he picked up the papers and resumed his work, wondering idly what delights his new wife was concocting for him. This marriage thing wasn't so bad, after all. Once you got the hang of it.

Still, no sense letting on that he was elated over her effort to please him. Might give her the wrong idea.

Hell, might give her the right idea.

Face it, this business arrangement idea was going nowhere fast. He'd tried his best to stay brisk and businesslike today for their wedding. He really had. But from the moment he'd seen her walking toward him up the courthouse steps, he'd known the effort was doomed to failure.

He might not be able to love her, but every time he looked at his bride, so pretty and glowing, her shy glances filled with warmth and hope, her body carrying the evidence of a mutual attraction he'd be a fool to deny, his belief in a strictly platonic marriage was exposed as the impossibility it was.

He rested his head on the back of his easy chair and stared at the closed kitchen door. He and Rini had been dancing around each other all evening, ever since he'd insisted on carrying her over the threshold.

"Just a ritual," he'd assured her.

"Like when they threw the rice," she'd said as he lifted her into his arms. They looked at each other and then she quickly looked away, embarrassed.

"I didn't think we really needed that rice shower, did you?" he said, gently teasing. "Under the circumstances."

He let her down, but kept his arms around her, tipping her chin up when she continued to study his tie. "Welcome home, Rini." He kissed her softly.

Lifting her lips to his, she had timidly returned his kiss. "I want to make you happy, Cole." Her eyes were guileless and sincere. "I know this isn't what you wanted—"

"Hush, darlin'. You've already made me happy just by being here." He pulled her close. "We'll be fine. You'll see." He kissed her again, a little longer and a little harder. When he let the tip of his tongue graze the swell of her lower lip, she shied.

She backed away from him nervously, then glanced around the room. "Oh, Cole, you have a beautiful home."

With a sigh, he closed the door and propped himself against the back of it, following her movements. "It's a bit bare. I'm not here much. Maybe you can do something with it."

He watched her take in the room—the gleaming hardwood floors and adobe-colored walls, floor to ceiling bookshelves, the huge fireplace. A couple of canvas-covered couches and his big leather easy chair. Come to think of it, it did kind of resemble his office.

"No curtains?"

"Never got around to them." He shrugged and grinned. "Just don't walk around naked with the lights on."

She darted him an amused look. "Too bad I had to leave my sewing machine at David's. I could have made some."

He pushed off the door. "You sew?" At her nod, he wandered over and sat down on the arm of his easy chair. "You can use mine." She glanced up, surprised, and he chuckled. "I make regalia, remember? It's in the guest room when you need it."

She nodded, purposefully examining some of the books on the shelves. "That'll be convenient. Having it in the same room I'm in."

He took a fortifying breath. This was what he'd been waiting for. "You won't be in the guest room, Rini."

She shot him a panicky glance. "No?"

He slid off the chair arm and walked slowly toward her. "No."

"Where will I be, then?" Her gaze darted to the living room couch.

Reaching out, he pushed a stray lock of hair behind her ear. "In my room. A woman belongs in her husband's bed."

Her eyes widened and she let out a little gasp, crushing the small hope he'd begun to feel. He had so wanted her just to be looking for a little pressure, or a definite invitation, so she could let herself give in to him.

"But our agreement! You said…!"

He closed the distance between them, standing so close he was pressed into the baby, his face inches from hers. "Is that what you really want, Rini? To sleep alone in a cold, empty bed?"

When she wouldn't look at him, he slipped his fingers through her hair and gently pulled her head back, forcing her face up.

"Alone, night after night? When there's a man right here who wants you? Who'll make hot, sweet love to you whenever you like?"

Her fire eyes were slumberous and full of want as she watched him. The blue darkened to cobalt, and her lashes fluttered down to rest on her cheeks. "I don't know, Cole."

"You're my wife, Rini. And I know you want me just as much as I want you. Sooner or later you're going to ask me to come to you in that big, lonely bed."

She swallowed. "I need time to think."

After a moment, he forced himself to let her go. Turning to the fireplace, he flicked a switch. The natural-gas logs burst into bright, colorful flames. "Very well. But you're still sleeping in my bed."

Silently, her eyes pleaded with him.

At that moment he was sure if he just swept her off her feet and carried her to that bed, she wouldn't fight him. Much. He could tell she wanted him, and he definitely wanted her. That was enough, wasn't it? After all, they were married now. For a few long seconds he was sorely tempted, but then reluctantly came to his senses.

"The room's bigger, and when the baby comes, you'll need space for the crib and what have you. I've moved my things to the spare room." He gave her an ironic look. "I'll sleep in your old bed. If nothing else, I can be surrounded by the smell of you."

Her mouth dropped open. "But—"

"You're down at the end." He gestured to the hallway. "Make yourself at home. I'm going to change my clothes."

With that he had strolled down the hall to the guest room and gone in, carefully closing the door behind him.

Damn.

Gripping the arms of his easy chair, he brought himself out of the frustrating memory. That had been just a few short hours ago, and since then he'd been the model of a perfect gentleman. But her simple statement still hung between them, coloring every look, every accidental brush of their hands.

I need time to think.

How much time was she talking here? Minutes? Days? Months? *Until she graduated and could blow him off for good?*

He opened his eyes to the totally unexpected sight of her standing in front of his chair. "Jeez!" He jumped up, papers flying, and narrowly missed catapulting the tray in her hands to the floor.

"Oh, my gosh!" She hastily put the tray on the ottoman and knelt to pick up his scattered papers. "I didn't mean to startle you."

"Startle me? You scared the—" He halted and forced a grin. "Sorry. I'm just a little edgy tonight. Here, let me get those." He went down on his knees and started gathering the papers. She reached for one next to him, giving him a fine view of the upper curve of her breasts as they pressed against the fabric of the scoop-necked sweater she'd changed into earlier. He looked his fill. She caught him looking.

He winked, neatly straightening the stack of papers in his hands. "Hell, I'll take what I can get."

Coloring slightly, she handed him the papers in hers. "Are you hungry?"

He snagged her gaze with his and held on. "Oh, yeah."

"Good," she said, nibbling on her lip. "I, um, I made sandwiches. And banana bread."

He tore his eyes from her lips and looked hopefully at the tray. "Banana bread? How'd you know that's my favorite?"

"Lucky guess. Come on." Smiling, she patted the seat of his easy chair.

After she'd settled him comfortably with a turkey sandwich in one hand and a cup of coffee in the other, she sat down on the floor beside him, leaning her back against the solid, straight side of the chair.

"Rini! What are you doing?" He started to get up. "You take the chair."

She grabbed the leg of his sweatpants and pulled him back down. "I like it on the floor. My back feels wonderful against your chair. It's at just the right angle."

He looked at her dubiously.

"Honest."

"We'll get you a chair tomorrow."

"Don't bother. I like it down here."

"Stubborn."

She batted her lashes.

The corner of his mouth twitched. "At least you could sit between my legs. Give me a thrill on my wedding night."

He almost choked on his sandwich when she said, "Okay," then scooted around and settled into the vee between his legs, pushing the ottoman to one side. She leaned back with her sandwich and mug, and the ends of her hair curled into his lap. He stuffed his sandwich into his mouth to stifle a groan. *Great idea, compadre.* He thanked God for baggy sweatpants and prayed she didn't turn around anytime soon.

He'd just managed to relax when she looked around. "Ready for your banana bread?"

"You bet."

She set aside his napkin and mug, broke off a piece of the bread and placed it against his lips. "Open wide."

He blinked, his throat suddenly tightening. She was going to feed him.

She was sitting between his knees, her face practically in his lap, and she intended to feed him. *Ho boy.*

He opened wide.

She picked up another piece and waited while he finished the first one. He was having a hard time swallowing. "Aren't you going to have any?"

She hesitated, bit off half of the piece she was holding, then held up the rest for him. A low sound growled out of his throat. He grasped her wrist and drew her hand to his lips.

He watched her watching his mouth as he pulled the bit of bread into it, along with her fingers, working them with his tongue. She followed his Adam's apple as he swallowed, then let her gaze drift down his body, coming to a skittish halt at the juncture of his thighs. His erection strained against the soft fleece of his sweatpants, inches from her languorous eyes. They looked up at him, slumberous and heavy lidded. The sweater dropped seductively off her shoulder, and he knew he was in big trouble.

He had to taste her.

Summoning the steeliest restraint that had ever been required of him, he gently lifted her face and bent low, angling himself to meet her lips. Softly, softly, he pressed a kiss to them.

Sweet. She tasted like bananas and coffee and chocolate wedding cake. His arousal throbbed, and he had to clutch the arm of the chair mercilessly to keep from ripping that silly drooping sweater down to her wrists.

She ran her hand through his hair and kissed him back, her mouth warm and pliant. "It's been a long day. I think I'd better put these dishes away and get to bed."

Bed. Sounded like an excellent plan. Maybe she should just skip the dishes part. "No, you go ahead. It'll just take me a minute to clean up out here."

"Okay, thanks."

Emotions warring inside his chest, he watched her pad softly out of the living room. He wanted her. With the pent-up passion of an eight-month wait he wanted to be inside her. But he'd made a promise, and he never broke his word.

Closing his eyes, he listened for several minutes to the sounds of the night. Outside, leaves swirled around the cement driveway, carried on a light breeze. A car drove by. His bed creaked invitingly down the hall, calling him to his wife's embrace.

Damn, it would be so easy to love that woman. He wondered if, perhaps, he hadn't already started to.

Strangely, the prospect didn't alarm him. It seemed she genuinely cared for him, and she had told him she truly wanted their arrangement to work. Maybe Tanya was right and Rini was different from the others, and he could let down his guard. Maybe his heart would be safe with her, after all.

He smiled as he turned off the gas and watched the fire die. Mindlessly humming a Pueblo flute tune, he cleaned up and then strolled to the bathroom to get ready for bed.

A few minutes later he took a last glance at himself in the mirror. The face that gazed back looked happier and more content than it had in years. Husband, father and, with any luck, lover. He could do this. Rini would help him move on, help him leave the past with all its hurts and disappointments far behind.

He had been right to choose her at the powwow. She wouldn't abandon him now. Not after today. How could she?

Katarina had already unpacked all her things earlier, putting them away in the voluminous dresser Cole had emptied for her. So there was no way of stalling any longer.

She approached his bed with a combination of arousal and trepidation. It was big. Very big. Acres of rustic wool Pendleton blanket covered forest-green sheets on a rich, honey-colored wooden bed frame. She leaned the heels of her hands on it, testing the mattress. The bed protested with a light squeak. She snatched her hands away, glancing guiltily at the door, hoping Cole hadn't heard.

Cole, her husband.

Shaking herself mentally, she picked up her nightgown, then looked down at the sweater and leggings she had changed into after taking a calming shower this afternoon. She didn't feel much more composed now than she had then. The tender kiss he'd just given her was as disturbing as his bold words about sharing his bed had been.

Lifting the cotton gown to her cheek, she indulged herself in a little fantasy about Cole coming into the room later and slowly stripping it off her.

Suddenly, she realized what she was doing, and tossed the gown onto the bed. She really must banish these thoughts. This marriage was a business proposition and nothing more. Despite Cole's loving kiss earlier, love was not on his agenda. He'd made that abundantly clear all through their wedding day. On the other hand, it was hard to believe it was her less-than-hour-glass figure that was prodding him into making these overtures. She wondered briefly what his motives were.

Quietly, she found the bathroom and made her preparations for bed. As she walked back to her room, she stretched. Her back had started to ache and she wished she had a hot water bottle to tuck behind her tonight.

"Is your back hurting again?"

"Oh!" She jumped, finding Cole standing right in front of her. "A little. I don't suppose you have a hot water bottle?"

"Sorry." He appeared to think for a second. "But I'll go you one better. How about a back rub? You said it helped before."

She shook her head, a bit too vigorously, vividly remembering exactly how good she had felt the last time he'd given her a massage. And not just her back, either. "Thanks, but no."

"Just a back rub, Rini. Let me do this for you."

She reached for the wall behind her. "I, uh…" She faltered. This was a bad idea. A really bad idea. But it sure would be great to be able to fall asleep for once without that dull ache in her lower back. Wanting his hands on her body had nothing to do with it. Nothing whatsoever.

He took a step closer. "I don't like to think of you hurting."

"Well…" She inhaled sharply when he slid an arm around her waist and began to knead her spine with his fingers. She struggled to form words. "Just a back rub?" For a split second, as she looked up into his eyes, she forgot completely that she wanted him to answer yes.

He pulled her imperceptibly closer. "You have my word I won't even try to kiss you—" the corner of his mouth kicked up "—first."

A frisson of desire sparked down her spine. "First?"

"You're in charge. You lead, I follow."

How did he know that putting her in control of things would practically guarantee she'd be putty in his hands? "You play dirty, you know that, Counsellor?" she whispered.

He gave her a roguish grin, worthy of a Barbary Coast pirate. "You have no idea."

She cleared her throat, hoping the action would somehow clear the sensual fog clouding her brain, too. "You need your eyes checked, Cole. I'm eight months pregnant."

He slowly ran a thumb along her jaw. "And every bit as sexy as the day I got you that way."

She blinked several times, flustered, a warm pressure building behind her eyes. *Hormones,* she thought desperately—she even cried at milk commercials these days. She lowered her eyes and chewed her lip. "Now I know you need glasses."

He smiled at her tenderly and tipped her chin up. Their gazes locked. She expected to be kissed, but he didn't lower his mouth to hers.

"Going to make me wait, Rini?"

She swallowed. *Right.* She was in control. Swallowing again, she nodded, still uncertain of what she wanted to happen next. She nervously searched his face for a sign of anger or frustration, but found none. Instead, an amused grin formed on his lips.

"Okay, darlin'. I can wait." He stepped back and swept an arm toward her bedroom. "In the meantime, would you like to slip into something more comfortable?"

Now, there was the sixty-four-thousand-dollar question. She eyed him uncertainly. "Just how comfortable did you have in mind?"

He flashed that grin again. "Naked?"

She closed her eyes against the surge of raw desire that swept through her body. *Moment of truth.*

Was this what she wanted? *More than anything.* Should she consent? *God, no.* She'd be a fool to put herself through any more heartache because of this man. She opened her eyes. "I don't think this massage thing is a very good idea."

She started to back away, but he caught her fingers in his.

"Joking aside, Rini. You've had to put up with so much during these months, all on your own. I want to help now. Even if it's just easing your sore muscles. Trust me. I'll be as good as you want me to be."

Sincerity was written on his every feature. She took a deep, cleansing breath. Why, oh, why was she so darned gullible?

"I trust you, Cole." She gave him a weak smile and murmured, "It's me I'm not sure I can trust."

His brow rose along with the corners of his mouth. "Mmm. I like the sound of that." At her withering glance he raised one hand in mock surrender. "Kidding."

He started backing into her bedroom, pulling her gently with him. When she resisted, he cocked his head. "Coming?"

She cast a look down the hall, suddenly panicking. "Um, I think I…I, um, left my nightgown in the bathroom."

"Okay." He indicated her room. "I'll just wait in here."

She rushed back to the bathroom and closed the door, leaning against it. *Oh, Lord.* She wanted him. She couldn't deny it. But she wondered again what his reasons were for wanting her.

When she couldn't delay any longer, she reluctantly returned to her room. Pausing at the door, she caught her breath. Her old four-poster never looked quite so inviting as Cole's king-sized bed did at that moment. He had piled her mound of extra pillows onto it and was stretched out beside them, arms stacked under his head, eyes closed. Her nightgown hung tidily over the foot rail of the bed. His sensual lips were turned up at the corners— the smile of a buccaneer with treasure on his mind.

Katarina's gaze traveled across his broad shoulders and skimmed down his tapered torso, snagging at the junction of his muscular thighs. Even in repose he was powerfully masculine. Her throat tightened, her blood growing thick and hot in her limbs. It was all she could do to keep from melting on the spot.

"Look at me like that much longer and I might get to thinking you enjoy the view."

She jerked her gaze away and felt her cheeks burn. "Sorry."

Rolling to his side, he lifted up on an elbow. "Sweetheart, you can look at me anytime you want." The heat in his eyes made her think he wanted to say more, but he just sat up and tipped his head at her nightgown. "That what you were looking for?"

She gave a weak smile and nodded.

He patted the bed beside him. "Come on over here, Mrs. Lonetree."

She glanced nervously at the quilt where his hand rested, and inched her way toward the bed. *Mrs. Lonetree?* She noticed that he'd turned on the lamp on the nightstand, and it cast a cozy glow over the linens.

"Scared?"

Her chin went up a notch and she shook her head. "No, of course not."

He smiled. "Liar." Sliding off the bed, he gestured at the pillows. "I'll get out of your way so you can arrange them how you want."

She climbed up into bed and hugged the top pillow to her chest. A loud click sounded behind her and she whirled around.

Cole had closed the door she'd deliberately left open, and he was leaning against it, arms folded at his waist, one ankle crossed negligently over the other. He flicked off the overhead light. "Do you have any baby oil?"

Her eyes strayed to the mirrored dresser and back to him. "No. Why?"

He pushed away from the door and strolled to the dresser, then, one by one, slowly examined the few personal items she had set on it earlier. Still hugging the pillow, she watched in the mirror as he ran his fingers across the brushes and bows, lifting her two perfume containers to his nose. When he found her small bottle of fragrant oil he twisted off the cap and rubbed a drop into his palm, testing the scent.

"Gardenia." His eyes met hers in the mirror.

"It's my only vice. Terribly expensive, but I can't make myself stop buying it."

He walked over and set the bottle on the nightstand next to the lamp. "I'll replace what we use."

She frowned at it, then looked up. "But…" It dawned on her what he had in mind and her lips parted. She shook her head.

He shrugged, grinning. "Whatever. Your call." He sat on the edge of the bed. "Lie down."

She ignored the flock of butterflies flying stunt tricks in her stomach, and turned back to position the pillows. She changed her mind several times about their arrangement, until his deep, rich chuckle sounded in her ear. "I swear, Rini, if you'd been this nervous back in May, we'd never be having this baby. Relax." He grasped her shoulders gently. "It's just a back rub."

Just a back rub. *Just a back rub.*

Who was he kidding?

She felt as nervous as a sixteen-year-old awaiting her first kiss.

The wood of the old bed creaked comfortingly as she eased herself down at an angle onto the mound of pillows. She felt a tickle of warm breath on her neck.

"Ready?"

She assumed it was a rhetorical question since his hands

alighted softly on her back and ran all the way down her spine and then up again. She shivered in delight.

Lost.

She was lost in a world of velvet caresses and soft moans. He worked her aching muscles until they were as supple as warm taffy. Until she glowed with the heat of his hands and tingled with anticipation of more intimate touches. When he slipped his hands under her sweater, her body shuddered from head to toe.

"You like that?" he murmured behind her, caressing her back.

She was beyond speech, so she hummed her answer on a sigh. "Mmm-hmm."

"How do you want me to touch you, sweetheart?" He pulled her sweater up to her waist and then a little farther.

"Take it off, Cole," she whispered. Shocked at her own scandalous suggestion, she nevertheless lifted up a bit to help him.

A low sound came from his chest when he swept the sweater up her midriff, grazing the sides of her bare breasts, and pulled it over her head. The sweater hit the floor with a poof. A strand of hair fell across her upturned cheek, and he lifted it behind her ear with his finger.

"So beautiful," he whispered, and her heart swelled with joy.

The sound of his hands rubbing together was followed by a waft of gardenia in the air around them. Tentatively at first, then more boldly, he massaged the light oil into the skin of her back, stroking it on with slow, sensual movements.

Her body was liquid fire. A steady throb of desire between her legs pulsed deeper with every heartbeat. Even the slight contractions she felt around the baby pulled the coil of tension in her woman's center that much tighter.

"Turn over, lover, so I can do the other side."

His words hit her like an erotic wave. Without letting herself think, she obeyed. He sat on his knees, watching her turn, his eyes hooded, his face taut. His gaze brushed over her bare breasts. "Oh, God, Rini."

He tossed a few of the pillows aside, then poured more oil into an unsteady palm, and smoothed his hands together. Starting with her fingers and hands, he worked up her arms, placing them above her head when he was done.

Her heartbeat sped as he spilled a few more drops of oil onto his hands. Her already hard nipples tightened eagerly, craving his touch. Her eyelids fluttered shut.

He drew his fingers along her jaw, then gently stroked down her neck and applied the oil to her upper chest. Her tortured breasts ached for his caress, but his hands skimmed by them, smoothing down her sides and ribs until they hit the top of her leggings. He hooked his fingers under the elastic, and her body arched.

"Shall I do your legs?" His voice sounded raw, almost hoarse.

She opened her eyes and looked into his. Reckless hunger, want and steely determination were what she saw. Blood surged rhythmically through a vein in his temple.

If Cole could take it, so could she.

"I'd like that," she whispered, mewling softly when he quickly drew her leggings and panties off in a single motion. She turned her head shyly, not daring to watch his reaction to her swollen body.

"Woman, you are so incredibly beautiful."

Slowly, she turned back. She lay before him, naked beneath his ravenous gaze. Over eight months pregnant, forty pounds heavier than usual, and she'd never in her life felt as sexy or alluring as he made her feel at that very moment.

A muscle jumped in his clamped jaw. A light sheen of perspiration coated his forehead. He reached for the bottle of oil and drizzled a thin line from her foot to her trembling thigh. With strong, clever fingers he massaged her ankle and calf, moving slowly up past her knee to her thigh. She could feel the back of his hand brush the curls between her legs, but maddeningly, frustratingly, he came no closer to the place where she most wanted him.

He started on the other leg. By the time he reached her upper thigh, she was a witless mass of molten desire. Wantonly, she parted her legs slightly, inviting his intimate caress. She nearly groaned in frustration when he took a deep breath and started on her belly. Lord above, he had to run out of safe territory soon.

Suddenly it hit her. He was waiting for her to tell him what she wanted. He'd promised a massage and nothing more, unless she said so. The man must be a saint.

"Cole?"

"Yeah, babe?" A rivulet of sweat trickled from his cheek down his neck and disappeared into a stain spreading on the front of his white T-shirt.

"You missed a few spots."

Chapter 11

Kneeling beside her, Cole swallowed heavily. "That right?"

Katarina nodded, loving the effect her words were having on him. "Uh-huh." *Loving him.*

She deliberately shifted her body, stretching her arms above her head, subtly thrusting her breasts out. Cole caught his breath. *Oh, yes.* She could deny it no longer. She was in love with her husband and longed to show him just how much.

"Where did I miss?" he asked in a strangled voice.

"My earlobes," she said teasingly.

She watched his jaw clench, the muscle twitching wildly. "Okay."

He moistened his fingertips with oil and gently kneaded the sensitive lobes between them. A moan of pleasure escaped her.

"Anywhere else?"

"My lips."

His gaze dropped to her mouth, his teeth clamped tightly. "Right."

Using his thumb, he stroked oil onto her lips, easing back and forth across her lower lip, smoothing over the bow of her upper lip.

"Wonder how it tastes," she murmured, then swiped her tongue over his thumb. "Hmm."

"Well?" His eyes were black as midnight, his face a study in painful restraint.

She licked her lips. "Not too bad. You should try it."

He blinked a couple of times, his eyes on her mouth. Without lifting his gaze, he sucked on his thumb where it had touched her lips. "Mmm. Spicy."

The air between them sizzled and cracked with electricity. Cole's chest heaved with labored breaths. Her own was tight with want.

His eyes locked on hers. "Rini, are we done here?"

She shook her head. "Almost. Just one more place."

He exhaled slowly. "All right. Where?"

She caught the front of his T-shirt in her fingers and gave it a little tug. "Come closer and I'll tell you."

He slid his legs down the bed and stretched out beside her, holding himself up on his forearm, bending his head to hers. She turned to him and pulled him closer yet, so their noses were end-to-end, their parted lips nearly touching.

"The tips of my breasts," she whispered into his mouth.

His nostrils flared and his tongue dragged across his lower lip. Wordlessly, he sat up and poured a small amount of oil into the cap of the bottle. He rolled her so she was on her back again.

Excruciatingly slowly, he let one drop fall from the cap onto her right nipple. She gasped at the impact, savoring the slippery warmth that spread down the hard point.

He toyed with her for a moment, poising the cap above her left breast, making her wait for the precious liquid to fall. She tried to hold perfectly still so it wouldn't miss, but her heart pounded so hard it made her breast bounce slightly with every beat.

"Please, Cole." Her voice cracked.

When the drop finally fell, hitting the tightly knotted bud, she cried out, her control snapping. She grasped his T-shirt and pulled him to her, covering his mouth with hers, swallowing his answering groan, savaging him with kisses.

"Cole." She whispered his name, keening in pleasure when his hands closed around her breasts.

"Oh, woman." His tongue met hers and stroked boldly into her mouth. "God, how I want you."

She grabbed his T-shirt and yanked it up his chest. "I want you, too," she urged. "I've dreamed of nothing else since May." She couldn't believe her dreams were about to come true.

He helped her slip it over his head, then slid his arm under her and awkwardly pulled her close. "Will it be okay? The baby?"

"Just be gentle."

"I will, sweetheart." Joining his lips with hers again, he spread her legs apart. "So silky," he breathed into her mouth. "So wet. Like a flower in the rain." He tested her depths with his fingers. "Rini, the baby's right there. I'm so hard for you I'm afraid I'll hurt one of you."

"Please don't stop, Cole. I'll guide you." She reached for the waistband of his sweats.

He stroked her intimately and whispered in her ear, "I want to be inside you."

Katarina's heart filled with happiness and she threw her arms around his neck, kissing him deeply. "Oh, Cole, I'm so happy. It's going to be okay, isn't it—our marriage?"

"Shh, of course it is."

"And you will love me, won't you? Swear you will...."

She felt him go still. Then he held her away from his chest and looked into her face.

"Rini," he said quietly.

"Because I couldn't stand it if I thought you wouldn't learn to love me, eventually."

"Honey—"

Katarina's words continued to spill out, regardless of her growing uneasiness. "I understand it'll take time. But we're together now. A family. You and me and our son. I'm pretty sure I could love you." *I already do.* "You could love me one day—" she nestled against him, waiting for reassurance...or something else "—couldn't you?"

Anything... *Please!*

"Rini. Honey…"

With a feeling of impending doom, she looked up into his eyes, and her heart shattered in a million pieces. "Oh, God."

"Sweetheart, don't—" The look of profound guilt and confusion on his face told her everything his words didn't.

She squeezed her eyes shut. "You don't want that."

"It's not that I don't… It's not that simple. I—"

"Alex was right. You don't really want me at all."

"That's not true. I've never wanted anyone more in my life, Rini."

"For sex. Just sex. And the baby." She pulled her arms from him and buried her face in her hands. "Oh, what have I done?"

She turned her back and curled into herself, hugging the child in her womb. How could she have misjudged the situation so completely? How could she have deceived herself into thinking he could ever love her, or even accept that she might love him?

He put his arms around her from behind. "I'm so sorry, darlin'. I thought love was the last thing on your mind."

"Cole, I'm having your baby! What did you think was on my mind? Just a quick roll in the hay and then back to our business proposition? I thought… Oh, I'm such an idiot."

Pain stabbed through her chest and a single tear fought its way past her tightly squeezed lids. She had to get control of herself. She would not cry in front of him. She wouldn't give him the satisfaction. "Please leave me alone."

She felt his hand on her arm. "Rini…"

She jerked away, unable to bear being touched by him. Shame burned in her face. "Go away. Please, just go away."

She could sense the reluctance in his movements, but he got up, grabbed his T-shirt and left without another word.

Katarina trembled with guilt and disappointment, frustration and dashed hopes. She thought with bitterness of her mother's scorn, of David's cruelty, and now this ultimate humiliation from the man she had married. She swallowed furiously, refusing to let herself cry. Why didn't he want to love her?

She took a long, shuddering breath. She knew she had to reach deep inside herself for the strength to go on hoping.

"I've been such a fool," she whispered to herself. "He

doesn't love me. He doesn't even want to. But for my baby's sake, somehow, some way, I have to change his mind.''

Katarina sang softly as she gathered ingredients to make French toast. Glancing at the multipaned window of Cole's kitchen—her kitchen now, she reminded herself—she caught the reflection of the determined look that refused to leave her face that morning.

She was married. And he was a good man, she knew, despite... Well, anyway, in a few short weeks she would have his baby, and they would be a real family.

After a long, sleepless night of soul-searching, she had decided the situation was definitely worth salvaging.

Sure, they had a few problems to iron out. Like the fact that he had no intention of ever falling in love with her, for instance. But she would work on that. She could find a way. Under the circumstances, she felt justified in her course of action. It was obvious he was very attracted to her, sexually. She was certain he could grow to love her, too. She had to believe it was possible. For her own sanity.

In the meantime, she'd be careful to keep him at arm's length. No repeats of her weakness of last night, that was for sure. She couldn't let herself get close enough to be susceptible to his heated looks and erotic caresses. That would be her downfall.

Grabbing a bowl, she cracked eggs and dipped bread. This had to be strictly platonic. Just until he realized he loved her, of course. But that was only a matter of time. Humming, Katarina poured Cole's coffee, hot and black just as he liked it. She'd take such good care of him, he wouldn't know what hit him.

She had just finished piling his plate high with French toast when she heard him stride down the hall toward the kitchen. She smoothed her dress, brushing at a splotch of powdered sugar, then turned to greet him.

He blew into the kitchen like a storm cloud. Her smile faltered, but she quickly repossessed it. "Good morning."

"Morning." He strode directly to the table and grabbed his coffee. It sloshed over the side of the cup onto his hand. "Damn!"

She hurried over with a cloth to wipe off the hot liquid. When she touched him he flinched worse than when the scalding coffee had hit his flesh. He jerked his hand away.

"Cole!"

"I'm fine. Don't fuss." He turned to the table.

She stared at his back, unaccountably hurt. "Okay." She pushed the hurt away and fetched the maple syrup from the counter. "Have some breakfast. I've made French toast."

"I don't eat breakfast. Coffee's fine."

She gripped the edge of a chair. "At least sit down."

He shook his head. "I have to get to the office."

Her heart stalled. What was wrong with him? "But...it's Saturday. I thought..." Was he mad about last night? What possible reason did *he* have to be mad? *She* was the one—

"I have a case coming up next week. I need to prepare."

Pulling out a kitchen drawer, he extracted an envelope and ripped it open, then lined up the contents on the table between their rapidly cooling breakfasts.

"Before I go, here is a house key, car keys, checkbook, credit card. There's a thousand dollars in the checking account and a two-thousand-dollar limit on the card. Another thousand will be transferred into the checking account on the first of every month. I know it's not much, but I'll have to cut back on work when the baby comes, and liquidating some of my stocks will take time, so I'm playing it safe for now. Later on there'll be plenty."

She gaped at him as he counted out another five hundred in cash onto the table.

"This is for food and other household expenses in the meantime. Enough?"

Mutely, she nodded. Pain curled around her stomach, spreading through her whole body with each beat of her stinging heart.

He picked up the car keys. "I'd prefer you didn't drive your own car all the way to UCLA and back every day. Brad says it's falling apart and it's a miracle it has lasted this long. These keys are to the Camaro. It's yours if you want it. Oh, yeah..." He pulled out his wallet and tossed another credit card onto the table. "Here's a gas card." He looked at her levelly. "Did I miss anything?"

Not trusting her voice, she gave her head a small shake.

He drained his coffee. "In that case, I'll be going."

His hand was reaching for the back door when she finally broke through the paralysis that held her in its grip. "I'm sorry about last night, Cole. I was upset. I've known all along you don't love me, and I have no right to expect anything more. Please—"

He stopped, then swung around, his face a study in cool indifference. She took a step back and hit the counter.

Memories of the way David had changed as soon as she'd moved into his condo crashed through her mind—memories of the way, almost overnight, a seemingly affectionate, considerate man had become the detestable bastard who'd flung biting, hurtful sarcasm at her every time she made a decision he didn't like. Which was nearly always.

Bracing herself for the ego-numbing abuse that was sure to follow, she recoiled from Cole's scrutiny. When he spoke, it was in a low voice, insinuating itself like a virus into her already frazzled nerves.

"No, Rini. You have every right to expect love from a husband. But don't ask me for it. I simply don't have it in me to give."

His eyes seared her almost painfully. "Physically, I want you like crazy, and I'm going to continue to want you. I'll honor our agreement, Rini, but I'm only human. Do me a big favor and from now on just stay out of my way. It'll be easier on both of us." He spun on a heel then and stalked out the door, slamming it shut.

Katarina's whole body reverberated with the weight of that slam. Her legs finally gave out and she slid down the cubboard to the floor, where she sat staring after him in a daze.

She supposed she had been dreaming to think their life could be anywhere close to normal, given their platonic relationship.

She glanced around the neat, simple kitchen, battling the despair in her heart. It would look nice painted yellow, she thought bleakly. With pretty white, lacy curtains. And white trim, too. Yes, he'd like white trim.

She bit her lip, tasting copper.

He hadn't ripped her to shreds, but he hadn't given her a chance, either. She closed her eyes and ran a shaky hand over the baby as he moved inside her. What would she do? She'd lost Cole before she'd even had a fair shot at winning him.

He just didn't understand. She'd already shared the bed of one man who didn't love her. It was just too painful to expose herself to that kind of hurt again. She'd come too far to go back to that place.

For a long time she sat there on the floor, only her hand on the baby moving. Cole had been very, very angry. But still, he hadn't made her feel like she was a a subhuman moron. In her misery, that thought nurtured a small seed of hope.

Finally, she roused herself. Shuddering out a sigh, she glanced up. Maybe she'd stencil a border around the walls up by the ceiling, too.

Yes. She'd like that.

Cole stumbled in after midnight, and the house was dark. The door to his bedroom stood wide open. Dog tired, he nearly collapsed into his bed, momentarily forgetting he no longer resided in the master bedroom. At the last minute he spied Rini there, ensconced in a pile of pillows and his Pendleton blanket.

He stood over her, torn between feelings of anger and frustration, and those of sadness and longing. He didn't know what had possessed him that morning. Maybe it had been the thought of having to live under the same roof with her, still furious with her—hell, with himself. Still wanting her. Unable to do anything about either. Knowing he had every right to. Knowing he had no right at all.

Damn, he was confused.

But he did feel a little better after a grueling day of self-punishment at the office, working through his feelings of being so thoroughly and unjustly rejected by her last night. After all, she'd known how he felt about love, long before letting him into that bed with her.

But Rini's apology this morning had told him loud and clear

that she hadn't intended to hurt him. She was just trying to work through her own private horrors. She had no way of knowing about his sensitivity to rejection. And he wasn't about to talk about it. Maybe in twenty or thirty years...

Rini moved in her sleep, hugging the pillow she held to her chest even tighter, softly murmuring words he couldn't quite hear. He was still angry, but even so, he had to stop himself from climbing in with her. He sighed, wondering when his body would get the message.

He turned and trailed into the guest room, emptying his jacket pockets as he went. Tossing his wallet and change onto the dresser, he stripped off his shirt and headed to the bathroom. Suddenly, he caught the smell of fresh paint.

Frowning, he turned and followed the smell into the chilly kitchen. A cold breeze blew in through open windows. Flicking on the light, he was floored to see what Rini had done. Instead of dull beige, the walls were now a bright, cheerful yellow, with glossy white trim.

"Like it?" Rini's sleepy voice sounded behind him.

He turned to the sight of her tousled hair falling over the lapels of his old flannel robe. "It's never looked so good," he said, momentarily unsure of whether he meant the kitchen or the robe.

She smiled tentatively. "I'm glad you like it."

He brought his wandering mind to heel. "But you shouldn't be painting."

She looked at her feet. "Dr. Morris said it was okay if I opened all the windows."

"That's not what I meant."

She didn't have to say a thing. The expression on her face said it all. She wanted to appease him.

He thought of his ex-wife's son, Jeff, who'd written him that heartbreaking letter, and of how things could have turned out just as badly with his own son and Rini if he hadn't made the effort to gather them to him. Silently, he thanked God for giving him the chance.

Guiltily, he shook his head. "Look, Rini, I'm sorry about this morning. I had no right coming down on you like a ton of bricks.''

She bit her lip. "I didn't mean to make you angry last night. I just—"

"I know," he said, more gruffly than he intended. "Apology's not necessary. And you don't have to earn your keep." He cut her a look. "In any way."

Eyes still on the floor, she nodded.

He glanced around the kitchen. "I don't want you doing so much. You just take care of yourself and the baby."

She looked up at him imploringly. "I need to feel useful. Let me do a few things around the house, at least." She laid her hand on his arm. "Please, Cole."

The way her eyes pleaded with him, he couldn't find it in his heart to refuse. Before he did something he'd regret, he moved his arm out from under her hand and started toward the living room. "Just be careful and don't overdo it, okay? Now, get back to bed. You'll catch your death with all these windows open."

When the office phone rang for the fifth time, Cole looked up irately from the papers he was working on. There weren't all that many days left to tie up loose ends before the birth. He'd wanted to finish this one last brief before going home, and the phone had been ringing nonstop since he'd gotten to his office three hours ago. A headache drilled into his brain.

"Lonetree," he snapped into the mouthpiece.

"Cole, sweetie, is that any way to greet your wife?"

He was in no mood for jokes. "No, but that's not a problem, since you're not my wife."

"Oh, but I am," the smug feminine voice purred. "This is Lindsay. I'm crushed you didn't recognize me."

Lindsay! That was just what he needed right now. *Not.*

"What the hell do you want?" When he hadn't heard from her after getting the letter from Jeff a couple of weeks ago, he'd thought her silence was too good to be true.

"It's nice to hear your voice, too. How are you?"

"Lindsay, I'm very busy, so you'll excuse me if I hang up."

"That wouldn't be a very good idea, sweetie. What would

your pretty new wife say if she found out her husband has a fourteen-year-old son?''

He drilled a hand through his hair, scowling furiously. ''Sorry, won't work. I never touched you and you know it.''

''Yes, well. There's just your word on that, isn't there?''

''Ever heard of DNA testing?'' Cole rubbed his aching temple. ''You've got a screw loose, Lindsay. I've already talked to Jeff and he knows I'm not his father. Stop hassling me, and don't even think about contacting my wife.''

She was silent for a moment, then sighed defeatedly. ''Give me a break, okay? I gave the kid up for adoption, and now he's found me. He's 'looking for his roots,''' she mimicked, groaning. ''He's only interested in his Native half. He can barely bring himself to speak to me. I remember what you went through when you were young. I just thought…''

Cole stifled his knee-jerk reaction to the subject of his own adoption. He had already told Jeff he'd take him to the next powwow and introduce him around the local Indian community. Teach him a few things. But Lindsay didn't need to know that. ''What do you want from me?''

''Can't you call him back and tell him you're his father?''

''Are you out of your mind?'' he shouted before getting hold of his temper. ''Besides being immoral and an outright lie, it wouldn't be fair to the boy. He deserves to find his real father.''

He heard a muffled female sniffle. *Great.*

He turned and sat against his desk, massaging his neck. ''Lindsay, I really don't need this bullshit right now.''

''Help me, Cole. Daddy will disown me if he finds out. He thought I was away at college. I have no idea who the kid's father was, except he was obviously Indian. Help me find out. Please?''

Cole smoothed down his tie and let out a long breath, cursing long and hard. Damn. Damn. Damn. This was way more involved than he wanted to get. But when he thought of the boy, his heart just wouldn't let him turn his back.

''Send me a list of potential candidates. No promises, but I'll see what I can find out.''

* * *

Katarina bit off the thread after finishing one last throw pillow, tossed it next to its mates on the sofa and stood back to admire her handiwork.

The worn area rug in the living room had been replaced with a new handmade one she had bought at a local weaving guild. She'd looked everywhere for coordinating fabric and, when she found the perfect match, had sewn curtains for all six windows, and today she had finished a dozen cozy throw pillows for the sofas and Cole's chair. The room looked even better than the guest room, which she'd redone last week. She smiled in satisfaction.

She checked the clock on the mantel. She had an hour to spare before she had to start dinner. Today she was trying her hand at fajitas—Cole had mentioned a few days ago how much he liked them. But they seemed pretty easy to make, so maybe she should get in some study time beforehand. Or maybe...

Her gaze skittered to the phone in the kitchen, and instantly she was deluged with uneasy emotions. She had put off this call as long as she could, but it couldn't be put off any longer. Her hand shook slightly at the thought of dialing the familiar number. But today, when she felt so good and had accomplished so much, surely today she would be strong enough to do it.

Resolutely, she walked to the phone, picked it up and dialed. All too quickly a brisk, feminine voice said, "Hello," sounding like she was next door instead of three thousand miles away.

"Hi, Mama."

"Katarina, is that you?"

"Yes, Mother."

"You'll have to make it fast, dear. I'm just on my way out the door. Frazer is taking me to the opening of that new show everyone's raving about. You've seen it, of course, since it was in L.A. last month. I have a fabulous new—"

"Mama, I got married a few weeks ago. I just thought you might like—"

"Married! Well, congratulations, dear, it's about time you came to your senses and married David. After all, you've been with him for years now—"

"I told you I left David last year. My husband's name is Colton Lonetree."

"Don't be ridiculous. David was perfect for you. He gave you direction. Left him? How could you? He was practically the most eligible bachelor in Los—"

"He didn't love me."

"Love? Pshaw. There are more important— This is just typical of you, Katarina. You never think before you leap into something. So tell me, who is this man you've married? Hilton something? What does he do? And why wasn't your own mother invited?"

"It's Cole. Colton Lonetree. He's a—"

"Is he some sort of foreigner? Lonetree doesn't sound like an English name to me."

"You'd like him. He's very nice. Handsome, too. He's Native American, from down—"

"Native American! You mean a…a—"

"A lawyer, Mama. You always wanted me to marry a lawyer. And now I have."

"Well. Then I guess he must be—"

"I'm going to have a baby, too. Isn't that wonder—"

"A baby!?"

"—ful? It's a boy and he's due next week. We're so thrilled…. Mother?"

"When did you say you got married?"

"A few weeks ago. I'm sorry I didn't call sooner—it was all pretty sudden. It was a courthouse wedding, but very nice. Alex had everyone back to the house afterward and she made this delicious chocolate wedding cake—"

"Oh, Katarina, what have you done?"

"It would be really nice if you could come out after the baby's born and meet him and Cole. I know you'll like—"

"I just can't believe it. Forced to get married in this day and age. Well, you'll simply have to do the best with the situation you've made for yourself. I only hope to God you won't be too miserable. At least he's a lawyer."

"His house is really cute, too. It has the prettiest yellow kitchen. With white trim. Just like we used to have when Daddy was—"

"It sounds delightful, dear. Uh-oh, I hear Frazer calling. Got to run. Congratulations, Katarina. I hope you'll be very happy. You'll let me know how it goes, won't you? Ta ta for now!"

"Bye, Mama. I love you."

Chapter 12

Cole pulled the truck into the driveway and parked behind the Camaro. He jumped out and strode up the walk, wondering what surprises were in store for him today.

Rini always had something going—in three weeks she'd practically redecorated his entire house. He was worried that she was endangering her health, but besides that, he honestly didn't know when she found time to do it all, between classes and studying half the night. He'd never seen anyone work so hard in all his life.

He hadn't meant for it to be like this. He didn't like it. But the more he tried to discourage her, the more she would do.

He flung open the front door and called out, "Rini?"

"In here," she called from his room. Her room. Whoseever the hell room it was.

Sighing, he slipped off his shoes and tossed his briefcase onto the easy chair before going to her. He stopped in the doorway. Except for their wedding night and those few minutes the second night, he hadn't set foot in his old room since she'd moved into it. "Hi."

"Hi. I got some things."

"So I see."

His bed was piled high with baby things. On the floor sat an infant car seat and a big narrow box containing an unassembled crib. Rini had scrounged up his toolbox from the garage and now sat next to it, ripping open the carton. She looked mighty uncomfortable.

"Here—" he quickly squatted down by her "—let me help."

"It's okay, I can manage."

He grasped her hands. "No one doubts that, darlin'. Why don't you relax on the bed and watch?"

Her fingers tightened briefly around his and she squeezed her eyes shut. He could see the dark smudges under them.

"The stuff for fajitas is ready. I should set the table."

"Dinner can wait. Come on. Sit." He led her to the bed and cleared a spot. "Are you having more contractions?"

She lifted a shoulder. "The usual. But my back is killing me. Too much shopping, I guess."

"Doing too much everything, I guess. I'll run a nice warm bath for you tonight." Before she leaned back against the headboard, he propped pillows behind her. "I've been wondering when you were going to get baby things."

She lowered her gaze as she rubbed her stomach. "I was hoping you'd go with me. But you've been so busy."

He stopped and looked at her, guilt washing over him once more. "You should have said something."

"I know you're trying to tie things up at the office before next week. I didn't want to be a bother."

"You're not a bother, Rini. Ever." He cleared his throat. "Look, I know we didn't exactly get off on the right foot, but we're a family now." He got up and paced over to the box holding the crib. "We have to learn to work together. For the baby's sake."

When he glanced back, Rini's eyes were closed and there was a hint of melancholy in her face. "I know. You're right."

He shrugged off his jacket and hung it over the doorknob, then opened the carton and began taking out crib pieces. Her gaze followed him as he worked. He put the crib together and then set it up in a corner of the room.

"Nice crib." He surveyed his finished handiwork and watched her pull a thick pad and sheet out of a bag. He took them and made up the miniature mattress. Rini fastened some colorful bumpers around the perimeter. He couldn't believe that soon a new baby would be sleeping there. His baby.

He slipped his arm around Rini and they both stood for several minutes gazing at the crib, contemplating what was to come. Without thinking, he reached over and put his hand on her stomach. He felt the muscles ripple, growing rock hard under his fingers. "Another contraction?"

She nodded. "How about some dinner? I'm starved. Then I need to get all this stuff put away. I should do some studying, too, but I'd like to get that baby quilt finished."

He shook his head. "What you need is some sleep."

She smiled, heading for the kitchen. "Too much to do."

The next morning Cole woke to the sound of Rini's moans. He opened his eyes and stared at the pillow in the still-strange bed for a moment, getting his bearings. The moans fit right into the pleasant dream he'd been having, but when he reached for his wife she was nowhere in sight. When another soft moan floated down the hall, he shot out of bed and ran to her room.

"Are you all right?" He approached the bed where she lay tangled in the sheet, the Pendleton blanket in a heap on the floor beside her.

Her eyes had been closed but sprang open at his words. "Cole!" Her hand went to her brow. "I had the strangest dream. I dreamed a Sherman tank was driving laps over my stomach. Ow!"

"What's happening?" He leaned over the bed, alarmed by the expression of surprise and pain on her face. "Woman, talk to me!"

"I'm awake, but the tank is still there." Her eyes widened and she clutched her stomach. "Oh, Cole. I think this is it."

He looked at her, shocked. "You're kidding, right? Tell me this isn't happening a week early."

She shook her head, obviously reluctant to believe it herself. "No. First babies never come early. Besides, it can't be time. I haven't even packed." She lifted her hands tentatively, then smiled. "See? All gone."

Breathing a sigh of relief, he plunked himself down on the side of the bed. "Had me worried for a minute there." He glanced at the alarm clock on her nightstand. "Time to get up, anyway. Feel like some breakfast?"

She scooted to a sitting position, pulling the sheet with her, and grimaced. "Oh, man. Do the tread marks show?"

He shot her a look, frowning. "Still hurt?"

She smiled weakly. "Only when I breathe." She held out her hands. "Help me up? Maybe I can walk the kinks out."

This was not good. Something was wrong; he just knew it. "Maybe you should call the doctor."

"I'll have a walk around the house first. Are you making eggs? I'm starving."

Grinning, he rose. "I'll take that as a good sign. Scrambled okay?" He helped her to her feet and caught her staring at his attire.

"Silk boxers?" She reached out and fingered the fabric.

He felt his grin turn lopsided. He loved the feel of the cool, slippery material against his bare skin, found it extremely soothing and sensual, but hadn't ever admitted it to anyone before. "Why should women have all the fun?"

She grabbed his arm to steady herself, her face scrunching up in a wince of pain. "Yeah, this is fun. I'll trade you anytime."

Instantly, the playfulness was forgotten. "Rini, these contractions are coming pretty close together. Are you sure it isn't time?"

After a moment, she took a deep breath and smiled bravely. "Yeah, it's time. Time for breakfast."

He chuckled and headed for the kitchen. "Yes, ma'am." If there was one thing he'd learned in the past weeks, it was if she was hungry, the kid didn't stand a chance. Baby might as well make himself comfortable and wait out breakfast.

As he prepared the eggs and set the table, Cole could hear her moving around, to the bathroom and back to her room, then walking in circles in the living room. He seemed to recall something from childbirth class about changing activities to determine if labor was real or false. Since she had been lying down, walking around should either make the contractions go away or speed them up. Either way they'd know.

He scrubbed his face with his hands. Hell. He wasn't ready for this. He went out to get her. "Breakfast is ready."

"Cole?"

He sought her eyes. "Yeah, babe?"

"They're not going away."

Cole nodded numbly. "Okay. What do we do now?"

"Eat," Rini answered.

He cleared his throat. "Right. I'll be right there." Splashing his face with water in the bathroom, he took a good look in the mirror. "Hey, Dad." He squeezed his eyes shut and groaned. Nope. He definitely was not ready for this.

When he joined Rini in the kitchen, she was helping herself to a second plate of eggs.

"Should you be eating?"

"I have a feeling I'll be needing all the energy I can get. Besides, this could take days."

He looked at her nervously. "Have you called Alex?"

"Yeah." She bit her lip. "Brad says she's on her way to San Diego for a business meeting."

His fork clattered to the plate. "Get her back!"

Rini shook her head. "She doesn't have a car phone. I left a message in San Diego, but by the time she makes the three-hour drive, gets the message and turns around, it could be all over."

"Aw, hell."

She looked up. "You can do it, Cole. You went to class."

"Me?" He surged forward. "I went *one* time! My God, Rini! I don't know the first thing!" He fell back into his chair, running a hand over his forehead. "What if I screw up?"

She raised a brow at him, then wrapped her arms around her stomach as another contraction took hold. "Comfort and encouragement," she rasped. "That's all you need to think about."

He was on his knees at her side in a second, anxiously searching for something useful to do to help her. He couldn't even hold her hand because she was busy using it to rub her belly.

He drilled his fingers through the sides of his hair. "Relax, take a deep breath and think about waves."

"I think it's a little early for that, Cole. I still have to pack."

"What?" He looked at her uncomprehendingly. "Oh." He grinned sheepishly. "I was talking to myself, not you."

She let her breath out in a laugh. "Jerk."

He parried her teasing smack on the shoulder and caught her hand in his. "Do me a favor?"

She nodded, her face glowing with the quiet excitement of what was happening.

"Pack your damn bag so we can get to the hospital? I'd just as soon not have to deliver this baby myself."

With his help she stood, then reached up and gave him a quick hug and a kiss on the cheek. "As soon as I take a shower."

He groaned.

After pacing for what seemed like hours, Cole at last hefted the small overnight bag Rini had thrown together before getting in the shower. "Finally! Is this everything?"

"Got the car seat?"

"Yep."

"Blanket and an outfit for him?"

"From the dresser like you said." Putting a hand on the small of her back, he firmly guided her toward the front door. Even after a warm shower, she looked drawn and pale, with lines of discomfort etched around her mouth. "Come on, let's go. The contractions are practically knocking you over now." He was about to have a nervous breakdown trying to get her to the car. Every time they got close, she'd remember something else. He had visions of having the baby on the corner of Colorado and Fair Oaks.

She gasped loudly.

He dropped the bag and grabbed her. "What? Are you okay?"

"My legs!"

"What about them? Do they hurt?"

"I forgot to shave my legs!"

He dropped his forehead to hers in relief, desperately fighting back the aggravation. "The baby won't care, and I promise not to look.'' He retrieved the bag from the floor. ''We're going now.''

She clutched his arm, the pain in her face evident. ''But I—''

''Now, Rini. We're leaving *now.*''

She stopped walking for a minute, closing her eyes and breathing through the contraction, leaning into him. ''I guess I can't put it off any longer. But I'm scared, Cole. So scared.''

He swallowed hard and put his arms around her. ''I know, honey. I'm here for you. I'll take care of you and the baby, you can count on that.'' He lifted her into his arms and carried her the rest of the way to the truck, then hurried around to the driver's side before remembering. ''Jeez, the pillows.''

It was a nightmare seeing her work so hard. It definitely put a whole new perspective on those hours of pleasure they had enjoyed nine months earlier. It was a wonder women ever wanted to have sex.

Cole sat on the hospital bed with Rini in his lap, just as they'd learned in childbirth class, coaxing her to relax her back against him between the steadily mounting waves of contractions. The bandanna he'd tied around his forehead to catch the stinging drops of perspiration before they hit his eyes was soaked.

Suddenly, she demanded, ''Dammit, Cole, how could you do this to me?'' She went limp in his arms, grabbing a short time to rest. ''Why the hell didn't you use protection?'' Her tone was sharp and accusatory.

Stunned, he saw the two delivery nurses glance covertly at each other in amusement. One of them checked her watch, while the other hurried out of the room. ''I…'' He cleared his throat, unable to think of an appropriate response. *Hell of a time to bring up this topic.* ''I…''

''Oh, now there's a brilliant comeback.'' Rini's voice, dripping with sarcasm, tightened along with her stomach muscles. ''Well, I hope it was worth it, sweet cakes. Seducing an inno-cent— Aaahhh!'' She moaned as the next contraction hit.

What the blazes was with her, anyway? Suddenly he remembered the instructor's words. *When she starts swearing and calling you names...* He nearly drooped with relief. "Almost through, darlin'. Just hang in there for a few more minutes." He kissed the top of her head and counted slowly as she struggled to relax through the peak.

"*You* hang in there if you want to," she gasped. "I want a C-section."

The door swung open and Dr. Morris stepped smartly over to the bed. "What's this nonsense about a C-section?" She checked the array of monitors, then stood with her arms crossed and a stern smile on her face. "You're doing great. This'll be over in no time."

"Easy for you to say," Rini grumbled, collapsing against Cole's chest.

The back of her hospital gown was damp with sweat, as were her face and neck. The fragrance of her shampoo mingled with the sweet tangy scent of hard physical work. He held her close, supporting her as she caught her breath, and gradually realized that her horrific contractions had slowed considerably. It had been several moments since her body had clenched in pain.

"Oh, man," she said unnaturally loudly. "Oh my God, I have to push!"

Dr. Morris had positioned her stool at the end of the bed, and now started issuing orders fast and furiously, first to the nurses and then to Rini. "Okay, Rini, slide down here. That's right. Next contraction, go ahead and push!"

They hadn't done this in the class Cole had attended, so after he hopped off the bed, the nurse showed him how to help Rini hold her position with a hand on her shoulder and one under her knee as she strained to push the baby out, then support her back in between. After a few times he felt fairly competent, but his strength was flagging miserably. He couldn't even begin to imagine how Rini felt.

"Cole! Let's see the top of your head."

He glanced up from his weary concentration when Dr. Morris addressed him. He wondered why she wanted to see the top of his head, but was too exhausted to ask. He bowed down.

"Yep, so far he looks just like you."

Cole blinked, then met Rini's wide-eyed gaze. They both burst out laughing at the same time. "Oh, Lord," she giggled, and winced at the same time. "Don't make me laugh! Oh, my...oh, God!"

She doubled over in a tremendous effort. Cole could feel his face drain of blood just watching his wife's intense mask of concentration. When would this torture cease? A muscle under his right eye ticked and he literally had to bite his tongue to keep from yelling at the doctor to just *do* something to end her agony.

Rini's body melted back over his arm as she panted in huge breaths. He grabbed a cool cloth and lovingly sponged her face. When he tried to whisper some word of encouragement, his voice tripped over a lump in his throat, cracking the word into bits. Swallowing heavily, he kissed her temple.

"Baby's crowning!" called Dr. Morris. "Hold back, Rini. Wait...wait...wait... Okay, push!"

Cole filled with panic when Rini shouted like a longshoreman lifting a bale, her body trembling with exertion. He glanced desperately at the two nurses, inwardly cursing their calm, rational demeanor. Couldn't they see she was dying?

"Rini!" he choked out when she collapsed onto her back, her head limp, her eyes closed. Shaking her gently, he opened his mouth to yell for help, when suddenly the air was pierced by a small hiccuping cry. Her eyes opened, and she smiled up at him then, all the former exhaustion in her face turning to radiant happiness.

"It's a boy." Dr. Morris' voice cut through the haze in his brain. "But then, you knew that. Cole?"

He tore his gaze from Rini's and looked toward the doctor. In her hands she held his son, red-faced and wailing, a perfect bundle of wiggling life. Cole's eyes filled and he looked at Rini. Gathering her in his arms, he rocked her as the tears he was unable to stop trickled down his cheeks. "You did it, sweetheart," he whispered hoarsely.

At that moment, he knew he would do anything in the world for this woman—his beautiful wife who had just given him the most precious gift of a lifetime. He vowed right then to try his

damnedest to put his mistrust behind him and learn to give her
what she wanted—what she deserved. His unconditional love.
He looked into her fire eyes and then tenderly kissed her.

"Thank you," he whispered, gathering her close.

Rini smiled and accepted another kiss from Cole. Poor man.
He looked like he'd been through a war. She reached up and
smoothed a trail of moisture from his cheek before he turned to
Dr. Morris. A tear? Surely not. His bandanna must have over-
flowed.

"Cole? Would you like to cut the cord?"

She watched her husband nod happily and move into the hub
of activity at the end of the table. His eyes scarcely left their
tiny son as the doctor and nurses swabbed, clamped, wiped and
swaddled. Rini lay back on the pillows, tired but content.

Their son. Hers and Cole's.

When they placed the baby in Cole's arms, the look on his
face was worth every bit of the pain she'd just gone through.
He murmured soothing words to the crying infant, caressing his
plump rosy cheek. The little one quieted and turned his face to
Cole's, grasping his daddy's finger and pulling it to his mouth.

Katarina's heart melted at the sight. Father and son had
bonded instantly, the love between them evident to everyone in
the room. She let out a little sigh, banishing the involuntary wish
that, just once, Cole might look at her with such utter devotion.

He brought the baby to her, carefully unwrapping his blanket
and laying him skin to skin at her breast. She scarcely dared to
hold him for fear of squeezing the little mite. But when he nuzzled her breast, seeking the nipple, she hugged him close and
lost her heart completely. She looked up at Cole, who stood
watching, a funny smile on his face.

He pushed a stray lock of hair from her temple, his fingers
lingering on her face. "I'm so proud of you. You were wonderful."

She felt warm all over and basked in his praise. "I couldn't
have done it without you. Thanks." She giggled then, giddy with
happiness. "Sorry I swore at you."

Grinning, he dropped down beside her, stroking the baby's

head as he nursed. "I probably deserved it." Cole's gaze softened to mush as it glided over her cradling the baby to her
breast. "But I have to tell you, seeing you like this—I may never
want to use protection again."

After being moved to her room, Katarina lay back in bed,
watching Cole hold the baby in a rocking chair the nurse had
brought in. There was a knock, and Alex appeared in the doorway.

"Rini! I can't believe this!" Her sister rushed into the room
and hugged her madly. "The one day I was gone! How could
you?" She laughed and hugged her some more. "Are you okay?
Where is he, the little darling?"

Alex glanced around the room expectantly and caught sight
of Cole. "Oh. Cole." She straightened, folding her arms over
the double-breasted jacket of her designer suit. "Thank you for
taking care of Rini."

He gave a tight smile. "She's my wife, Alex. It's my job to
take care of her. Hi Brad, Kenny," he said, rising as the two
walked in.

"Hey, man, congratulations!" Brad came over and slapped
him on the arm that cradled the baby. "Let's see the little guy.
Aw, if he isn't the cutest—Rini! You outdid yourself!" He
leaned over the bed and planted a smack on her cheek.

"Thanks, Brad. He is kind of cute, isn't he?" Katarina
couldn't believe that less than twelve hours ago he'd been snug
inside her body. It was amazing. "Al, aren't you going to look
at him?"

Alex squeezed her arm. "Of course I am." She got up and
glanced hesitatingly at Cole. Rubbing her hands down her skirt,
she approached.

Cole's eyes remained neutral while Alex reached one finger
up and moved the blanket away from the baby's cheek. Something flitted across her face, something that could have been
sadness, but she schooled her features quickly.

"He's beautiful," Alex murmured softly.

Katarina could feel her face begin to crumble when Cole carefully lifted him, offering the baby to Alex. At Alex's surprise, he nodded. "Go ahead, if you like."

Her sister held the baby with the gentle awe of a woman who longed for a child of her own with all her heart. "Oh, Rini, he's perfect."

Cole walked over and stood next to the bed. For a moment his fingers danced lightly on Katarina's shoulder, then he slipped his arm around her, pulling her close. She sighed, feeling at once warm and secure, surrounded as she was by her family—the people who loved her. She leaned her head against Cole's side. Well, most of them loved her.

But it was a start.

Alex cooed at the baby, stroking his tiny nose and chin, then gave him a kiss on the forehead. She looked up then, her eyes shiny, a tremulous smile on her lips. "He looks just like you, Cole." Swallowing heavily, she gingerly passed him back to his father.

Katarina watched the emotions pass over Alex's face, ending with a single tear, which her sister quickly dashed away.

"I'm an aunt!" Laughing, she plopped onto the bed and hugged Rini again.

"What's his name?" Kenny asked, peering into the face of his new cousin. Alex and Brad looked expectantly at Katarina.

"Gosh, I don't know." Her eyes met Cole's. "We haven't really talked about it yet. What do you think?"

Seating himself on the bed, he let her take the baby from him. "I've got a good friend named Roman. Always liked that name."

Rini considered. Roman was nice. She could live with that.

"What name would you choose?"

"Me?" Cole's question knocked her off balance. "Well," she ventured hesitantly, "I've been thinking maybe I'd like to call him Chance."

She looked down at the baby in her arms and smiled. He was her big chance. Her chance to make her life into something really good, after all she'd gone through. Through him, she'd gotten a second chance with Cole, with school, and ultimately, with herself.

Cole adjusted the blanket around the baby. "I like that. Chance it is."

Her jaw dropped. "Really? Just like that?"

"Sure, why not? It fits. Chance Lonetree. Sounds good."

Kenny nodded seriously. "Major cool name."

Chance did nothing but eat and sleep. Well, and poop. Chuckling, Cole changed his fourth diaper that afternoon. He loved it. He loved everything that brought him in contact with his baby boy.

Rini was napping, exhausted after a week of feeding Chance every two hours. How she would be able to start back to class on Monday Cole had no idea.

He shook his head, smiling wryly at Chance as he slipped his romper back on. "You've got one very stubborn mama, little one. She's determined to get this nursing degree." Lifting him in the air, he winked and kissed his nose. "Guess you'll just have to put up with your old man feeding you when she has classes."

Chance let out a belch, and Cole laughed out loud. "Yeah, I know. If I had the choice of sucking from those beautiful, round—" He stopped abruptly, clearing his throat. "Well, anyway. I'll enjoy feeding you."

It had been pure torture watching Rini breast-feed. Her already perfect breasts had become even fuller and her nipples were dark and inviting. His mouth watered every time she shyly pulled aside her top, conscious of his gaze, but thankfully unaware of his ravenous hunger.

At first he'd tried not to watch, but seldom succeeded. So he'd gone out and bought a gorgeous antique rocker for her, positioning it in front of the fireplace across from his easy chair, where he had a perfect view.

He'd gotten into the habit of bringing her a warm, damp cloth after Chance had finished, then taking the contented baby to his crib while she got herself together. If he didn't leave the room, he was sure he'd slip up and ask if she needed help, bringing all their sexual electricity crackling to the surface again. Bad idea.

The doctor had told them no sex for six weeks after the delivery. But of course, that advice was academic. Rini obviously didn't plan on letting it happen, even after the six weeks were up.

Cole had already come to crave her presence in so many other ways—for her sunny smile first thing in the morning, her loving glances when she thought he wasn't looking, their long talks in front of the fireplace. He told himself to be strong, to fight his physical need for her. Opening himself like that would surely be begging for a heartache. For until she took that final step herself, with no pressure from him, Cole couldn't be sure she was committed to staying with him. So he kept his emotions locked down tight.

Rini appeared in the bedroom doorway wearing his flannel robe all a-kilter, her face flushed and hair mussed like she'd just come from beneath him. The sight of her sleepy smile hit him right below the belt.

He took a deep breath. Aw, hell, who was he kidding? At that moment he knew he wouldn't rest until he'd made love to her. He'd face the heartache—if and when it came.

"Hi. Good nap?"

"Mmm. Wonderful. Everything okay?"

"Four poopy diapers and he stuck his tongue out at me three times." His favorite game with Chance was stick-your-tongue-out-at-the-other-guy.

Laughing softly, she let her loving gaze drift from his face to the baby in his arms. "You're such a goof." Tilting her head, she stepped over to them and drew a finger down Chance's cheek. She smelled wonderful, like his Pendleton blanket and baby powder and tantalizing woman, all rolled into one.

The robe's front hung slightly open, revealing the lush curve of her breasts. It was all Cole could do to tear his eyes away. *Four more weeks.*

"Mom called to see how you were," he said to distract himself. "I asked them to dinner tomorrow night."

"Sounds nice. I can make—"

"I'll make dinner." He passed Chance to Rini when the baby

started to fuss. "You've got enough to worry about feeding this greedy little fella."

She landed a quick kiss on the side of Cole's mouth. "You're spoiling me rotten, you know."

"About time someone did." He leaned toward her, thinking about a lingering return kiss. Chance started wailing in earnest. Cole chuffed out a breath. The kid's timing definitely needed work.

Chapter 13

"He's such an angel," Cole's mom, Julia, whispered to Rini before dinner the next night as they bent over the sleeping baby. "You must be so happy."

Rini sighed with contentment. "Unbelievably. I keep pinching myself to be sure it's all real."

They quietly went out and Julia took her hand. "Rini, Ted and I have known you for only a few weeks, but I want you to know we already love you like a daughter. And we are so grateful to you for Chance. He's a dream come true for us."

When Julia gave her a hug, she knew it was heartfelt. "I feel just the same about you and Ted."

"I wish you would call us Mom and Dad."

"I'd like that." A warm glow spread through her. This woman had given her more love and support in the past few weeks than her own mother had in thirty-one years. Smiling, she linked her arm through Julia's. "I'd like that very much."

When they walked into the living room with their arms affectionately around each other, Cole raised a questioning brow.

Katarina grinned. "Sorry, I've stolen your mom and dad. They're mine now."

Rising from the couch, he mocked a frown. "Is that so?"

"Yep."

He ushered them all toward the dining room, shaking his head. "I'm sure there's a word for that."

"Yeah. It's *family.*"

At that, he turned and regarded her while his parents seated themselves at the table, an odd look on his face.

"I'm beginning to find out what I've been missing," she said.

"And?"

"I like it. I think I might stick around," she teased.

He reached out and grasped her arms, and for a moment Katarina thought he would say something more, something important. But instead he just kissed her forehead. "Good choice."

There was that damn word again. Just when she thought she'd finally gotten over her fear of making decisions, he went and said something like that. She knew Cole was nothing like David. He'd never once questioned any of her choices and had always given her his full support. But the word still made her very nervous.

As she took her seat next to him, she scolded herself soundly. She was being ridiculous. Cole wasn't going to change into some controlling macho man overnight. He'd proven that time and again.

She reached for a platter. "This all looks wonderful! I had no idea you were such a gourmet cook."

"Hidden talents." He grinned roguishly. "You'd be surprised how many I have."

It was impossible to miss his meaning. He had that pirate look about him that had nearly undone her once before. She felt her cheeks grow warm. He winked.

Oh, Lord. She passed the roast to Ted and thought about how the temperature in the house had gone up several degrees in the past twenty-four hours. She wondered what had caused the sudden rise. For the first time since their wedding night, Cole was actually flirting with her again. She snatched up the potatoes, scooping a mountain onto her plate.

"Hungry, darlin'?" The wicked gleam in his eye belied his mild smile.

Katarina glanced at Ted and Julia. But if they knew what was going on they gave no indication, instead heaping Cole's delicious meal onto their plates.

Ted broke into the charged silence. "So, you been to any powwows lately?"

Cole's knife clattered to his plate and he stared at his father. "Excuse me?"

Ted's brows went up. "Powwows. You know. Big party, dance circle, lots of feathers. I seem to recall you going to a couple hundred in the past decade."

Cole didn't look at Katarina once as he coughed a little and retrieved his knife. "No, I, uh, haven't been to any in quite a while."

His mother gave him a puzzled look. "Oh? But dancing was so important to you. What happened?"

Thoughtfully, Katarina watched him grope for the tie he wasn't wearing, recognizing the nervous gesture.

"Just got busy." He glanced at her. "I was actually thinking of taking Rini and the baby to one pretty soon. Sort of introduce them around."

Katarina felt a surge of alarm. Irrational as she knew it was, the thought of meeting all those pretty women he claimed were just students didn't appeal to her at all. She couldn't stand it if he flirted with them. "I don't know if that's such a good idea—"

"Sure it is. Once word gets out, everyone will be dying to meet you and see the baby. And I sort of promised this kid... Mom?"

The sudden concern in his eyes made Katarina glance over at Julia. She was staring wide-eyed at her plate, her hands at her throat, looking like she was struggling with something.

Cole was at her side in a split second, calling in panic, "Mom! What's wrong? Mom!" He grasped her shoulders and shook her. She didn't appear to notice him, but stared fixedly at the table in front of her, hands grabbing at her throat. He glanced to his dad in desperation.

Julia's eyelids began to flutter.

"My God! She can't breathe!" Katarina jumped up, seizing

Cole's wrist as he was about to slap his mother on the back. "No! That will just make it worse!"

"But you said she can't breathe!"

"I know, let me—"

"I have to do some—"

"Cole, please! Move aside!" Katarina put a hand on his biceps and pushed him out of her way, none too gently. She had to hurry, Julia was already unnaturally pale. Rushing to the back of her chair, she put her arms around her mother-in-law's chest, linking her hands just under the ribs. Then she gave a big pull, trying to force the air out of Julia's lungs, bringing the obstruction with it.

It didn't work! She could feel Julia starting to slump from lack of oxygen.

Once more she pulled with all her might. There was a pop and a wheezing sound, and suddenly Julia sputtered and was racked with coughs, sucking in air, tears streaming from her eyes.

Thank God!

Julia gave a final cough and groaned, but finally responded to Cole's frantic queries. "I'm fine. Thanks to Rini."

"You did it!" Cole's eyes met Katarina's as he held his mom, respect and profound gratitude shining through. "You saved her life!"

She smiled self-consciously. "All in a day's work for a nurse."

Once Julia's breathing was back to normal, they helped her to the couch and urged her to lie down, then Ted called the paramedics.

"Rini? Thank you." Her mother-in-law's voice was raw and full of emotion. "I was so frightened. I was so sure I was going to die. I couldn't breathe and—"

"It's over now. You're fine." Katarina put her hand on Julia's and gave her a reassuring smile to stem the horror in the older woman's eyes. "Rest now."

Cole pulled her up into his embrace. He clung to her, his hands kneading her back. "I nearly lost it there. Thanks for taking over."

She hugged him back. "I'm just glad I could do something. Sorry I pushed you."

"Are you kidding? I was about to make things worse. Don't ever worry about my reaction. You just do what you have to do. I trust your judgment, Rini. I trust it with my life." He sighed as he watched his parents over her shoulder.

Tears came to her eyes from the sudden release of stress and because of his words. He trusted her decisions. She held him tightly, happiness and relief coursing through her body. It was like an enormous stone had been lifted from her whole being. He had actually said he trusted her choices.

A few days later, Cole sat with his ex-wife in a small restaurant. She'd wanted to meet to discuss Jeff, but Cole figured it was more to torment him.

"Tell me what you've done about the boy," she demanded.

Cole drove his fingers through his hair and tugged hard on the strands to prevent himself from grabbing her by the neck over the table between them and squeezing.

"These things take time, Lindsay. It's not like I can just stroll up to every Indian guy you ever slept with and make him take a DNA test. I'm working on it in my own way."

"I need results. I can't risk having the boy show up on my doorstep at an inopportune moment, asking questions."

Cole sighed at her unmotherly attitude. "Jeff's a good kid, Lindsay. You should accept him. Let him into your life."

She snorted. "Like you accepted your own mother?"

He sliced her a deadly look.

Her lips thinned. "It's best this way. For everyone. And he doesn't seem to care, anyway."

Cole crossed his arms over his chest. "He cares. Believe me, your son cares." He knew he was fighting a losing battle. "Look, I'm doing what I can. Be patient."

She tossed back the last of her wine and stood. She leaned over and put an arm around his neck, giving him a bitchy smile. "Yes, dear." She kissed his cheek, nearly choking him with her cloying perfume, then flounced out of the restaurant. He wiped his cheek with the back of his hand in disgust. And decided if she called him again making demands, he'd cheerfully wring her snooty little neck.

In the days that followed, Katarina caught Cole silently watching her at the strangest times—while she fed Chance, as he had been doing from the beginning, but also when she washed dishes, pored over her textbooks or weeded the garden. She'd look up and there he'd sit, chin in hand, a finger saving his place in the legal papers spread before him, or a strip of leather and an awl resting on his knee.

She would give him a little smile and suddenly he'd realize what he was doing. He'd grin back sheepishly and pretend to resume whatever project he was working on. But usually when he was in one of those moods, she'd look up five minutes later and he'd be back at it. It was kind of cute.

It made her think maybe she had a chance with him. That maybe he was beginning to fall in love with her, after all. The thought warmed her to the furthest reaches of her heart. Soon, she thought. *Soon.*

She no longer searched to find things to do that would please him. After his heartfelt words about her saving Julia's life, she had realized to her chagrin what she'd been doing since the wedding. In her anxiety over their uncertain relationship, she'd lapsed back into the old pattern of seeking approval.

One of these days she hoped with all her heart that his feelings would progress from affection to love. That he would tell her he loved her, so they could truly be husband and wife. But until that happened, she vowed not to push herself, or him. Love couldn't be hurried, no matter how much one longed for it.

Humming a little tune, she put the finishing touches on a snack tray she planned to carry out to Cole. She glanced up through the kitchen window, catching sight of him leaning under the hood of her old, beat-up compact. The driveway around it was scattered with tools and bottles of various automotive fluids.

Shirtless and wearing jeans with more holes than fabric, Cole's burnished body presented a delectable sight in the warm afternoon sunshine. She'd never quite gotten used to the capricious California weather, but at the moment she was enjoying its benefits to the fullest.

She checked on Chance, asleep in a bassinet in the living room. Then, sticking sprigs of fresh mint from the garden into two tall paper cups of iced tea, she picked up the tray and headed for the backyard.

Cole was now lying on his back on an ancient blanket under the engine. She put the tray on the grass near the driveway and sat down next to it. She knew better than to disturb him in the middle of some intricate maneuver under there. She'd learned restraint at an early age when her father had ended up with a face full of motor oil after she'd inadvertently startled him once. She grinned at the memory. Boy, had he been mad. But they'd ended up rolling on the grass in fits of laughter in the end, both covered in oil. Her mother, of course, had put an end to that bit of dirty nonsense.

Katarina had a great view of Cole's legs. Long and athletic under his bleached-out jeans, bent knees sloping to bare feet, they invited her glance to linger. The distinctive odor of motor oil mingled with the earthy scents of early spring and the tang of fresh strawberries. She sighed as she let her gaze wander slowly up Cole's body, caressing every inch of compact muscle as it went, until his lean, bare torso disappeared behind the jacked up wheel of her car.

The waistband of his jeans rode low on his narrow hips; his concave belly gleamed with sweat and a light spattering of grease. Lazily allowing her gaze to ride those hips awhile, she smiled to herself and popped a grape from the tray into her mouth. This was just what she'd always thought marriage would be like.

Except for that one small detail...

"You want me to take them off?"

She started at the sound of Cole's chuckle coming from under the car. "What?"

"My jeans. You want me to take them off? Seems like it might make all that fantasizing you're doing a whole lot easier."

Her face blazed in the warm sun. Oh, brother, caught red-handed. Or rather, red faced. His pirate's grin taunted her from around the front of the tire. She launched a grape at the cocky bastard.

"Ow!" He rubbed the spot on his thigh where it had bounced off. "Good thing your aim is off."

She stuck out her tongue. "Says who? That was just a warning shot."

"What was it, anyhow?"

"Grape. I brought refreshments."

"What a charming and delightful wife I have."

"Thank you."

"When she's not armed and dangerous." He slid out from under the car and sprawled on the ground on the other side of the tray, accepting the cup she offered him. "Paper?"

"So you don't have to wash your hands. My dad always hated interrupting his projects to clean up for a snack. So we worked out this system."

She followed his approving eyes as they traveled over the tray of grapes and early strawberries, cheese cubes and bread sticks, along with the small pile of toothpicks next to them.

"Toothpicks. Good idea. But what about the bread sticks?" His brow quirked.

"My dad used to smoke cigars. He'd just chomp on the bread sticks like stogies."

Cole nodded, watching her carefully. "Used to?"

Tamping down a quick sting of pain in her heart, she dropped her gaze to her hands. "He died of throat cancer while I was in college."

"I'm sorry." Cole sipped his tea, and a light, warm wind ruffled her hair. "You loved him very much." It wasn't a question. More like a quiet observation.

Sighing, she lay back on the springy grass and reached for a handful of cheese cubes. "Yeah—and the best part was he loved me back."

The apricot and plum trees that ringed the lawn were just breaking out in fragrant blossom, and the flowers shimmered in the breeze. Occasionally, one of the petals broke loose and floated slowly down to the lush grass. Katarina pulled in a big lungful of springtime.

"That's how I know," she murmured.

How she knew it was possible for a man to love her. Her father had never had a problem saying "I love you." The memory of his loving looks and hugs made her want to hold out for the real thing, even while it was breaking her heart to do so.

"How you know what?"

She glanced at Cole, who had rolled onto his stomach and lay with his chin on his arms, gazing out over the back garden, a toothpick hanging from his mouth.

"How I know to use paper cups," she said, covering her unwitting slip.

He glanced over but didn't challenge her. Instead, he went back to his survey of the budding perennials.

She studied his profile—the aristocratic nose, high angular cheekbones, square jaw and full, sensual lips. She watched as he sucked on the end of the toothpick, her imagination suddenly working overtime.

The ample muscles in his broad shoulders bunched and shifted as he reached for a bread stick, pulling the pick from his mouth. Closing her eyes, she had visions of those bronze shoulders hovering naked above hers, the corded muscles of his biceps working in an ancient rhythm as he moved over her. For the first time she saw the attraction of having mirrors over a bed. She had to stifle a groan.

Her eyes shot wide-open, she was so horrified at her errant thoughts. She grabbed her iced tea and gulped down half of it.

Cole's wicked chuckle drifted over the lawn. "What's the matter, darlin'? Gettin' too hot for you?" He sat up and tossed a couple of grapes into his mouth. In a supple movement he rose to his feet, then lithely, leisurely, stretched his body like a magnificent giant cat. A black-haired puma, the beautiful, dangerous mountain lion that roamed the arid hills of his native southern California.

She stared in fascination, holding her breath when it appeared that the loose waistband of his jeans would slide down over his slim hips and keep going.

"No such luck, babe," he teased, as if he could read her thoughts, "they seem to be caught on something."

She drew herself up, barely able to keep a straight face. "I can't imagine what you're talking about."

"Oh, you can imagine plenty, I'd wager." Arms folded across his powerful chest, he strolled over and stood before her. "The six weeks are nearly up, you know. After that I'm available anytime."

"In your dreams, *hombre*. Remember our agreement."

"I remember." His gaze was lit with a hunger that shook her. "But I've also seen the way you look at me."

She swallowed heavily.

Kneeling down, he leaned over and brushed his lips across hers. Just a whisper of a touch, light as the breeze soughing through the blossoms overhead. She shivered.

"I still want you," he said, his voice low and sultry.

She closed her eyes, expecting his lips to come crashing down on hers. When they didn't, she swayed imperceptibly toward him. He smelled of fresh grass and oil and grapes and Cole. She breathed in, savoring his nearness.

"You want me," he murmured.

The words tumbled softly over her hair and into her ears. She could feel his hot breath slide down the front of her dress, curling between her breasts. His finger traced a lazy path along her jaw. She realized she was trembling like a leaf.

"Open your eyes, Rini."

She obeyed, looking up into the liquid midnight of his.

"Admit it to yourself, if not to me." Again he brushed his velvet lips over hers, tenderly, longingly. Seductively. When he reached the corner of her mouth he increased the pressure just a shade, pressing a wisp of a kiss into her imagination. He whispered, "You want me, Fire Eyes."

You want me, Fire Eyes.

Katarina still shivered at the memory of him whispering those words seductively in her ear over two weeks ago.

She leaned heavily against the bathroom sink and contemplated her face in the mirror. *Panic.* That's what she saw. Pure, unadulterated terror.

It had been nearly six weeks since Chance's birth.

Cole had been a model of decorum, but she could see impatience in his eyes now, every time he looked at her. He was counting the days just as diligently as she was. But for entirely different reasons.

What would she do?

"Rini! Have you fallen in or what?" Alex's voice held mostly pique and only the barest hint of concern.

Katarina opened the door and smiled sheepishly. "Sorry."

"What is with you, anyway? You've been acting weird all afternoon, and I know it's not the wine. You've hardly touched yours."

She'd touched it just enough to blurt out in response, "It's Cole. He wants sex."

Alex's brow rose, and she smiled mischievously. "Imagine that. When does the doctor say it's okay?"

Katarina let out an exasperated breath and led Alex back to the living room. "No, you don't understand."

"So tell." Her sister flopped down on the sofa.

Reluctant to talk, but knowing she had to confide in someone or go nuts, Katarina leaned back against the cool brick of the fireplace. "We haven't had sex since Chance was—"

"Born. Right. I understand that's standard procedure."

"No. Since Chance was conceived."

"What!" Alex's eyes were the size of saucers. "But you're married! Why on earth not?"

"And now I'm afraid I'm going to give in to him, and I don't know what to do."

"Give in?" Alex refilled her wineglass and sank back against the sofa, taking a long swallow. "Rini," she said in a deadly calm voice. "Are you out of your mind?"

"I know I should stick to my principles, but he's just so damned...sexy."

"Principles?" Alex groaned, speaking to the floor lamp across room. "She's married to the hunk of the western world and she doesn't let him touch her."

Katarina looked up sharply. She'd noticed her sister's thaw toward Cole since the baby's birth, but until now Alex had never actually said anything to indicate her change of heart. "Since when are you on his side?"

"I know I thought he was scum-eating slime when I first met him, but I'm not too proud to admit I was wrong." She met Katarina's gaze directly. "I've seen how he treats you. He's a guy most women would kill to have. He's smart, good-looking, kind, generous, and he changes diapers."

"He had Obsession perfume on his shirt when he came home last week."

Alex looked up. Katarina knew exactly what she was thinking, but, to her credit, she didn't say it. Since discovering David's chronic infidelities, Katarina was prone to jealousy and suspicion at the least provocation. With David it had been deserved. With Cole her jealousy had cost her months of suffering, at the very least, and had nearly cost her her baby's father and her happiness.

"Attorneys' clients have been known to wear perfume now and then," Alex said comfortingly.

Katarina fiddled with a fingernail, a stubborn pout on her lips. "Anyway. He doesn't love me."

"Oh, honey. Give him a chance."

She couldn't even smile at the unintended pun. "Oh, Alex, I have!"

Tears of frustration spilled over her eyelashes. "I tried everything. I cooked his favorite meals, kept the house spotless, decorated it the way he likes. I even typed his stupid papers when Charlie was out sick."

Alex sighed. "Never worked with Mother, either, did it?"

Katarina scowled into her lap.

"Maybe Cole doesn't want a housekeeper or a secretary. Maybe he wants a wife. A companion... Sex."

Katarina looked up and wiped her eyes determinedly. "I want him to love me first."

Her sister stretched out her arms to her. "Maybe he does. Maybe he just has a hard time saying it."

Katarina shook her head and accepted a hug as she sat down. "He tells Chance every day."

Alex sighed. "I know how important this is to you. But

whether or not he loves you, he's trying his damnedest to do right by you.''

"I know he is, Alex. But it's just not enough. I want his love."

Tanya was spending the weekend with her family at Rincon, and she asked Cole and Rini to bring the baby and come down for a neighborhood barbecue. After checking with T., Cole called up Jeff and invited him, too. They'd talked several times on the phone, but had never met face-to-face. It was long past time. Since Jeff lived down that way, they arranged to meet at Tanya's.

On Saturday morning, Cole loaded the car seat and diaper bag into the truck and settled behind the wheel, with Rini close beside him and Chance's car seat buckled next to her.

He shot her a wink and shifted into Reverse, deliberately sliding the stick shift under her skirt. She quickly scooted her knees to the side and clamped them together. Chuckling, he gave her an evil grin.

She was so teasable, and he loved doing it. From the first moment he'd laid eyes on her, he'd been hopelessly attracted to her innocent sensuality. Her guileless fluster at his sexual innuendos never ceased to delight him, inflaming him to taut arousal. He couldn't wait to get her into his bed, naked and purring.

He squirmed in his seat, his hip brushing hers as he tried to make more room in his suddenly tight jeans. Her gaze dropped, landing squarely on the obviously swollen ridge of his sex.

"Forget it, sweetness," he quipped. "A couple more days and you can have your wicked way with me. But until then, it's no dice. Doctor's orders."

Her mouth quirked in a failed attempt at looking stern. He imagined how it would taste if he just leaned over and covered that luscious mouth with his. The tip of her tongue brushed the succulent swell of her lower lip. He looked up into her pretty blue fire eyes, watching them lower shyly to his lips. He steeled himself against the urge to kiss her, nearly losing it when the truck hit the bottom of the driveway and her curves jostled softly against his side.

He jammed the truck into gear and took off with a lurch. Could it be Rini was reconsidering their agreement?

It was a long drive to Rincon, nearly two and a half hours, even clipping along the inland route and avoiding the beach crowds. The California freeways were fast and efficient that morning. Colorful magenta ice plant and yellow daisies grew along the sloping sides, in riotous spring bloom.

Cole rolled down his window, slipped a slow, mellow jazz CD into the player and stretched his right arm out along the seat back. With his black truck freshly waxed, his woman nestled by his side and the smell of talcum powder wafting over from his slumbering baby boy, Cole figured life couldn't get much better than this.

Rini's head dropped gently against his shoulder and he circled his arm around her, pulling her close as she fell into an untroubled sleep. Well, he mused, maybe life could get a little better. But he was working on that.

He glanced over at her and Chance—his family. He'd found a peace and contentment during the past weeks that he would never have imagined possible. All because of this woman. He couldn't conceive of life without her anymore. Even without sex, Rini had shown him more love and devotion than any lover had even come close to giving.

In a hot rush of panic he realized just how much she had come to mean to him, how much he needed her. Every day and in every way. He couldn't take it if she left him.

He hoped like hell if he could get Rini to make love with him, he could bind her to him forever. That had to be the key. Mark her again and again as his, and only his. Make her dependent upon his touch, fill her body with a need so potent she couldn't sleep at night if he hadn't relieved it first. Only him. He would give her such pleasure she'd never, ever think of leaving him.

She stirred at his shoulder, rubbing her cheek against the soft nap of his shirt, and instinctively his hand moved to caress her hair and neck. He wondered what it might be like if he could really open his heart and allow himself to love her. The thought terrified him, but he had made a vow to try. He owed her that much.

Irrational fear crawled up his spine. She had abandoned him once. And she'd barred him from her bed. How could he trust her with his heart? Still, he was determined to face his demons. For her.

As he held her tight against him, he told himself he could surely trust her, now. She had married him and had thrown herself into caring for him and the baby without a backward glance. He knew she loved Chance with all her heart, and on their wedding night she'd hinted that she loved him, too.

He pulled into Tanya's driveway filled with new resolve. He had to make Rini need him. Just him.

Only then would he feel safe enough to love her.

Chapter 14

When Cole swung open the wooden screen door to his cousin's house, grabbed Katarina's hand and walked in carrying Chance, the entire Proudhomme clan descended like locusts.

"They're here!"

Katarina's pulse zipped in panic. She hadn't seen so many people of varying sizes, shapes and ages crammed into that small a space since the high school graduation party her father had thrown for her. If Cole hadn't had such a firm grip on her hand she would have turned tail and run.

She could feel her palm grow sweaty against his. Would they like her? Would they ignore her? Would they make comments behind her back?

"Cole! Rini! You made it!" Tanya burst out of a door on the other side of the living room and elbowed her way through the throng, throwing her arms around Katarina in a hug. "Perfect timing! We just lit up the grills. How are you? Everyone, this is Cole's wife, Rini. And this little *kihaat*—" she swept the baby from Cole's arms before he could protest "—is their son, Chance."

Instantly, Katarina was surrounded. Cousins, nephews and

neighbors pressed in to clasp her hand, yelling hellos and congratulations over the din. Their friendliness was overwhelming, and she felt her fear and hesitation fall away like a cocoon.

Glancing up, she saw Cole gauging her reaction as he was also besieged by well-wishers. She grinned. Obviously pleased with that, he winked, then was swallowed up in a swarm of pretty young women.

Katarina fought a sickening surge of jealousy and rotten memories. Suddenly it was like a bad rerun. Giggling, the women crowded close to Cole and whispered in his ear, all the while casting furtive glances at her.

Unable to watch, she swallowed heavily and turned her back. *Damn it anyway!* She knew she was being irrational. He'd vowed to be faithful to her, and she believed him, in spite of the voice inside asking what reason had she given him to want to be.

Who could blame the girls for flirting? A woman would have to be dead not to react to Cole's tempting virility. Katarina tried not to think about the strange perfume she had smelled on his shirt twice now while doing laundry. Each time she'd firmly dismissed it, telling herself it had been a client or another lawyer he'd brushed up against. But seeing him now, surrounded by women, the old fears flared back to life.

She frowned as he was dragged by the coquettes out into the backyard, where the men were tending the grills and playing soccer. By the time he joined the game they had stripped him of the diaper bag, as well as his shirt, and had formed a cheering squad along the sidelines.

"This is his home," an old woman said, following Rini's troubled gaze out the back window. "It is good that he found us. Good that he brings his family now."

Katarina pulled herself together and looked at the woman. "He found you?"

She smiled, showing a full set of large sturdy teeth. "He was one stubborn *chacho*. He didn't give up till the agency told him where he came from."

"Yes, he told me he was adopted."

The woman nodded slowly. "One day he will heal." Her wise

old eyes searched the room and found Chance, who was being passed around from cooing grandmother to tickling aunt. "Perhaps he has already."

Katarina studied the wrinkled face for a moment, wondering what relation, if any, she now had to the woman behind it. Could this be Chance's biological grandmother or great-grandmother? She didn't dare ask, for fear of overstepping some unknown boundary. If the woman wanted her to know, she would have said something.

But there was one thing she would risk asking. "I know Tanya is Cole's real cousin, and her parents are his biological aunt and uncle. But what about his mother and father? What happened to them?"

With a sad expression the old woman looked away, then rose. "I think they could use our help in the kitchen, *hija.*" She shuffled toward the back of the house.

The back door swung open, and Cole strode into the room, grinning, his arm slung around another man. She checked behind him and sighed with relief. No women.

"Rini!" Cole beckoned her. "You remember my brother, Billy."

"Of course. You were at the wedding. How are you?"

"Came to see my nephew! Where is that little rascal?"

Suddenly, there was a commotion at the front door. Someone was admitted to the house amid a murmur of exclamations.

"That must be Jeff," Cole said with a quick glance at Rini. "The kid I told you about—the one I'm helping to find his father."

Katarina nodded. She thought it was great that he was helping the boy. Before knowing Cole, she'd had no idea how traumatic it could be for a child who obviously belonged to a culture different from the one in which he was raised. From the stories he told of how lost Jeff felt, she knew it was important that Cole ease this child's way back to his own culture.

The exclamations became louder as Cole and Billy pressed into the crowd surrounding the new arrival.

"Oh, my God!" Cole and Billy said in unison, catching sight

of the boy at the same time. Cole turned and stared incredulously at his brother.

Curious, Katarina glanced down the path that had parted in front of them. "He looks just like Billy!" she murmured in astonishment. An uneasy hush settled over the group.

Cole recovered and came forward, extending his hand. "You must be Jeff. Welcome. I'm Cole."

The boy smiled shyly and mumbled a greeting, but his eyes kept darting to Billy.

Cole stepped aside. "Jeff, this is my brother, Billy." He looked his brother right in the eye. "Jeff's mother is Lindsay Walker."

Billy blanched, and looked from Cole to Jeff and back. "Who, uh..." He dragged a hand across his mouth. "He yours?"

Katarina gasped, her own hand flying to her mouth.

"No." Cole's growled answer was instant and certain.

She sagged with relief, then caught sight of Jeff and chastised herself. The poor kid looked like he wanted nothing more than to run out the door. Or fly into Billy's arms.

Cole moved to the boy's side and put a supportive hand on his shoulder, facing his brother. "So, *nupeet,* were you seeing Lindsay about fifteen years ago? You know, about the time I married her?"

Rini's brows shot up of their own volition. *That* Lindsay? His ex-wife's son! Was that why Cole was upset?

The crowd stirred and a murmur rose and fell as Billy put up his hands in a defensive gesture. "Cole, it wasn't like that at all. You were long gone to grad school. Do the math, big brother."

Cole took a deep breath and squeezed Jeff's shoulder. "Could this boy be your son?"

Billy looked as though he would fall over in a stiff breeze. He nodded. "I suppose he could. I had no idea," he added in a whisper.

Jeff's face became a jumble of emotion. He shuffled from one foot to the other and stuck his hands in his pockets. "Cool," he croaked out, sounding anything but.

Katarina and everyone else in the room smiled. Suddenly,

Billy had his arms around Jeff, and they were both laughing and hugging, trying valiantly to hold back tears.

Grinning, Cole propelled them toward the back door. "Bro, I think we've got a few things to discuss. In private." He glanced back at her. "Will you be okay for a few minutes, honey?"

Still smiling, she nodded. "Go ahead. I'll be helping in the kitchen."

She joined the whirl of gossip and activity in the kitchen, preparing platters of spicy chicken, pots of aromatic beans, corn on the cob, salsa and tortillas, happy to have someone else be the center of speculation.

But she couldn't miss the occasional whispered exchange among the women, usually accompanied by a furtive glance her way. It started her wondering why Cole had failed to mention to her that Jeff was his ex-wife's son. Was there something more to this Lindsay than he was telling her?

Katarina finally sat down at one of the many picnic tables that had been gathered from the neighboring houses. Cole slid onto the bench across from her.

"How'd it go?" she asked.

His face split in a smile from ear to ear. "Great. Jeff and Billy are both still in shock, but I can tell they're going to hit it off like chili and cheese." He tipped his chin toward a table where the two were sitting, laughing and talking, but never taking their eyes off each other.

Her heart melted. "What a perfect ending."

"Beginning, I'd say."

She looked back at him and her heart melted a little more. "Oh, Cole. What a beautiful thing to say."

And speaking of beautiful… He was still without a shirt, his bare chest drawing the eye of every woman from nine to ninety. His hair was tousled and he had a cute smudge of barbecue sauce on one cheek. A warm curl of love wound around Katarina's insides. He was so damned sexy. And so damned…good. And she was so much in love with him it hurt.

Unable to stop herself, she leaned across the table to wipe off the barbecue sauce, but found her fingers lingering over the masculine angles of his cheekbone and jaw. He winked.

He was the kindest, most honorable and best-looking man there by far, and he was all hers. She sighed. Let the other women flirt. She knew she'd be the one going home with him.

As if he could read her thoughts, he reached up and caught her hand, caressing her palm slowly with his thumb. Heat pooled in his eyes. She couldn't have torn her gaze from his to save her life. She was utterly mesmerized by the look of desire in it, even as she sensed the people around them grinning and poking each other in the ribs.

Slowly, he brought her fingers to his mouth and lingeringly kissed each one in turn. Every bone in her body grew weak with yearning for this deeply sensual man. He wanted her; it was plain. There was something very primitive and powerful about a man laying such intimate claim to her in front of all those people. If he swept her away to bed at that moment she doubted she would have the will to stop him. Lord knew she wanted him desperately.

Should she give in? Could the secret to his love be that simple? Had the one thing that could ensure his love been staring her in the face all along? It hadn't helped with David. But she was realizing more and more each day that her husband bore no resemblance whatsoever to her former fiancé.

Katarina was still dizzy from the impact of Cole's heated looks and the questions in her heart an hour later when Chance woke up demanding to be fed. Excusing herself, she took the opportunity to retreat with her whirling thoughts into the house.

In a back bedroom, she settled on the bed and tried to concentrate on feeding Chance.

A quiet knock sounded and several female heads peeked in. *Oh, no!* It was *them*—the girls who'd been flirting with Cole earlier! What should she do? Could she face them?

"May we come in?"

Without waiting for her answer, five or six young women tumbled into the room and approached her on the bed. Exposed as she was, she felt terribly vulnerable. Fear and uncertainty reared up, unbidden.

In her panic, it didn't quite register that they were all smiling and chattering cheerfully, until they plopped down around her and started oohing and aahing over Chance.

"He is the cutest baby! He looks just like Uncle Cole!"

"Thank you," she murmured, frowning in confusion. They were also much younger than she'd first thought. Why, they were barely out of high school, if that! Suddenly, it struck her. "Uncle Cole?"

"We call him that out of respect. He's not really our uncle."

"He's my second cousin," declared a plump girl with glasses and a long braid. "I'm Marie."

"Well, he's not my cousin, for all the good it did me," said an older girl with a pout. "Rini, you are so lucky to have caught him. He's the dreamiest."

Katarina's brows raised. "Well, I—"

"I'll say," said another with a sigh, a row of silver hoops in her ear glittering in the sun streaming in the window. "Such a hunk." She glanced up and smiled. "For an old guy."

Katarina nearly choked. "He's not really all that old—"

The girl with the earrings nodded solemnly. "Oh, yes. He's way over thirty, you know. Didn't he tell you?"

She couldn't help grinning. Her foolish jealousy evaporated in a puff of welcome and, she hoped, permanent sanity. "He did mention it, yes."

"Well, I still think he's sexy," persisted the pouty one.

"Tell us how you met?" asked another girl.

"Oh, yes! It's sooo romantic!"

Katarina felt a tingle of alarm. "Met? I'm not sure—"

"Tanya said you met in a tepee and it was love at first sight," Marie said. There was a chorus of giggles.

Katarina could feel herself going crimson. She would have to kill Tanya for this.

"We were at that powwow, you know, when he told everyone he'd met the woman of his dreams."

Katarina's jaw dropped in dismay. "He said that?" She had run away and left him standing there alone after he'd told these women she was the woman of his dreams? Tears welled up in her eyes.

"Oh, yes. We were all so excited."

"But Uncle Cole had been in his war paint when you were together." Marie grinned knowingly. "So after the dancing you didn't find each other," she continued in a fairy tale voice. The girls all gazed at Rini forlornly. "But he kept searching for you everywhere, for months and months. Finally, he found you by accident—"

Katarina put a trembling hand to her mouth.

"It wasn't an accident," said Earrings, with the conviction of youth. "He was meant to find her. It was fate. Kismet."

The girls gazed up at Katarina, stars in their young eyes. She could almost taste the dreams behind every pair that studied her with hushed awe. *Oh, Cole!*

"Do you love him very much?" Marie asked.

The innocent question caught her by surprise. She struggled with the giant lump in her throat, swallowing down the need to cry. "Yes, I do. So very much."

The girls let out a long collective sigh.

The pouty girl's pout deepened. "I suppose this means he'll be too busy to keep giving us dance lessons." The fantasy mood was shattered by her accusing tone. "He hasn't been for ages."

Katarina shook herself mentally. *Dance lessons.* Just as he'd said—but she hadn't believed him, not deep in her heart. Katarina felt like crawling into a hole. Instead she wiped her eyes, drew herself up and looked squarely at the girl. "I'll make sure he starts coming again. Chance and I can come, too. I'd really like to get to know everyone here better. You all mean a lot to Cole."

The girls beamed with pride, and even Pouty perked up. "We like him, too. He's a great teacher."

"Rini, maybe you could talk him into moving back!"

There was a general buzz of excitement over that idea. "Yeah! You're a nurse, right?"

"Well, soon—"

"There's a job for a nurse at the health service that Dr. Red-cloud can't fill. You could apply!"

Katarina smiled warmly, shaking her head. "I don't think so. Cole has his practice up in L.A. But thank you for asking. You've all made me feel so welcome."

Two of the girls reached over and hugged her, and soon she and Chance were being hugged by all. Her heart was ready to burst. How could she ever have thought these sweet girls were out to steal Cole away? She was so ashamed of herself.

"Come on, let's take Chance for a walk and show Rini the sights!"

Laughing, she allowed herself to be dragged by the giggling mob to the front door, passing an astonished Cole.

"Hey, where're you going?"

Katarina lifted her arms in an expansive shrug and smiled. "We're off to see the sights!"

The girls commandeered one of the half-dozen baby carriages sitting in front of the house and settled Chance into it, all snug and cozy.

"Shouldn't we ask the owner?"

"Nah," Katarina was assured. "This is Luz's. She won't mind."

She was beginning to get a feel for what it was like with Cole's people. There was a real sense of community, of sharing, that she found herself unbelievably drawn to. For the first time in her life, she saw the possibility of belonging to something larger than one small isolated household. The thought was more than appealing. Too bad Cole's practice prevented him from moving back here. She would enjoy getting to know these people.

The day was glorious. A cascade of sunshine tumbled over Mount Palomar into the narrow green valley that surrounded the lazy San Luis Rey River. A scattering of puffy white clouds floated by overhead as the group strolled along the gravel shoulder of the road, heading for Route 76. They passed a miniature orchard of stately trees filled with fragrant white blossoms.

"That's Tanya's macadamias," Marie said. "You'll no doubt get a bagful at holiday time. Tani hasn't bought a Christmas present in over ten years."

Katarina chuckled. "I think I've already gotten a taste. Cole's mom sent me some delicious nut-covered cookies this year."

The plump cousin looked puzzled for a moment. "She sent you Christmas cookies?"

She nodded. "Cole delivered them Christmas Eve. We took a walk and I nearly went into labor."

They all wanted to hear the story, and by the time she'd finished telling of her and Cole's whirlwind courtship, they had passed a mushroom farm and a chapel with two tepee-shaped outhouses, and had reached a tiny grocery store. Some of the girls went in for sodas while Katarina stayed outside with Chance and Marie. An older woman came out of the store.

"Oh, look! There's Mrs. Padilla. Hello, Aunt Lanie!" Marie called out, motioning her over to where she and Katarina stood.

Leaning over the crib, the woman exclaimed, "Oh, what a beautiful little boy." She glanced up curiously, her eyes obviously comparing Katarina's pale blond looks with Chance's dark coloring. "He's yours?"

Marie introduced them. "Mrs. Padilla, this is Rini Lonetree, Cole's wife. And this is their son, Chance."

"Cole's wife?" Shock and surprise momentarily paralyzed the older woman. Then her eyes strayed back to the carriage. "And his son?" They softened as she reached in to pull the blanket from Chance's face. "Yes. Yes, I can see that now." She looked up. "Rini, I am so happy to meet you and Chance. I didn't think Cole would ever get married again." Once again her eyes were drawn to the carriage, and she reached out to stroke Chance's tiny arm. "May I?"

Katarina nodded.

Chance gurgled and cooed in Mrs. Padilla's arms as they chatted, waiting for the girls to come out of the store. He grasped the end of her long black braid, pulling it until Katarina thought she would surely put him down. But the woman just beamed and hummed and rocked him in her embrace. She had the patience of a saint.

When they were ready to go, she handed Chance back with obvious reluctance. "He's such a dear one. If you ever need a baby-sitter, you call me, okay? Marie has my number."

By the time they got back to Tanya's the sun was low in the sky, and Chance had fallen asleep again.

"What did you guys do, hike to the top of Palomar?" Cole

teased when she came out after putting Chance down. He gave her a quick hug and kissed her forehead. "I missed you."

She melted into his embrace, breathing in the delicious male scent of him. "Missed you, too."

Her pulse quickened when he pulled her tight against his still shirtless body. She made a low purring sound into his neck, tempted to slip her tongue out and taste his smooth, dusky skin. He was as tantalizing as a mocha fudge cheesecake. She longed to indulge in his rich sinfulness.

Groaning in frustration, she pulled away. This would never do. The man was seducing her. Worse, she was seducing herself!

"Come on. Let's go for a drive." He grabbed her hand and tugged her toward the door.

"But Chance—"

"I asked the girls to keep an eye on him. Come with me. There's a place I want to show you."

Katarina relaxed as Cole steered the truck through the village, then turned onto a dirt road leading up into the rugged hills. Dark green chaparral covered the hillsides, interspersed with some kind of bright purple flowering shrub. The smell of sage and moist, clean earth permeated the air.

They parked at the side of the track and Cole slowly led her on foot up a steep, nearly nonexistent animal trail. They hiked past huge granite boulders that lay scattered about as if a giant had poured a bag of irregular gray marbles on the peaks and watched them roll down.

By the time they reached the top, Katarina was panting. She flopped down on a clear patch of sandy ground below a giant marble and collapsed onto her back, catching her breath. Even Cole was winded. But as he lay down on the slope next to her she couldn't miss his peaceful expression.

"Did you come up here when you were young?"

"Yeah." He stacked his hands under his head and peered down over the valley. "After I found my biological family and moved to Rincon, life got pretty intense. Sometimes I just needed a place to be alone and think."

"Must have been tough for you, jumping into the middle of things like that."

He shrugged. "Yes and no. Tanya and my aunt and uncle were great. Billy, too. He made sure I was accepted and learned everything I needed to know. He was very protective of me." A smile crinkled the corners of his eyes. "He'll be good with Jeff."

"Who else looked after you?"

He laughed. "Pretty much everybody. I was a community project."

"What about your mom and dad? I mean your biological parents?"

His face went stony. "What about them?"

"Did they help you?"

"No."

"Are they still around?"

"I never asked."

Katarina wondered at the venom in Cole's voice. As important as family was to him, it was strange that he hadn't attempted to see his own mother or father. But it was obviously not a subject open for discussion. "Do you miss living here?"

His expression softened a bit. "Yeah. Especially on days like today. But it's not always like this."

"No?"

"This place is like a family. We love each other, but we fight, and it can get nasty and petty. We gossip, get jealous. Mostly it's good, but it's like living in a glass house."

She chuckled. "Is that why you didn't have any curtains in your house? To make up for moving away?"

He shot her an amused glance. "Ha ha ha." He rolled onto his side and scooted closer. "But you fixed that, didn't you?"

She knew she was in trouble when she turned to him and his pirate's grin flashed back at her. She could practically taste the mocha fudge. *Lord have mercy.*

He reached out and drew a finger down her cheek. "You going to let your husband kiss you, Rini?"

She licked her lips. "I don't think that would be such a good idea…" Her gaze was caught by his sensual mouth—the corners upturned in a predator's smile, the bottom lip full and kissable— already parting in anticipation.

"Oh, I disagree," he murmured, pulling her onto her side to face him, running his hand down the length of her body and then back up again, turning her resistance to quicksilver. "I think it's a good idea." He slid his fingers into her hair and tugged her closer. "A very good idea."

Poised, waiting, searching her eyes, he held her there. Waiting while her limbs grew slack and her blood pounded. Waiting while her mind emptied of objections and filled with longing. Without realizing what she was doing, she lifted her face and moved toward him.

He tightened his grip and held her so she could go neither forward nor back. "Tell me, Rini. Tell me you want to kiss me."

His hot breath fanned across her face, tickling the nerve endings in her cheeks. Her throat tightened and she had to swallow to keep the desire from overwhelming her. "Kiss me, Cole," she managed to whisper. "Kiss me or I'll die."

With a low groan his mouth consumed hers. All her pent-up yearning and hunger exploded when she opened to him and tasted his tongue on hers. She moaned in surrender and fell back, twining her arms around his neck. He followed, covering her upper body, pressing her into the sandy ground.

She closed her eyes and her world was reduced to the taste of barbecue and salsa and male. "Oh, Cole," she moaned.

One large hand cradled the back of her head, the other roamed her body, igniting blazes wherever it touched. She arched up when it skimmed her tender breast.

He broke the kiss, rubbing his finger along the lacy garment under her blouse. "Damn, I can't get used to you wearing a bra."

She dug her fingers into his shoulders and tried to pull him back. Her excitement settled right in the tips of her heavy breasts. "Trust me, it's better this way."

"Why's that?" His clever fingers were already unbuttoning her blouse.

"Never mind." She gasped when he pulled the front of her blouse out of her skirt and bared her to his ravenous gaze.

"So damned beautiful," he murmured hotly, bending down

to run his tongue along the upper curve of her bra, dipping into the deep valley between her breasts.

It felt so good she didn't know what to do with the small voice telling her she shouldn't be letting him do this. It felt so right that when the voice told her her hands should be pushing him away, she instead made them hold him tighter. It felt so arousing when he slid his hand behind her and unclasped her bra that the little voice was thoroughly drowned out by her moans.

"Cole..."

Her loosened breasts swelled and tingled. She glanced down and saw him watch a drop of milk seep from her nipple and run slowly down the side of her breast. The heated intent in his eyes was obvious even before he had moved a muscle.

Her eyes widened. "I don't—"

He leaned forward and drew his tongue up her breast, gathering the droplet as he went. "Mmm. So good."

"Cole, stop," she moaned, mortified.

He nestled closer. "Every time I watch Chance suckle at your breast, I'm so damned jealous. I want to curl up beside him, have you stroke my head and sing softly to me, too."

His gaze burned into her eyes, igniting her to the core, making her forget all modesty. She slowly became aware of his fingers sliding up and down the sensitive skin of her inner thigh.

"Oh, babe, I want to touch you." He slipped them past the elastic of her panties and into her waiting flesh.

There was no earth, no sky, no wind, no sun. There was only Cole. Cole was the solid strength that grounded her, the shelter covering her, the ragged breath catching in her lungs, and the heat scorching her body.

She surrendered completely to the skill of his tongue and the art of his fingers. Her breath came in gasps. Her body shuddered and she sang out moans of ecstasy.

"Oh, darlin', I love how you sing for me."

He paused to tug off her panties, pushing her flowing skirt up to her waist. He spread her legs wide, then knelt between her naked thighs.

She looked up at him, backlit like a Hollywood god, his

square jaw set, his sweat-shiny muscles rippling in the sun. She wanted him. Lord above, she wanted him. Posed as she was to accept his sexual demands, she wished like hell he'd just unzip his pants and thrust into her.

For a moment it looked like he might do just that. But then he gave her a slow, sultry smile and hooked his arms under her knees, raising them as he lowered his body. When his hips rested just above hers, the fabric of his jeans brushing the small cloud of hair between her legs, he stopped. He smelled tangy, like fresh sage and hot skin and molten desire.

Soft as a feather, his lips brushed hers, gliding smoothly over them like an eagle riding a thermal. She trembled at the raw strength that lay behind his deceptively gentle touch, and yielded to the predatory fierceness that had scattered her objections to the wind.

She was his, completely.

And Cole knew it. Today Rini would refuse him nothing. "Tell me what you want," he urged, his chest swelling with hope.

She searched his eyes for a long moment, a moment that felt like an eternity to his heart. Finally, she whispered, "I want my husband."

Her words filled him with elation. "You're sure?" He laid his forehead against hers. "If we do this, I won't go back to what it was before." Not that he possibly could even now. Not after tasting her again.

"I'm sure." She kissed him, a sweet yearning kiss filled with promise for their future. "Make love to me, Cole."

He nestled down onto her, feeling every lush curve and soft inviting mound under him. He held her quaking body tight and claimed her lips with his, exploring her surrender with infinite joy and delight.

His tongue teased and tasted, drawing more moans and shudders from her as he plumbed the depths of her warm, welcoming mouth. So sweet. So giving. So perfect.

She began to move under him, subtly spurring him to deeper intimacy. His hand moved down over her hip, then up again, dipping into her waist, sliding up to her breast. "Think the doctor will scold us? There are still two days to go."

"I'm sure she—"

Whatever Rini was going to say was lost in a sigh when he burrowed his face between her breasts, kissing and licking her, then dipped his tongue lower, skipping over her skirt to kiss and caress her tummy. Her belly wasn't concave as it had been before, but he loved the little swell that reminded him of the small miracle that was sleeping contentedly back at Tanya's.

A warm feeling of possessiveness flowed through him. God, he wanted Rini. He wanted to keep her and cherish her forever. Never let her go.

He couldn't wait any longer to make her his. He rose, and with eager hands Rini helped unfasten his jeans and pull them down his thighs, then she held out her arms to him. With a low sound deep in his throat he lowered himself over her.

He felt her legs wind around his waist, pulling him closer. Poised on the brink of joining, he looked into her eyes and caught his breath at the love and happiness he saw in them. Holding her gaze with his, he eased his aching manhood into the silken heat that beckoned. He groaned at the lightning quick, welcoming pleasure of being surrounded by her.

If there was a heaven, he'd found it.

At his entry, Katarina's mind simply ceased to function. Her body took over. She melded with Cole, and their joining became the center of her swirling universe. He filled her and quietly held her and whispered sweet words until she was bursting with emotion.

"Are you doing okay?" he asked. "Does it hurt?"

"You feel wonderful," she managed to answer on a sigh.

He let out a breath and started moving. Slowly at first, then more boldly, he rocked deep into her. His mouth came down over hers, his tongue matching the long, measured thrusts of his pelvis.

With every new stroke she burned hotter and wilder. More than ten endless months she had waited for this, and now she was finally his. She dug her fingernails into his back and hung on, drowning in the ecstasy of his hard, strong body claiming hers again and again.

Much too soon, she felt herself hurtling toward the brink of oblivion. She melted under him, into him, lost herself in the torrent of sensation flooding over her. She twisted and turned, crying out as he buried himself in her once, twice, three times.

Then she was over the edge. Pulsing and bursting in an explosion of pleasure. Calling to him, over and over. He crushed her in a tight embrace, moving against her quickly, urgently. Then he arched up, throwing his head back like a magnificent beast, and she heard the echo of her name, torn from his throat, on a gust of wind.

He collapsed onto her and laced his fingers through hers. They lay like that, chests heaving, hearts soaring.

Cole rubbed his cheek in her hair and whispered, "Oh, Fire Eyes. You take my breath away." Lifting onto his elbows, he smiled down at her. He pulled her left hand to his mouth and kissed her wedding ring. "You're mine now. Only mine." He gave her a searching look for several moments. "You wouldn't leave me, would you?"

Katarina's heart stopped. She shook her head. She didn't want to leave him. Not ever.

Now that they'd shared so much, surely he would say the words she longed to hear. Winding her arms around his neck, she held him close.

"Tell me you love me, Fire Eyes," he whispered into her hair. "Say you'll stay with me always."

Emotion burned behind her eyes. She shut them tightly and clung to him with all her heart. "I love you, Cole. And I never want to leave you. Ever."

She held him and waited for him to say it back. That he loved her, too. But the moment passed. Disappointment stabbed through her.

Give him a chance, Alex had once said to her. A sigh fluttered past her lips. And she prayed she wouldn't have to wait too long.

Chapter 15

Cole studied the pattern emerging on the piece of butter-soft buckskin in Rini's hands and smiled. "That's really pretty." The red, blue and yellow geometrical shapes looked like they'd been woven, the beads were placed so tightly and precisely together. "You're a pro at this. Are you sure you've never done beadwork before?"

He was putting together a buckskin vest and pair of moccasins for a friend's regalia, and he had decided to make Chance a set at the same time. When Rini had sat quietly watching him, he'd invited her to decorate the back of Chance's vest. At first she'd resisted, but he explained that it didn't matter how it turned out, it was the love behind it that counted, and she'd given it a try.

She returned his smile with a slight blush on her cheeks. "First time, honest. It's an old Finnish pattern I remember from a table runner in my grandmother's house before she died." She sighed. "I wonder what ever happened to it."

"That's great. Chance's regalia should reflect his whole heritage, not just my part."

Cole watched her work for a moment, noting that the purple smudges under her eyes were lighter today. He'd made her go back to sleep after they'd made love that morning, and he'd threatened to burn her books if she so much as glanced at them before dinner. With all her classes, endless studying, Chance's feedings and his own attentions, he knew she must be running on empty.

But he wasn't about to give up the incredible physical relationship they'd enjoyed for the past few weeks, ever since the trip to Rincon. She had taken him to heights he'd never known possible, and he'd given her pleasures she'd confessed to only dreaming of.

He wagered she wasn't about to give it up, either. Her body was so in tune with his that all it took was a glance and she was ready—hot and trembling and wet with desire. Desire that only he could satisfy. And he did. Every night and most mornings, too.

No, neither of them would give up this newfound passion, so he had to make damn sure she didn't collapse from exhaustion. Getting her involved in making Chance's regalia for the upcoming powwow seemed like a perfect way to get her to slow down and relax awhile.

They sat cross-legged on a large circle of leather on the living room floor, buckskin and tools, needles and tubes of beads surrounding them. She looked so beautiful sitting there across from him, her pale hair cascading onto her shoulders in waves, her tongue peeking out from between her lips as she concentrated on her stitching. As had happened so often over the weeks since Chance's birth, his heart contracted in his chest.

He'd made a vow to try to love her unconditionally, and he'd tried. Honest to God he had done his best. There had been times when he was sure his heart would break from the pain of not being able to let go, of not being able to make that last free fall into mindless, soul-deep love, as he so yearned to do.

But something always held him back. The dark, cynical part of his mind that always lectured him on the perfidy of women— that they would love you one day and be gone the next. The mocking skeptic in him that kept reminding him she wouldn't need him anymore once she'd gotten her degree and could support herself and Chance. The voice that never failed to point out as evidence her refusal to say she would never leave him.

Since that first time at Rincon, he'd continued to ask. And she always said she never wanted to leave him. Never *wanted* to leave him. But there was a world of difference between those statements. And he was just the man to pick up on it.

He'd gambled that making love would prompt her to take the final step to committing herself fully to him. It hadn't. But it *had* made him start waking up in a cold sweat at night groping at the empty space in his bed where she should have been—only to realize she was seeing to Chance. He would feel like a fool, but only after the heart-pounding panic and the headlong rushing of blood through his veins had slowed enough to allow him to reason logically.

It was torture, and the only way it would be eased was when she could look him in the eye and tell him she would never leave. Until then, he knew he would not be able to let down the barriers he'd carried with him for so many, many years, no matter how much he wished he could.

She looked up from her stitching and caught him watching her. She tipped her head in that cute way she had when she found him staring—part curious, part pleased, part shy. With a breaking heart, he leaned over and kissed her, scattering beads and awls over the floor as he went.

How he wished he could just say the words.

Katarina scowled and determinedly returned her concentration to the top of the page she was attempting to memorize. Only two more days till finals. She couldn't afford to daydream. Everything depended on her getting this nursing degree. For the past month, things had been wonderful between her and Cole. Wonderful and horrible. She didn't know what to do.

He had moved back into his room with her, and the spare room had become Chance's nursery. Every night they would make hot, passionate love, or slow, easy love, or intense, stormy love, until they were both exhausted and replete. Then he would gather her in his arms and they would sleep, entwined like the lovers they were.

And still he did not love her.

She had so hoped that making love to him would be the key to opening his heart. He seemed happy. He complimented her unfailingly on everything she did, encouraged and helped with her studies, watched with a smile when she fed Chance. Cole seemed content.

And yet, he did not love her.

She could feel the emotional barrier between them just as solid as a brick wall. To be sure, there were places where the mortar had crumbled so she could peek through that wall. But whenever she did, he would always retreat just out of reach, closing himself off behind that breezy affection or blazing passion with a determination that nearly broke her heart.

What if he never grew to love her? What would she do? Should she take Chance now and leave Cole, before she totally lost herself in a dead-end relationship once again? Now, before Chance's tiny heart would be broken by seeing his daddy only on weekends?

She didn't want to think about the possibility of having to leave the man who had come to mean the world to her. But she could not spend her life with a man who didn't love her. And she had to be prepared for the eventuality that he never would.

That meant she had to graduate, and to graduate she had to pass her finals. Which meant memorizing the damned book she couldn't seem to focus on.

There was a loud pounding on the door, and she groaned. It couldn't be Cole—he'd gone into the office for a few hours. Besides, he would never knock like that for fear of waking Chance. She cast a glance at the closed door to the nursery, hurried over to the front door and opened it wide, ready to give whoever it was what for.

In a blur of black and chains, a huge man lurched past, shoving her aside. Stunned speechless, she found her attention seized by the large silver gun he clutched in his hand. It was pointed at the ceiling, but the eyes in his bruised and bloody face were staring right at her.

She glanced desperately toward the nursery, then groped behind her for the door. He turned and looked around as if crazed, his wild, long hair flying. A confused frown creased his face. He looked back, catching her inching backward. Grabbing her arm, he yanked her into the living room and slammed the door shut.

"No!" She struggled against his iron grip. "No!"

Resting his weight against the wall, he tugged her closer, almost cradling her against his black leather jacket. She could smell sweat and the open road and a hint of exotic perfume. Suddenly, his expression changed subtly, softening.

"Fire Eyes," he croaked, then slid down the wall and lay unconscious, a battered heap at her feet.

Cole leaned across Lindsay's desk and gave her his most menacing scowl. "He wants to see you. God knows why, but he does. You owe him that much."

Lindsay paled. "I told you, I can't. Daddy would never speak to me again if he found out."

Cole bit back a curse.

"And he'd probably kill Billy."

"Let him try," Cole growled.

She put her hand over his on the desk. "Billy can tell Jeff anything he needs to—"

"You're pathetic! He's your own flesh and blood!"

Lindsay jumped up. "And my father isn't?" She whipped around the desk, stalked up to him and grabbed his lapels, pressing up against his chest. "Jeff already has an adoptive mother who loves him! But what happens to me if I lose my only dad? After I satisfy Jeff's curiosity will he hang around to comfort me?" She backed off, waving a hand. "No way. He's made it clear what he thinks of me."

Cole sighed and pulled out a card on which he'd written Jeff's address and phone number. "Call him, Lindsay. Just once, think of someone besides yourself." He pressed the card into her hand.

The office door opened and Lindsay's secretary poked her head in. "There's a call for Mr. Lonetree from his office, on line one."

He looked up worriedly. "Thanks." How did Charlie know where he was? More importantly, what emergency had prompted him to call? Cole picked up the phone and punched the flashing button. "What's wrong?"

"Rini called. Some guy broke into your house."

Cole burst through the front door and immediately spotted the man lying prone on the sofa. "Renegade!" He came to a sliding halt on his knees by the couch, first relieved, then alarmed at the sight of his bruised and battered friend.

"Hey, *compadre*." White patches where Rini had bandaged his face shifted when Renegade smiled up at him. "Hell of a woman you've got yourself."

Cole grasped his hand, then quickly let it go at the wince that distorted his friend's already swollen face.

"Stubborn as a mule," Rini muttered. She stood at one end of the sofa, holding a cup of tea and looking stern.

Renegade winked at Cole. "Thanks for the hospitality. I'll be out of your hair by morning."

"He's in no shape to travel," Rini said firmly. "I saw that contraption he's riding, and—"

Chuckling, Cole rose and gave her a kiss. "No use, darlin'. He's rattled out any brains he ever had a long time ago. One trip more or less won't make any difference." He took the cup from her hands. "You did good. Thanks for taking care of him. And for calling me."

Worriedly, he watched Renegade struggle to sit up and lean stiffly against the back cushion, his eyes closed.

Rini glanced at the man on their couch. "Um, I've got to get back to my studying. If there's anything you need, I'll be in the bedroom."

Cole gave her a squeeze. "Thanks."

After she'd closed the door behind her, he handed Renegade the tea. "Drink. Then you can tell me just what the hell is going on."

He took a long pull of the green liquid and grimaced. "What is this stuff, anyway?"

"Something to help recover from childbirth, I think." His friend looked up in alarm, and for a second Cole thought he might spit it out. He laughed. "Tough guy."

Renegade shrugged and slugged back the rest in one gulp. Setting the cup down, he let out a long, weary breath. "I found her." Cole didn't need to be told he meant RaeAnne. Renegade reached for the leather jacket Rini had folded over the back of the couch and pulled out an envelope. "Can you keep this safe?"

Cole nodded. "Of course." He knew better than to ask what was in it or how sweet RaeAnne Sommarby was involved in something that had left his best friend looking like this. But it was useless to speculate. The man was as tight-lipped as they came about work, even if it involved his long-lost love.

His friend leaned back and sighed, his face easing as if a heavy burden had been lifted from his back. "I want to see your baby boy." Renegade pushed to his feet and gave him a care-worn smile. "Glad you gave Rini a second chance. She's quite a lady."

"She's pretty amazing, all right." He led his friend to the nursery and together they leaned over the crib, speaking in hushed voices.

"He's beautiful. You're a lucky guy."

"Better believe it." Cole turned to his friend. "What about you and RaeAnne?"

Renegade's jaw hardened. "She's mixed up with some creep." He glanced up, looking Cole straight in the eye. "If he hurts her, I'll kill the bastard."

He was dead serious. Cole knew what doing something like that, even in the line of duty, would mean to his friend's career, his life. "You'd do that?"

"Yeah."

He gazed down at his sleeping son, knowing he'd do the same for him. "Would she thank you?"

"She loves me."

Cole gripped the side of the crib. "How can you be so sure? How do you know she won't just let you solve her problems and then run off?"

Renegade regarded Cole closely. "I don't. I just have to trust that what I see and feel is real." He laid his bandaged hand on Cole's arm. "If you can't imagine life without her, it's real. If she's the first thing you think of in the morning and the last thing before you fall asleep, it's real. If you watch her eyes when you tell her you love her and they go all soft and mushy, it's real.''

Cole tore his gaze from his friend's.

"You haven't told her."

He shook his head.

Renegade reached out and smoothed a finger through Chance's hair. "You're an idiot, *compadre*."

"She won't stay. I can feel it."

Straightening, Renegade stuck his fists on his hips. "Any reason she should leave?"

He swallowed heavily, facing the one man in the world who knew him best. "None of the others had any reason, either."

The big man before him spoke with a voice as soft and gentle as dandelions in the wind. "There's always a reason, Cole. You just got caught in the middle. You've got to stop blaming yourself for things you had no control over."

He made a deprecating sound.

His friend continued to study him. "You know, it was you who gave me the nickname Renegade, but it would suit you a whole lot better. You reject everything and anyone that threatens to get too close—your adoptive family, your real mom. You set yourself up for failure by marrying that Lindsay woman…"

Cole's jaw set.

"You deny your white upbringing, yet here you are out in the 'burbs in your little bungalow, Mr. yuppie lawyer. You play the roll of the great warrior at powwows, but when was the last time you went to a sweat lodge?"

Cole touched the front of his shirt, seeking the soothing reassurance of his silk tie, but came up with a fistful of cotton. "You're full of crap, Roman."

"Am I? The name you chose for yourself tells it all. *Lonetree.* I'm surprised you didn't take the middle initial A. Then you could be Cole A-Lone tree. *A* for Alienated." Renegade sighed and slung an arm around his shoulders. "You've got a fine family here. This is the real thing, *compadre*. If you blow this one you'll regret it. Take it from someone who knows."

* * *

"Speaking." Katarina juggled the phone on her shoulder as she adjusted Chance's romper.

"This is Dr. Redcloud from the Rincon Health Service. My niece, Marie, met you at a barbecue several weeks ago at Tanya's."

"Oh, Marie! Yes, how is she?" Katarina smiled, thinking of the day.

"She's fine. She mentioned to me that you are a nurse."

"Well, almost. I'll be graduating in a week or so, if I pass all my finals. Then I'll need to take the R.N. exam."

"Close enough. How would you like a job?"

Katarina's hands stilled. "At Rincon?"

"You could start Monday after graduation."

She squeezed the snaps closed on Chance's romper and set him on a blanket on the floor. "I'm flattered to be asked, and I wish I could, but Cole's practice... We really can't move."

Dr. Redcloud sighed. "I was afraid of that. Well, it was worth a shot. Do me a favor?"

"Of course."

"Talk to him about it? We would do everything we could to help make the transition. Find you a place to live, a baby-sitter for your son."

She laughed. "You must really want me."

"Desperately." Dr. Redcloud laughed, too, but Katarina could hear the seriousness in her voice. "It's not often there's someone qualified who also has connections here at Rincon and might consider us over the big hospitals in the county."

"Well, I'll let you know what Cole says, but I don't think he'll go for it."

"I understand, and thanks for thinking about it."

After Katarina said her goodbyes, she couldn't help but fantasize about the possibilities. She'd always dreamed of finding a small place in the country. And now with Chance to consider, it sounded even better than before. He could grow up among flowers and fresh air instead of pollution and crime. As she walked to the utility room, she smiled at the image of hanging her wash out on a clothesline to dry in the sun and wind.

Her smile faded when she couldn't picture Cole's clothes hanging alongside her own.

Cole had been unapproachable ever since his friend had dropped in out of nowhere a week ago. Short-tempered and moody, Cole hadn't said more than ten words to her the whole time since. It was so bad that she was actually relieved when he'd gone into the office this morning.

As she dumped the clothes out of the laundry hamper and sorted them, she wondered sadly what had made Cole so broody. They hadn't even made love since then. She didn't want to think it was her fault, but the change in him was so great she couldn't help thinking it must be. Now that she had given herself to him, had he just gotten tired of her? After seeing his free-and-easy friend, was he regretting having a wife and child to support?

Picking up one of his cotton shirts, she caught a whiff of perfume. She frowned and put the shirt to her nose. *Obsession.* Her legs suddenly felt weak. Her hand shook as she ran it over the cotton and then threw the shirt into the washer. She shoved the rest of the whites into the tub. Just because she knew Cole wasn't seeing any clients right now didn't mean a thing. There could be any number of explanations.

And she wouldn't—couldn't—believe that he had already grown bored after only a few weeks of making love to her, and had found someone else.

No! There was no one else, she told herself sternly. She was imagining the whole thing. It was just the jealous tendencies caused by David's philandering that were sneaking out again. But she'd learned her lesson. She would not give in to them. Cole was different.

Resolutely, she poured detergent into the washer and spun the dial. She trusted him. Her husband would never betray her with another woman. He just wouldn't do it.

Even if he didn't love her.

Cole tugged the soft flannel blanket up to Chance's chin and smoothed a hand over his cheek. The room was dark, as was the whole house, but moonlight poured in through a gap in the curtain. Crickets chirped a homey lullaby outside the window.

Cole sighed, feeling a pull on his heartstrings he wouldn't have believed possible just a few short months ago. How he loved his son! And as much as it scared him witless, he knew Renegade was right. He loved Rini, too.

Admitting it, even silently to himself, had launched him into a tailspin of panic after his friend had driven off a week ago. Since then, Cole had meticulously avoided being close to Rini. He couldn't look into her eyes without feeling abject terror at the vulnerability he suddenly experienced.

When she sought him out about some household thing he'd snap at her. When she touched him, he'd shrink away in fear that he would blurt out everything. And he wasn't ready to do that yet.

He padded barefoot down the hall and stood in the doorway to their room, watching her sleep. He knew he had to deal with it—this love he'd be a fool to deny. He should tell her. And deep down, he wanted to tell her. To share it—that giddy helplessness of having one's heart held so precariously in another's keeping, the heady vertigo from the plunge into trust that he'd taken without quite realizing what he was doing.

Rini's chest rose and fell under his wool blanket. He longed to slip into bed with her. Just hold her tight. Throw caution to the wind and whisper the words in her ear.

But he didn't have the guts.

Besides, she'd be taking her last exam in the morning. She was dead tired from studying all day. She needed to sleep—more than she needed to hear the pleas of a lovesick man whose only thought was to bury himself deep inside her and tell her he loved her again and again until sunlight trickled through the windowpanes.

It would wait. Just a couple of days. Until she'd finished with studying and tests and graduation rehearsals.

Then he'd tell her.

She'd be rested and happy. He'd cook her an extra special dinner and buy her something really nice. Then he'd look at her over the lighted candles and tell her he loved her.

He wouldn't worry about her abandoning him one day. He'd

just say it. *I love you, Rini,* he'd say. Then she'd tell him she loved him, too.

And she'd never leave him. Ever.

"Cole?" Rini rose up on one elbow.

He started. "What? Go back to sleep!"

Her face wasn't visible in the dark, but he saw her chin wobble. "Aren't you coming to bed?" Her voice was a thready whisper.

"I, uh…" He took a step toward the bed and then halted. "I, uh, need to finish up something." He shot a hand through his hair. "In the, uh, living room. I'll be back in a few minutes. You go to sleep."

She didn't move. He backed out of the room and quietly pulled the door closed. *Ho boy.* He stood with his sweaty palm on the doorknob and took several deep breaths. He'd nearly lost it.

His stomach was knotted almost as hard as his— *Aw, hell.* He turned stiffly and headed for the guest room. If he made it through the rest of the week with his sanity intact it would be a pure damned miracle.

Cole shot out of bed and groaned. It was Rini's graduation day and he was late. He rubbed the heels of his hands over his eyes, wincing at the rocks and gravel that ground into his eyeballs. Hell, he had to get some sleep soon.

Thank goodness the waiting would soon be over. Ready or not, today was the day. His pulse pounded in terror at the mere thought of what he was going to do later.

Rini had already left for the early morning graduation festivities. He had fallen back to sleep after being up much of the night with Chance, who seemed to have acquired colic at an age when other babies were just getting over it. And now Cole had overslept by a mile.

His nerves were nearly shot by the time he and Chance peeled into a parking garage at UCLA. Chance had wailed for the whole forty-minute ride, only falling asleep as they got off the freeway in Westwood. But when Cole lifted him from the car seat, the baby woke up and started again with gusto.

Two old ladies scowled as he slid into an empty spot next to them. He killed the impulse to glare back and instead gave them a helpless shrug, jiggling his screaming son on one knee.

The sun was merciless, Chance was miserable, the ceremony was interminable and Cole hadn't even had his coffee. He sighed and slumped down on the hard seat.

He was so damned proud of Rini, sitting out there somewhere in the sea of black and gold. This was what she had worked so hard for. He should be excited for her. Irritatedly, he pushed back the traitorous thought that now she could make it on her own with no help from him.

No. She wouldn't leave him. Not after tonight.

The names of the graduates droned on.

Damn, he needed to get himself into a better mood. How was a man supposed to feel romantic with a splitting headache and a cranky kid squirming in his arms?

He stuck a bottle in Chance's mouth and went over what he had to do before tonight. The steaks were marinating and he'd already made the lemon meringue pie, so he just needed to stop at the Chinese grocery to pick up spring rolls, and the bakery for crusty French bread. He had a nice bottle of *Pouilly-Fuissé* chilling, and hazelnut chocolate coffee beans waiting in the freezer. Thinking about the nice dinner he'd planned eased the throb in his head somewhat.

What else?

He had to remember to hide the box containing the pearl earrings he'd bought her somewhere handy, near the fireplace. A corner of his mouth lifted in anticipation.

He hoisted the baby to his shoulder and patted him. Chance let out a gurgly belch and warm milk spewed down the back of Cole's shirt. He clenched his teeth in frustration. The day could only get better.

After the ceremony, Katarina accepted a kiss from Cole and gave Chance a hug. The little guy appeared positively wrung out, and the big guy didn't look much better. The masculine angles of his face seemed pinched and she couldn't for the life of her figure out how his beautiful bronze skin could possibly have turned that dreadful shade of pinkish gray.

"Rough morning?"

"A bit. Congratulations, honey. You done good."

"Thanks." She looked down at her graduation gown billowing in the breeze. He was always so supportive and encouraging. She glanced up. "Shall I take Chance home with me?"

"I've got the car seat. Why don't you just feed him before we go? Most of his last bottle is on the back of my shirt."

They settled under a shady tree while she fed Chance. Cole looked tired. But oh, so handsome. His hair was getting longer. She wondered if he planned on growing it past his shoulders again, like it had been when she first saw him. She sighed, imagining running her fingers through its coarse silkiness.

Cole unscrolled her diploma and studied it. Her gaze trailed across his broad shoulders, admiring how his male frame stretched his knit shirt as he held the parchment up to view. Looking from him to the diploma, she blinked back the tears that suddenly swelled in her eyes.

It wasn't until she was alone in the car driving home that she allowed them to fall freely. In her heart, she wasn't sure whether they were from finally fulfilling her lifelong dream, or from the knowledge that she could do nothing but watch as she slowly lost the only man she had ever loved.

Chapter 16

Two hours later, Cole finally pulled his truck into the driveway, fuming like a geyser ready to blow. Rini ran to meet him. When she caught sight of him, she stopped dead. He knew his shirt was torn and he was covered from head to toe with dirt and streaks of black grease. Judging from her reaction, he must look as angry as he felt.

"Cole, are you okay?"

Reining in his instinctive retort, he rubbed a hand over the middle of his chest, then scratched agitatedly at his knit shirt. "Do me a favor and don't ask," he said wearily. "Can you get Chance?"

Thankfully, she bit back her questions, nodded and hurried to gather the crying baby and diaper bag out of the truck's cab. The instant Chance's head hit her shoulder he fell into an exhausted sleep. He ground his teeth. Figured.

"I'll just put him in his crib," she murmured.

A blissful silence reigned over the house as Cole made his way to the kitchen and grabbed a bottle of beer. His Adam's apple bobbed gratefully as he swallowed the cold liquid, and he swiped over his eyes wearily.

Rini walked in. "He's out like a light."

Cole peered over at her. "I don't know what's gotten into him lately. For the past few days he's done nothing but cry. My nerves are about to snap."

She averted her gaze. "Probably just picking up on all the stress. From finals and graduation," she said quickly. Too quickly, he thought. "You have a flat tire or something?"

He took a long swallow from the bottle, wondering what was making her so jumpy. "Or something."

"On the freeway?"

Another pull. "Uh-huh."

She walked to the kitchen counter and poured herself a glass of wine. "The police hassle you?"

He paused in middraft. "What do you think?"

"Chance scream the whole time?"

"Yep. Amazing they didn't arrest me for suspected child abuse." He was still wound tight as a spring and his head pounded. It didn't get much worse than changing the truck's tire on the side of a freeway with a baby screaming in one ear and a redneck California Highway Patrol officer making thinly veiled racist remarks in the other.

"I'm sorry."

He grunted, opened the cupboard, popped three aspirin and eyed the pretty white, eyelet-lace sundress Rini had changed into. All the adrenaline that had been rushing around his bloodstream for the whole rotten day zeroed right in on his groin. He was instantly hard.

"God, you're gorgeous." How could she wear something like that and not expect him to ravish her on the spot?

Her smile faltered when she spotted the huge, straining erection his jeans did nothing to hide. The worn denim couldn't begin to disguise the throbbing length he longed to impale her on. Damn, he needed her badly.

He allowed her to take one hesitant sip of her wine. Two. A gulp. Then he moved in. He captured her mouth hungrily, pushing his tongue between her lips. She stiffened, but after a second or two her body sagged against his. A soft moan escaped from her throat. Groping toward the counter, he set aside his bottle, then did the same with her glass.

He ravaged her mouth, all the frustrations of the day pouring out into his passionate assault. She tasted so good; she felt so right in his arms. "Oh, Rini, honey." He crushed her to him, reveling in her heated response. "I've missed you so. Missed this."

Her lips pulled away when he grasped her breast. "Wait—"

"Oh, woman, I want you."

Now. Right here. Hot and wet and frenetic on the kitchen table. No, the table was too far. The counter. He leaned in and covered her mouth again. His hands worked under the hem of her dress and up to the top of her panties and tugged. Down to her ankles they slid.

"Cole," she groaned. "I need to ask you something."

"What's the matter?" he murmured heatedly as he raised her dress to her waist and lifted her bare bottom onto the counter. "Don't you want your husband?" In a twinkling he had her dress unzipped and the clasp of her bra undone.

"Yes, more than anything, but—"

"Good."

He pushed the sleeves and straps off her shoulders, baring her breasts, then bent to lock his mouth around a pointed tip. Rini gasped and pulled his head tightly to her. The nipple lengthened on his tongue, and he gently stroked it. He wanted her so badly his throat ached. He moved down her body, taking pleasure in licking and sucking and nipping her into a writhing, panting mass of frustrated need.

Need for him.

He felt her fingers in his hair, grasping and tugging. "Cole, please—"

"I'm coming, baby." He yanked down his zipper, struggled to release the snap at his waist.

"No, you don't understand." She pushed at his shoulders, breathing heavily as he jerked his jeans down his hips.

"What?" He could hardly think at all for the piercing agony of need and desire pulsing between his legs. He parted her thighs and stepped between them. His sex was perfectly aligned with the wet, silky sheath he sought so desperately. "Put your legs around my waist," he rasped.

He grunted in satisfaction when her legs hooked around him despite a hesitation. Circling an arm behind her soft, round derriere, he moved closer, pressing the length of him against the burning hot woman's flesh at the juncture of her spread thighs. He rubbed up and down, stimulating the hard little point he knew would give her the greatest pleasure. "I want to make love with you," he urged in a gravelly whisper, adding his thumb to the persuasion.

She moaned, letting her head fall back for a moment. "Why?" she asked the ceiling, her voice strangled.

He paused, the physical torture mounting unbearably at her unaccountable resistance. He clamped his jaw tightly. Why couldn't she just melt in his arms? "Why what?"

"Why do you want to make love with me?"

Cole steeled himself against the urge to just ram home. What a question! He resumed moving his trembling thumb in a slow circle around the pearl of her desire. "Come on, baby. Let it go." She quivered and grew wet, but her eyes sought his, the question in them burning slightly brighter than her hunger for him.

He would not enter her without permission. But he was likely to cripple himself if she didn't give in soon.

"Answer," she whispered.

He pressed his thumb a little harder, patience hanging on by a thread. "Because I want to make you explode with pleasure. And if you don't let me, I'm going to explode with frustration. I need to be inside you, Rini. *Now.*"

Her eyes went limp and liquid. Shoving him aside, she lurched off the counter and stumbled away. "I can't do this anymore. I just can't."

Frustration had him crackling with anger. "What is your problem?"

"You! You're my problem!" She wrapped her arms around her middle. "You don't love me!"

He stared at her incredulously. If he'd had a less harrowing day, or his head hadn't been throbbing quite so badly, or if he hadn't been denying himself the pleasures of her body for more than a week, he might have been able to deal with her declaration more rationally. Known what to do. Taken her in his arms and soothed her with words he'd already planned to say.

As it was, he snapped, "Don't be ridiculous, Rini. I can't deal with this right now."

She sucked in a sharp breath. "That's it. I have to leave."

"Fine," he growled with an oath, and started to stalk away. "I'm taking a shower."

"I'll send for my things later."

His whole body went into red alert, his heart clutching as if grasped by a powerful fist. He spun back to her. "What the hell are you talking about?"

"Dr. Redcloud offered me a job at Rincon. I'll—"

"What!?" Anger roared through his veins.

"At the health service. You can see Chance on—"

The full impact of her statement hit him like a locomotive. His hands clenched into fists and he slammed one against a cupboard door so hard the glasses inside shook. "You're *leaving* me?" he shouted, unable to think of anything but her taking a job—and his son—that far away. "How can you do this to me?"

She was going to leave him!

Staggering under the cripplingly familiar pain of abandonment, he stalked to the opposite side of the kitchen, afraid to be within touching distance of her. "You said you loved me!"

"But you didn't!" she yelled back, and stormed out of the kitchen.

Didn't what? His mind reeling with numbing hurt, Cole stared after her, unable to wrap his brain around her nonsensical parting words.

How long had she been planning to leave him?

He grabbed the sides of his head, sure it would splinter from the pain. He leaned his forehead against the cool, solid wood of the cabinet in despair. Anguish clawed at his heart, rending it into shreds.

So much for the beginning of his new life and the new Colton Lonetree. So much for the man who was confident of his place in the world. The man who was not afraid to love.

He yanked his jeans closed, covering himself from deceitful eyes. Eyes that had gazed at him so lovingly, while all the while planning to use and discard him.

He had to get out. Go somewhere and think. Lick his wounds and decide what to do.

Katarina ran into the bedroom and slammed the door, then turned and locked it for good measure.

She flung herself onto the bed and lay staring at the ceiling, arms crossed tightly over her midriff, hot tears running down her cheeks onto the pillow. For a long time she couldn't move. The thoughts kept whirling about in her head.

How had this happened? She hadn't meant to leave him. Not like this, anyway. Certainly not today, which should have been a celebration of everything she'd worked so hard to achieve. And not in the accusatory manner in which she'd done it. He'd had such a bad day, and she'd been so unfair. She should have been calm, rational, given him a chance to respond calmly and rationally.

The situation struck home with sudden, searing pain. She'd told him she was leaving.

Oh, Lord. What would she do?

Cole steamed up the stairs to his office, craving the peace and solitude of his private sanctuary. He opened the outer door and ran right into Lindsay Walker.

"*You!*"

"Hi, Cole. Can we talk?"

"This isn't a good time, Lindsay."

"Please?" She looked up at him, and he noticed the red rims around her eyes. "I really need a shoulder."

"This *really* isn't a good time."

Her gaze dropped. "I met with Jeff."

Jetting out a breath, Cole shut his eyes for a moment. *Damn.* "All right. Let's grab a cup of coffee." Maybe listening to someone else's troubles for a few minutes would let him put himself back together.

They walked to a nearby café and chose a table for two at a window in the back. "So what happened?" he asked.

She stared into her coffee. "It was awful. He accused me of all sorts of things." Her shoulder lifted imperceptibly. "All of which were true, of course."

Cole leaned back and fingered his coffee cup. "Ouch."

Her eyes flitted to his, then around the room. "Sort of got me thinking, I guess."

He remained silent, letting her take the time she needed.

"There wasn't much I could say to defend the choices I've made in my life, but there was one thing I could do." Shakily, she lifted her cup and drank.

"And what was that?"

"I told my parents about Jeff."

He sat up straight. "Holy moly! How'd they react?"

"My father is nothing if not predictable." She sighed.

"Hell, Lindsay." Cole shook his head. He'd once hated her for what she'd done to him in their youth, and had come close again these past few months on her son's behalf, but now his heart went out to her. Nobody deserved to lose a parent's love over something like this. "I'm really sorry."

She looked up, her eyes glistening with tears. "You're a good man, Cole. The second biggest mistake I ever made was tricking you into marrying me."

His mouth twisted in a wry grimace. "What was the biggest? Jeff?"

"No. Letting you go."

His brows rose in surprise, then he relaxed in ironic laughter. Reaching out, he tapped the end of her nose. "Don't get caught in the nostalgia, darlin'. It would never have worked, and you know it."

That won a smile from her. "Yeah. I know." She put her hand over his and held it between them on the table. "You've found the love of your life, and it isn't me."

She had to remind him. "Found and lost."

"Lost? Did you have a fight?"

"She's leaving me."

"Oh, Cole." Lindsay took his face in her hands and stroked his hair away from his face. "Why?"

He braced himself against the hollow pain of Rini's betrayal. "Seems she no longer needs me. She graduated today. Got herself a new job and a new life. Without me."

Lindsay gazed at him contemplatively. "I don't believe it for a minute. You're too good a man to throw away like that. There has to be another explanation."

He snorted. "Right."

"Go to her, Cole. Tell her you love her and have no intention of letting her go. You do love her, don't you?"

"She doesn't care how I feel."

Lindsay rose from the table. "She cares. Believe me, your wife cares."

He tossed a few dollars on the table and got up, too, frowning to hear his own words quoted back at him. He searched Lindsay's face, wondering how their roles had suddenly switched. "Maybe. Will you be okay?"

She smiled and slipped into his embrace. "Yeah. I'll get through it. Dad'll come around. Both of them will."

"If you ever need anything…"

"Don't call you, right?"

He chuckled and kissed the top of her head. "Call me. I gotta go. Let me know how it goes with Jeff and your dad."

"I will." She looked up. "And Cole?"

"Yeah."

"Thanks." She kissed him lightly, her expression one of coming to terms with something she had been struggling over for a long, long time. "For everything."

He nodded, then turned and walked out.

To find Rini and find out what the hell was going on. Maybe Lindsay was right and he'd gotten it all wrong. Again.

Katarina finished her tea and rinsed out her cup. She had to admit, she felt better having forced herself to relax and observe the ritual of afternoon tea. Surely she hadn't blown it nearly as badly as she feared.

Gathering up Chance, she resolved to find Cole and talk things over. Maybe he'd convince her he really did love her, even if he couldn't say it.

Then again, maybe not.

Maybe she should take the opportunity to go away for awhile. Just to see how she really felt about him. About whether she could go on living with a man who didn't love her. Maybe it wouldn't be such a bad idea to take Dr. Redcloud up on her offer, if only for a few days or weeks.

But whatever Rini did, she needed to talk to Cole.

Figuring he was probably at his office, she drove straight there.

"Sorry, he hasn't been in today," Charlie told her.

"Any ideas?"

"Nope." He went back to his keyboard, his long braid dangling over one shoulder. She felt like yanking it. Lord, he was uncommunicative. And far too loyal to his boss.

Tamping down her aggravation, she hoisted Chance on a hip and headed for the door. Where to now?

Walking to the car, she scanned the street, looking for his truck. It was difficult to see for all the traffic, but there it was, about half a block up. She shifted Chance to the other hip and looked around again noticing the large, plate glass window of a café on the opposite corner. That seemed as good a place as any to start. She made her way across one street and waited for the light to change so she could cross the other.

It was then she saw them. Seated at a cozy window table, Cole and the woman were the only customers in the section. As the traffic light turned green and then red again, she watched in growing anguish. They talked intimately, their heads bowed together over the table.

Katarina clutched Chance to her, hurt tearing into her breast. This was not some product of misplaced jealousy. This was real. She had told Cole she was leaving, and he'd wasted no time in running straight to the comfort and sympathy of another woman. It was all Katarina could do not to flee.

With leaden legs, she forced herself to move down the line of parked cars, stopping directly across the street from the pair. They were holding hands over the table. Through tears, Katarina watched as the woman put her hands to Cole's face and tenderly caressed it. Far from objecting, he caught her hands in his fingers and held them. This must be his Obsession.

A strangled moan escaped her. She couldn't take any more. Whirling, she fled back to the corner. The only thing that kept her from plunging through traffic to the other side was Chance in her arms. Forced to wait for the light, she turned for one last look. Cole and the woman stood with their arms around each other.

When they kissed, Katarina's heart shattered completely.

"Rini, where are you?" Cole flung open the door and called out. "Honey, we need to talk!"

The sound of silence reverberated through the house like the bars clanging shut on a cell.

"Rini?"

Oh, God! She'd left!

He tore through the house, shouting her name and cursing. He slammed back the closet door and lost his breath when he saw it was nearly empty of her few belongings. Her toiletries were gone from the dresser.

Running to Chance's room, he nearly stumbled on a roll of garbage bags on the floor. No suitcases, he thought, a strange calm settling over him. He inspected the diaper table and jerked open the small chest of drawers. Bare.

He sat heavily on Rini's four-poster and buried his face in his hands. A thick, icy darkness slithered over him, wrapping itself around his heart, numbing his mind and deepest emotions.

So it was true. It had happened again.

Sitting there, feeling completely alone in the world, he just couldn't believe it. *Perfidious woman!* How could he ever have trusted her? How could he have been so stupid? The sun hadn't even set on her graduation day and she'd already abandoned him and taken away the child of his heart.

"Oh, Rini, Rini, how could you have done it?"

Katarina swiped at the rogue tear streaking down her cheek, and quickly stuck her handkerchief back into her white uniform pocket. It wouldn't do to be caught crying her first day on the job. Again.

Determinedly, she returned her attention to checking the charts Dr. Redcloud had requested for tomorrow morning's appointments. But with a will of its own, her mind wandered back to Cole and the ache in her heart. Tears threatened in earnest.

She was plagued with doubts. She missed him terribly and was miserable over what she had seen in that café. But the traitorous thought that she had surely gotten everything all wrong—just like last time—wouldn't leave her alone.

Yet even if she was wrong about the woman in the café, would it really make a difference? He still didn't love her.

"Rini, are you still here?" Gloria Redcloud stopped in front of her desk.

Rini dashed her hand surreptitiously at her damp cheek. "I just wanted to go over tomorrow morning's charts. I'm done now."

"You go on home to that little baby of yours. He's such a cutie."

Katarina smiled. "Yes, he is. I'm so lucky Mrs. Padilla is willing to watch him while I work. She's wonderful."

"I'm sure Lanie's thrilled to get the opportunity." Dr. Redcloud leaned against the edge of her desk. "How does Cole feel about that arrangement?"

"Cole?" Katarina busied herself closing up a chart and straightening the stack. She hadn't exactly told the whole truth when she'd shown up at the health service yesterday. "I, uh... He's caught up in court this week. I haven't been able to talk to him yet."

Dr. Redcloud studied her for a moment before heading for the lab. "Well, good luck," she said over her shoulder.

"Thanks," Katarina mumbled, watching her retreat. She didn't have time to ponder the odd comment, because at that moment Tanya burst through the door.

"Hey, Rin!"

"Hi, Tani." She gave her a hug. "What are you doing down here on a weeknight?"

"Had something to deliver to Mom, and I had to see for myself if the rumors were true."

"Uh-oh. Do I get a lecture or comfort?"

Tanya gave her a compassionate look. "Bit of both?"

Katarina smiled wistfully, grabbing her purse. "Comfort, please. I don't need you to tell me what a fool I am. I've already started to realize that."

"Yeah. A fool for thinking Cole doesn't love you."

Her smile faded. She shook her head as they walked to their cars. "Lust isn't the same as love."

"Tell me about it."

"And I saw him with another woman."

"Cole?" Tanya stared at her dubiously. "It wasn't what you think."

"They were kissing."

"It definitely wasn't what you think. I don't care what it looked like."

She sighed, knowing in her heart that Tanya was probably right. "How can you be so sure?"

"I know Colton Lonetree. If he wanted someone else, he'd divorce you first."

She made a deprecating noise. "Sure he would."

"He loves you, Rini."

She sighed again. "You're wrong. He doesn't love me."

"Bull."

"Then why does he refuse to say it? Why hasn't he called?"

"'Cause he's a flaming idiot."

"And what about the woman at the café?" she continued, attempting to ignore Tanya's sarcasm despite the smile she felt tugging at her lips. "You know, the one he was kissing?"

"I'm sure there's a reasonable explanation, if you'd just ask him."

She threw up her hands in exasperation because, God help her, she had reached the same conclusion.

Tanya stopped in the middle of the dusty parking area and took her arm. "Rini, if he told you he loved you, and you knew he meant it, would you go back to him?"

Katarina groaned, discouraged again. "In a hot minute. But

that's not going to happen. I gave him opening after opening, and he never took them. Even if this woman turns out to be his long-lost sister—'' she shook her head morosely ''—he doesn't love me, Tani. Without real love the attraction will eventually fade, and I'll be left with a husband who doesn't love me and no longer even desires me. He'll be unhappy, and he'll find fault with everything about me.''

''It sounds like you've had personal experience with this.''

''I have. And it would kill me to have to face the day Cole turned into another David. I've already lived through that once. I love him more than I can say, but I can't put myself through it again. I just have to accept the situation and try to move on.''

''I'm telling you, he loves you, Rini. If he isn't down here on his knees by the weekend I'll eat my hat.''

''You don't wear a hat,'' Katarina reminded her wryly. ''Wanna come with me to pick up Chance?'' she asked, putting an end to the depressing conversation.

Tanya checked her watch. ''Sorry. I promised Mom I'd bring her some applesauce before dinner. Who've you got watching him?''

''Lanie Padilla. She's been a godsend. I'm so—''

She halted. Tanya was staring at her slack-jawed, her face as pale as Katarina's own. ''What is it?'' Rini grew alarmed. ''Is there something wrong with her?''

''No! No, not at all.'' Tanya seemed to recover and turned to her car. ''Aunt Lanie's terrific. I'm just surprised she offered. Does, um, Cole know yet?''

Katarina lifted her chin. ''Everyone at Rincon must know by now. I expect he's heard through the grapevine.''

Unlocking the door, Tanya mumbled, ''I doubt it.''

Katarina got the distinct feeling there was something going on that everyone knew about except her. It made her very nervous. ''Wha—''

''Listen, Rini.'' Tanya cut her off, climbing into the car. ''Mom's waiting for that applesauce, but she wanted me to stop by and ask you and Chance to dinner. Come on over after you get him, okay? We can talk more then.''

Katarina nodded, waving to Tanya as she roared out of the lot.

"Heard you were at Rincon yesterday." Cole sank into one of the lumpy chairs in front of Tanya's desk at her office at the Southern California Native American Center.

"Yeah. Took Mom that photo of Charlie's I'd promised to frame for her." She looked at him expectantly.

Cole wasn't about to beg for information. Or demand to know if she'd seen Rini. Whether she'd asked about him...

He straightened. "Thanks for lending us the room here at the center."

Tanya lifted a brow, but didn't comment on his obvious evasion. "How'd it go?"

Jeff had called and asked if they could talk over some of the things he was going through. Cole had just come from that meeting and was feeling a bit vulnerable. The boy reminded him way too much of himself at that age.

How could Cole pretend to counsel someone else, when he still hadn't faced his own demons after all these years? He sighed. "He's a good kid, just real angry."

Tanya smirked. "Remind you of anyone you know?"

"Ha ha ha." He pinched the bridge of his nose. "Jeff and Lindsay have apparently been talking every day. He says her dad seems to be coming around a little."

"That's good. Hard to believe a father would consider disowning his own daughter over something like that nowadays."

He pursed his lips and shrugged. "Not so hard. Some parents don't give a damn. Some care too much."

"And which category do you fall into?"

He scowled. "Not funny, T."

Licking a finger, his cousin rubbed a coffee stain off her pristine desk. "Yeah, what the hell. You can always get to know Chance when he's fourteen."

He shot out of the chair. "Hey!" She was deliberately baiting him.

"Well?" she demanded, suddenly belligerent. "Just what is it going to take before you realize what a class-A fool you are?"

"I'm outta here. I don't need this from you, too." He grabbed his briefcase.

"That's right. Run away from it."

"Dammit, Tanya! I'm not the one who left! And I just spent the entire morning listening to Mom's sterling opinion of me, so don't you start, okay?" He had managed to control his temper with his mother, but he sure wasn't going to put up with any crap from his own cousin, best friend or no.

"You talk to Rini yet?"

He set his jaw, determined not to be taken in by any of Tanya's inevitable arguments—and ruthlessly throttled the flutter in his heart at the mere sound of Rini's name. "I have nothing to say to her."

Tanya snorted. "That was painfully obvious to everyone from the beginning. I'm just amazed she put up with your tight-lipped wounded warrior act for as long as she did."

He slammed the briefcase to the floor, glaring at her. "What the hell's that supposed to mean?"

She surged to her feet and drew herself up to her full height, braced her hands on the desk and leaned right into his face. "It means if just once in your wretched life you'd thought of someone else's feelings, if you'd just once opened that mouth and said 'I love you,' she'd still be with you! That's what it's supposed to mean!"

He ground his teeth. "You're on drugs, *chica*. Rini used me to get her degree, then took off. End of story."

"Well, isn't that convenient," Tanya mocked. "Spared once again from the dreadful ordeal of loving someone."

He grabbed his tie and straightened it, seeking its soothing texture. "That was a cheap shot, T. Especially coming from you."

She dropped abruptly into her chair, looking properly chastised. "Yes, well. It's not like I have anyone crying himself to sleep over me." Her statement was sharp, but the look in her eyes was sympathetic.

The wind knocked out of his sails, Cole fell back into the seat, propping his arms on his knees. "I miss Chance as much as he misses me," he said, deliberately misinterpreting her words. "I miss him like mad. And believe me, I'm going to fight—"

"I'm not talking about Chance and you know it."

He looked up, half wanting her to convince him Rini was miserable down at Rincon. "She's the one who left. If she's cryin', don't blame me."

"No, not you. Never you." Tanya sighed deeply. "Cole, all she wants is three little words. Is that so much to ask? You love her. You know you do!"

He lifted his chin. "It doesn't matter how I feel. I can't trust her. She took my son and abandoned me."

"And why do you think she did that?"

He shrugged uncomfortably, twisting his tie between his fingers. "Does she need a reason? It's what always happens."

Tanya rolled her eyes skyward. "Oh, puh-leeze. Not that old tune again. Rini wants to be loved by the man she married. Nothing less will do. Is that so hard to understand?"

He looked at his cousin, not quite believing what she was telling him. But knowing he had to find out. In the past few days he'd rediscovered what life was like without Rini. It wasn't worth living.

"You really think it's that simple?" he asked, hope stealing through him. "That she'll come back if I tell her I love her?"

Tanya smiled. "I know it is. That and an explanation of why you were kissing some woman in a café the day she left."

Cole's jaw dropped nearly to his knees. "Kissing—? You've got to be... That was Lindsay and we were just talking. Well, mostly," he added with a prick of guilt. Damn.

"Don't tell me, tell Rini."

There was a knock on the door and the receptionist stuck her head in. "Reeve Southwell to see you."

"Thanks, Lilly. Show him in." Tanya rose and looped her arm through Cole's as they turned to the door. "I want you at Rincon by the weekend, *nuyukssum*. No excuses."

"You're asking a lot of me, T."

"No more than you can handle. It's time to move on with your life. Put the past behind you and look ahead. I know you can do it."

He kissed her on the cheek. "I'll think about it, my cousin."

Chapter 17

Later that afternoon Cole was still thinking about what Tanya had said. He stretched out in his easy chair and bit into his bologna sandwich. It was the third time in a row he'd had that same pitiful dinner entrée after skipping lunch. He told himself he was too busy to make full hot meals like Rini always did, but he knew that was a crock. It was only three in the afternoon and he had nothing to do but mope. He simply had no appetite for anything she hadn't cooked.

Setting his beer on the ottoman, he picked up a small stack of stuff sitting there. One-handed, he sifted through the credit cards, receipts and checkbook Rini had left scattered on the kitchen table when she'd fled. He spent a long time contemplating each one. Staring at the name embossed on them.

Katarina Lonetree.

It sounded melodic and right. Just like a love song.

He shuffled the pile, picking up a picture he'd fished out of his desk drawer the day she'd left. The photo showed them at their wedding reception at Alex and Brad's, having been snapped just at the moment he'd suggested they take their leave.

The look on her face was enough to bring a grown man to his knees.

Insecurity, apprehension, even fear were all there in her eyes. But underlying everything was a look of pure adoration. It was obvious she thought the sun rose and set in the man she was looking at. Him—Cole Ace-Jerk Lonetree.

How could he have missed seeing that look all this time?

Was Tanya right? Had he waited and waited for a commitment from her when all it would have taken to ensure a lifetime of happiness was a commitment from himself? He closed his eyes and groaned out loud, holding the picture to his chest. *Oh, Rini, forgive me, darling. What a fool I've been.*

"Cole?"

Startled, he jerked his eyes open. "Rini?" He leaped up from the chair, scattering all but the picture he clutched in his fist. "Oh. Alex." Disappointment crushed him.

"Sorry, Cole. Just me. You didn't hear my knock."

He smiled bleakly and gave her a sincere hug. Since the day of Chance's birth, Alex had, for some reason, turned into his staunchest supporter. He wasn't quite sure what the test had been, but he was glad he'd passed. "A sight for sore eyes. What brings you to this sorry house?"

"The front door was open. I wasn't sure you'd let me in…"

"Of course I will. Want a beer?"

"No thanks. My stomach's been a bit jumpy since Rini…" Spotting the picture in his hand, her mouth curved up. She gestured to it. "Is this a good sign? Last I heard you still hadn't spoken."

He led her to the couch and perched beside her. "I want her back, Alex. I love her. Tanya has the crazy notion I'd never have lost her if I'd told her that."

Alex let out a breath and sank back into the cushions. "That about sums it up."

"Why the hell didn't you tell me this before?" He scrubbed his face with his hands. *He was whining.* He couldn't believe it.

She grinned. "None of my business. Besides, I figured you'd have plenty of time to come to your senses. Who'd ever guess

Rini would have the strength to leave as soon as she did? It took two years with David.''

''Just my luck she changed.''

Alex laid a hand on his arm. ''Yes. Your luck, and your doing. You're good for her, Cole. She blossomed with you. Now, go get her back before she takes root somewhere else.''

Suddenly, he had an awful, terrible thought. ''How does she like her new job?''

''Loves it. She can't stop talking about how great Dr. Redcloud is and—'' Alex stopped in midsentence, her mouth forming an O when she darted a glance at his crestfallen face. ''But I'm sure there are plenty of nursing jobs up here she'll like just as much.''

''Yeah. Sure.'' He stood, jamming his hands in his pockets. Maybe there was some flaw in her new routine he could use to convince her the job wasn't so great. That she'd be better off with him—just in case his declaration of love was too little, too late. ''Where's Chance while she's at work?''

Alex brightened. ''She found a wonderful woman who loves taking care of him. She lives just a couple of blocks from the health service. I sure hope I'll find someone as reliable as Mrs. Padilla when—''

He jerked to attention. ''Who?''

''Her name is Lanie Padilla. She's a treas—''

His jaw clamped and his eyes narrowed. ''She's got *that* woman watching my baby?''

She nodded uncertainly. ''Cole? What's wrong? Oh, God, is she an ax murderer or something?''

''Worse.'' *No way.* He grabbed his jacket and keys and stormed out. ''Lock the door when you leave, Alex,'' he shouted over his shoulder.

No way was that woman getting her hands on his son. Not after what she'd done to her own.

Smiling, Katarina hung back in the doorway for a moment and watched Mrs. Padilla and Chance, who were playing on a satiny quilt spread on her living room floor. The woman was remarkable. Katarina thanked God every day for sending her.

Chance spotted her standing there and squealed, kicking his plump little legs and arms in the air, a silly toothless grin smeared across his face.

"Hey there, little tiger," she cooed, stepping forward and scooping him up, squeezing him to her. "Did you miss your mommy?"

He gurgled in response.

"He hardly had time," Mrs. Padilla said, chuckling. "Between his two naps and you spending your entire lunch hour here with him."

"But Mommy misses her baby boy so much," she said in baby talk, tickling his tummy. Chance nuzzled her breast and she laughed. "I know what you missed."

"Would you like to sit down and feed him before you go? We can chat."

"Just for a few minutes, thanks, Mrs. Padilla. That would be nice."

"Please, call me Lanie. How about some tea?"

"Sounds wonderful. I've been running all day." She sank onto the sofa and stared down at her uniform, wondering what the best way to approach Chance's feeding would be.

Lanie dug a flannel receiving blanket out of the diaper bag and handed it to her. "There. In case my son comes in. The shock might kill him." She winked, her eyes sparkling, then went in to set water to boil.

Warmed by her thoughtfulness, Katarina watched Lanie move around the narrow galley kitchen, which was separated from the living room by a breakfast bar. "How old is he, your son?" she asked conversationally.

"Thirty-one."

"Oh!" Rini's eyes widened, then she burst out in giggles. "Yes, I see what you mean." She adjusted Chance at her breast. "How many kids do you have?"

Lanie halted with her hand on the whistling kettle, then jerked it away from the hot steam and dabbed at her fingers with a towel. "Two. I have two sons." She turned and stared intently at her. "What did your husband say when you told him I'd be watching the baby?"

"Why does everyone ask me that?" Katarina shifted uneasily under her scrutiny. "I'm sure he'll be as pleased as I am."

Lanie brought the tea tray in and set it on the low table in front of the sofa. She fiddled with the napkins a bit and twirled the plate of cookies on the tray so the big gooey ones were in front of Katarina. "He doesn't know, then."

Katarina picked up a cookie and nibbled on it. "It won't be a problem."

Lanie's brows lifted skeptically. "Don't count on that. My guess is when he finds out, he'll be storming through that door in record time."

Melancholy had seeped into the older woman's voice. But what possible reason could there be for...?

"You see, I'm—"

Oh, Lord. Their eyes met and Katarina realized with dawning horror that she was looking at the one woman on earth Cole would never allow within a mile of his son.

"I'm his biological mother."

Her heart sank. "Oh, Lanie! He'll kill me!"

"Me, more likely." She made an attempt at a light tone, but her voice cracked on the words.

Good Lord, Lanie Padilla was Chance's grandmother! "What are we going to do?" Katarina groaned and slumped down on the sofa. "We'll just have to reason with him, that's all."

Lanie patted her hand. "Somehow, *reason* is not a word I'd use in the same sentence with *Colton Lonetree* and *Lanie Padilla*."

"But why? I just don't understand this...this hang-up he's got about you. Lots of adopted kids are reunited with their birth parents and are thrilled about it."

"I don't know, Rini." She shook her head sadly. "I made every effort to see him when he came back to Rincon as a teenager. He would have nothing to do with me then, and he still won't. I guess my giving him away is something he just can't forgive."

They sat quietly for several minutes, the sound of Chance nursing contentedly blending with birdcalls and the rustle of leaves filtering in through the open front door.

Katarina thought about Cole not forgiving his mother. Forlornly, she finally understood why he had been so angry when he'd thought she was considering giving up their baby. And why he wouldn't ever forgive her after what she'd done to him, twice now. She had committed the one unpardonable sin—she'd abandoned him, just as his own mother had done. And she'd taken his child to boot. Colton Lonetree could never love a woman who had done these things.

She fought down a sob. Ever since she'd left him, she had been hoping and praying he would burst through the door at work or at home and sweep her into his arms. Beg her to come back, declaring he couldn't live without her.

Now she knew he would charge through the door, all right. But not to kiss her and tell her he loved her. She swallowed hard to hold back her burning tears, her heart tearing in two. She hadn't realized how desperately she wanted to go back to him.

She loved her job here, and the people were wonderful. But when she searched her soul, deep down, she knew she would never be truly happy without Cole. And now she knew her worst fears had come true. *He would never love her.* Katarina closed her watery eyes and shuddered out a sigh.

From the street outside came the screech of brakes and the loud rapport of a heavy door slamming.

And it looked like he was here to tell her so.

Cole brought the truck to a thundering halt in front of the small studio bungalow he knew belonged to Lanie Padilla. He catapulted out of the cab and stormed up the path. This was just the perfect end to a really perfect week. Yes, sir. He was mad as hell, and somebody was going to pay.

He slung open the screen door and shot through it. There sat Rini and the Padilla woman, cozy as could be, sipping tea on the couch. He searched frantically for Chance, spotting him lying on an odd, faded purple quilt at Rini's feet, sucking contentedly on a toy.

"What the hell do you think you're doing here?" he demanded, too irate to know which woman he was addressing.

Lanie Padilla set her tea mug shakily on a coffee table. "Hello, Cole," she said in a soft voice, rising to her feet.

He clenched his jaw tight, not wanting to speak to the woman at all. He'd managed to avoid it all these years, and it galled him to have to exchange words with her now. He turned to Rini. "How could you have done this behind my back?" he snapped through gritted teeth.

On the floor, Chance jerked, startled, and gazed wide-eyed at Cole, then burst into tears. *Just great.* Everyone was thrilled to see him.

He clamped an iron grip on his temper and reached down to snatch Chance up before Rini could get to him. "There, there, little one. Daddy didn't mean to scare you." He kissed his cheek and pulled him to his chest to comfort him.

Rini was watching him with shiny, doleful eyes. His heart melted, and for a split second he thought he might break down and draw her up into their embrace.

But he needed to know what was going on. "This arrangement is not acceptable, Rini. You should have asked before you hired this woman to watch my son."

Lanie Padilla looked at him levelly. "She didn't know who I was when she hired me. I just told her a few minutes ago."

He sneered. "Because you knew I'd be coming to put an end to it." He pinned his gaze on Rini, who looked about like Chance had—just before he'd erupted in tears. "You're coming with me. Get your stuff." He swung to the other woman. "You're fired. And don't ever talk to my wife or son again."

Rini's eyes darted up in surprise at the possessiveness in his tone, but then filled with a determination he'd never seen before. "Oh, no you don't, Colton Lonetree. You can't stomp in here like a caveman, shouting and giving orders. I won't have it!"

He stared at her, shocked speechless by the force of her statement and the flash of fire in her eyes. It was the first time she'd ever stood up to him on anything—the first time she'd ever even raised her voice that he could remember. He nearly grinned.

"She's your mother, Cole. Talk to her!"

That brought him back to reality with a bang, and he scowled.

"She may have given birth to me," he hissed, "but she is *not* my mother. Let's go."

"No." Rini crossed her arms over her chest and sat back resolutely. "If you're so sure you were the victim back then, you've got nothing to lose from hearing her side of the story." She narrowed her eyes in challenge.

He met her glare with one of his own. "Seems to me I'm holding all the cards," he said, glancing down at Chance, who had stuck the end of Cole's tie into his mouth. "I could just walk out the door and leave you here."

"And get charged with kidnapping," she retorted, the sparks practically shooting out of her eyes.

Her newfound self-assurance looked good on her. He felt absurdly aroused. Jeezus. Hell of a time to think about—

Abruptly he paced to the window and gazed out over the green valley, bouncing Chance on his arm. The majestic purple mountains rose in the background like a Hollywood set. They looked unreal. Sort of like this situation.

He loved Rini and wanted her back. If he left now, he could kiss that little scenario goodbye. But if he stayed, what would he be forced to endure?

Holding his face impassive as granite, he turned and leaned against the windowsill. "All right. I'm listening."

The woman who would be his mother clutched her hands together in front of her and suddenly looked scared to death. She hadn't moved an inch since rising, but now she stepped nervously away from the couch. Rini's eyes followed her every move, radiating support and encouragement. Cole didn't like that one bit.

When the woman spoke, he had to strain to hear her. "I'm not sure how much others have told you—"

"Nothing," he said loudly. "I made it clear I wasn't interested."

Rini frowned at him. He frowned back.

"I see," his birth mother said quietly. "Oh, Rini," she said in a rush, "I appreciate your trying to do this, but it won't work. Why don't you just go with him? I'll be okay." She hurried toward the back bedrooms.

Damn! He couldn't let her get away. Without quite realizing what he was doing, Cole strode over and caught hold of her. Her skittish gaze halted on his hand grasping her arm, then she peered uncertainly up at him.

He had to endure this. *For Rini.* He took a deep, cleansing breath, and hoped like hell he wasn't going to regret it. He let go of her arm. "No. Rini's right. This is way overdue. Tell me. Please. I want to know."

She looked into his eyes and must have seen the attempt he was making, and possibly what it cost him to do so. Swallowing, she moved away, walking a circuit around the room, touching a doily here, a pillow there, a picture frame on the mantel.

"I didn't give you up willingly, Cole. I want you to know that. If I'd had any kind of choice, I would never have let you go."

He'd probably known that all along, deep down. But hearing it from her like this, now, punched a hole in both his gut and his tenacious bitterness. With a sinking feeling, he nodded.

"I was fifteen when I got pregnant. Young and careless."

Where had he heard that before?

"Your father was from Pechanga Rez, right up the road. Joseph Perada was his name."

Cole's world suddenly tilted on its axis, his stomach doing a free fall. Dizzily, he watched Lanie clutch the edge of the mantel, her knuckles going white. He clung to Chance for dear life.

Her voice trembled. "I've never told anyone that before." She drew herself up and rubbed her arms. "He died in an accident shortly after. Who knows what might have happened if…"

Cole's head spun. His father was dead. *Joseph Perada. Your father.* His father was dead. *That's why he never came for you.* "A-accident?" he managed to stammer.

Lanie grasped the end of the thick braid flowing over her shoulder and twirled it around her finger. "He and some buddies were at a party. Drank too much. The usual story." Around and around.

"Did you…love him?" Somehow he already knew the answer, and his heart lodged thickly in his throat.

"We were young, but what we had was special." Her dark eyes—so much like his own, he reflected absently—softened. "Yeah, I loved him."

She cleared the rasp from her voice. "His folks didn't approve of me, of course, but we met whenever we could. His brother had an old Chevy he'd borrow to come down to see me, when he was supposed to be going to the library."

"Why didn't his family approve?" Rini interjected from the couch.

Cole switched Chance to the other arm and went to sit next to her. He'd heard stories about Lanie's parents. At the time, they had just helped confirm his low opinion of her.

"My mom was a drunk. Dad couldn't hold a job and was always in trouble for gambling. The social workers came around constantly, threatening to take me away—and did a few times—even though I had aunts and uncles willing to let me live with them." Her expression fell in defeat. "In the end, they took you instead."

He gritted his teeth, torn between anguish and anger. Through his work at the center, he knew the story was more than plausible.

"That's awful," Rini murmured. "How can they just take a woman's baby like that? It's inhuman."

Cole sighed, scrubbing his face with his hands. "Happens to us all the time. The Indian Child Welfare Act was enacted to make it possible for tribal councils to find foster or adoptive parents within the child's own tribe. But all too often, it was ignored."

"There was no ICWA passed when they took you." Lanie shook her head. "I'd tried my best. I quit school and went to work as a house cleaner. It was against the rules, but I took you with me to the houses where no one was home. I couldn't rely on Mom to be sober enough to remember to feed you."

He looked up in surprise. "But I thought… How old was I when…?"

"Nine months. One of the rich lawyers I cleaned house for came home unexpectedly while I was there with you. He felt it was his duty to report it. I lost my job, and Social Services stepped in.''

Cole's chest tightened as he watched his mother struggle to continue speaking.

''They didn't care that I had aunts and cousins who would help me out. They were determined to put you in foster care.'' She swallowed several times. ''I'd seen firsthand what happened to kids who went through that system, and I couldn't bear for it to happen to you. Someone suggested I call a private adoption agency to help me find a decent home where you could grow up with a real family. It seemed like the only way to keep you safe.''

Her hands came up to cover her face. A single sob escaped, then she wiped her cheeks with her palms. ''I'll never forget the day they came to take you away.

''Dad had gone to some dog race somewhere. Mom was drunk as usual. The social worker turned up her nose and wouldn't even come in the house. I cried and begged and pleaded to keep you. Nothing helped.''

Cole glanced over and saw a tear trickle down Rini's face. She reached out and took Chance from him, then rocked him back and forth, her cheek to his head, leaving a pool of wetness on his soft, black hair.

Cole didn't feel all that in control himself.

He grabbed for his tie and rose to pace to the window. ''Nine months. I can't believe they never told me I was that old. No wonder I felt abandoned.'' He turned, desperately fighting the vicious, bitter demon that threatened to eat his insides.

''You had an old silk quilt I'd picked up at the Goodwill and cut down for you. Purple silk. Must have had some history.'' She chuckled through her tears, walking slowly to the quilt on the floor. ''But you refused to sleep without it. Cried like a pup when it was in the wash.''

Her smile faded as she picked up the worn purple quilt and clasped it to her breast. ''They wouldn't take it. Said it was inappropriate for a child.''

He looked down, realizing he was still clutching his tie in his fist, frantically smoothing the fabric with his thumb. When she approached him with the outlandish little quilt and offered it to him, he lost it.

Grabbing the quilt in one arm and her in the other, he crushed them both to him, not bothering to stem the tears that leaked from behind his tightly squeezed lids. "Oh, Mother," he choked out, "I'm so sorry."

She sobbed in his embrace, her arms wound around his waist. For a long time they stood swaying back and forth, comforting each other in their misery and elation.

When he was able, his eyes sought Rini. She smiled at him, her red-rimmed eyes shining with joy. He extended a hand toward her in invitation. Wiping her flushed cheeks free of moisture, she got up with Chance, and all four of them joined in a big hug.

"Oh, C-Cole," she stammered.

Lanie pulled away slightly, her watery smile radiating the peace of having a great burden lifted. "Does this mean I'm not fired?" she asked with a hiccup.

"I guess it does." They laughed and hugged again, and Cole savored the moment as he had seldom before in his lifetime. His happiness was complete as he basked in the embrace of his beloved family. He kissed each one in turn, starting with his mother, then Chance, and ending with Rini.

His mouth sought the warmth of hers, lingering over its moist, soothing heat. Her lips responded lovingly, surprising him with their intimate caress.

Rini suddenly disentangled herself and put her fingers to her lips. "This is so wonderful. I'm so happy," she murmured.

But she didn't look happy. In fact, the expression on her face was miserable, a portrait of longing and sadness. Cole was instantly alarmed.

She took a step back, gnawing on her lip. "I, um…" She backed up another step. "I…"

His heart went into double-time. His mother looked almost as worried as he felt. "What is it?" *Oh, God.* "Rini, my heart can't take too much more excitement today, so if this is bad news, can it wait about a hundred years?"

She smiled bleakly. "No, I just…I'm sure you two have a lot

to talk about, and I, uh, promised Tanya…'' She took another step backward. ''So, I'll just be going….''

Like hell. He'd just gotten his mother back, and he realized with blinding certainty he wanted his wife back, too, even if it meant getting down on his knees and begging. She was the one woman who made his world complete and perfect, the one who made his life worth living. Without her, nothing else mattered.

In a single step he closed the distance she had created between them. ''Over my dead body.''

She had a death grip on the baby, so he took Chance from her and handed him to his mother, along with the quilt he still held.

Rini looked at him uncertainly. ''Cole—''

''You're not going anywhere.''

She blinked and tears glistened on her lashes. She looked so lost his heart ached. ''I'm not?''

''No.'' He took her hand, so small and delicate, but strong enough to work miracles, and cradled it between his. He took a deep breath. ''I want you back.''

Her mouth opened in disbelief.

He knit his brows together, feeling more vulnerable than he'd ever felt in his life. ''I knew before. But now, today, with my mother, the way you forced me to listen to her, to see how stupid and stubborn I was being, well, it just made me all the more certain.''

Rini stared at him, her eyes filling with hope and wonder. ''What are you saying?''

''Please, Rini, come back to me.'' He pulled her into his arms. ''Oh, Fire Eyes, I love you. You and Chance are my life. I love you so very much. I was a prize moron for not telling you every single day, but I'll make up for it for the rest of my life if you'll let me.''

If he had to, he'd plead and implore her to return. Tell her over and over how much he loved her. Beg her forgiveness for being such an unbelievable fool.

He kissed her eyes, her damp cheeks, her parted, trembling lips. ''I love you more than life itself. Marry me all over again, Rini, *really* marry me. Rini? Say something, please.''

She burst out in tears, but this time he could see they were tears of joy. "Oh, Cole! Do you mean it? Do you really mean it?"

"With all my heart."

She threw her arms around his neck. "I love you, Colton Lonetree. So very much. And yes, I'll marry you again."

Relief pouring through him, he grinned happily. "This time we'll do it right. With a dress and bridesmaids, the works. Would you like that?"

"Yes. Oh, yes, yes, yes!"

"And I want a dozen more children."

Her eyes popped open as wide as her happy smile. "A dozen?"

"Okay, two," he said, laughing and swinging her around.

"Deal." She kissed him, long and lovingly.

"Hey, Mom!" Cole heard his half brother's voice call out as the screen door was flung open behind him. "What's for— Cole!"

Turning, he grinned at Billy's obvious stupefaction at seeing him in his mother's house, smiling. "Hey, bro! Come in and join the celebration."

"But—but…"

"Relax, Billy. Lanie and I were just…" He glanced inquiringly at his mother, who stood happily next to his brother, beaming like a summer day, Chance snuggled in her arms. "Can I call you Lanie? Mom's sort of taken, and…"

She smiled broadly. "Lanie's just fine." She turned to Billy and said, "Cole and Rini are going to be married. Isn't that wonderful?"

Billy shook himself out of his shock and clapped Cole on the shoulder, a loopy smile on his face. "You bet! Wonderful! But I thought they were already… Oh, never mind. This is great! Cole, I…aw, heck." Billy threw an arm around his neck and gave him an embarrassed but heartfelt hug. "Welcome back, bro. We've missed you. All of us."

Cole squeezed him back and parried the mock punches his brother threw at him in an attempt to keep his face from crumbling. "Hell of a way of showing it, Bill," he laughed, grabbing him for another hug.

There were more embraces all around, and Billy finally flung himself onto the couch, pleased as a sultan surveying his domain. "This is great. First I get a son, and now a whole family! With a mom and kids and grandkids and everything. This is great!"

Billy's words jolted through Cole. It was true. This was exactly what he'd been looking for all along, too. Somewhere to belong. *Really belong.* Down to the roots of his ancestors.

He grabbed Rini by the arms. "I can't take you back to Pasadena with me."

She opened her mouth in bewilderment. "But—"

"I know how much you love your new job. I can't ask you to leave it."

"But I don't—"

"And I'd really like to cut down on my lawyering a bit. I've got a bank account full of money saved, and my portfolio should keep us going for a while. I'd like to teach dancing again, work more on crafting regalia. Stay home with Chance, like I was doing before."

"What are you saying?"

"Here, Rini. I want to live here, at Rincon. Is your house big enough for all of us?"

"I don't—"

"It doesn't matter, we can get another one. A giant house, with lots of room. For those two dozen kids you promised me."

Rini slapped a hand over her mouth and gasped, choking on laughter. "Two *dozen?*"

"What do you say?"

"To the two dozen kids or the house?"

"Making our home here."

She smiled, her pretty fire eyes radiating so much love he thought his knees might buckle. "You mean it's my choice?"

"Yep."

"Then I choose to be with you, Cole. Wherever you are, for the rest of my life, I choose to be there, too."

Epilogue

"**Y**ou've got to be kidding."

Hiking her heavy silk wedding gown up off the dirt path, Katarina burst out in a gale of laughter at the accommodations Cole was pointing to.

He looked offended. If he could possibly look anything but wildly sexy in his black tuxedo and starched pleated shirt. "I'm perfectly serious. If it was good enough for my ancestors, it's good enough for me. And you, too, woman."

She fought a losing battle to look stern. "I know for a fact Luiseños didn't use tepees, Cole. You told me so yourself."

When he'd suggested moving back to the rez, this wasn't quite what Katarina'd had in mind. Still, she couldn't help but giggle at the miffed expression on his face.

"Lodges. Besides, it's just for one night."

"Our *wedding* night," she reminded him with an exaggerated pout that threatened to dissolve into mirth.

"Well, what was I supposed to do? Throw your mother and Frazer out on their noses?"

She chuckled. "You could have made them sleep in the tepee—"

"Lodge."

"All right, *lodge,* and they'd have thanked you for the intense cultural experience. I've never seen anyone charm my mother quite as quickly and thoroughly as you managed to do. It was an amazing thing to behold."

He flashed her the old pirate smile, wiggling his eyebrows. "Darlin', you think that was amazing, just wait."

He reached for her and she demurred, ducking away quickly.

He put his hands on his hips and watched her retreat with a feral gaze. "And what about Alex? You'd make your pregnant sister sleep in some sleazy motel?"

She stopped in her tracks, aghast at what he was suggesting. "Of course not!" A smile spread over her whole being when she thought about Brad's announcement at the reception that evening. Alex was finally carrying the baby she so longed for, and she'd made it through the first trimester. It was all too perfect.

Including their primitive honeymoon suite. It brought back wonderful memories of a certain day in May... But of course, she wasn't going to let Cole know that. Just yet.

"That would be beastly. A pregnant woman!"

"All right then. Stop complaining and come here."

He looked at her hungrily. It was that same look he'd been giving her since she'd walked down the grass aisle in Tanya's backyard earlier, on the arm of his best man, Renegade Santangelo. Like he would eat her up in a single bite if she let him come too close.

He came closer.

She scampered away. She wanted him tied up in knots by the time they reached his lodge. Judging by the sizzling looks he was sending her, it appeared to be working.

She flashed him her most flirtatious smile. "Renegade looked particularly handsome today."

Cole grunted, stalking her steadily.

She sighed provokingly. "Black leather pants and frilly shirt. Very sexy. And that hair..."

"RaeAnne seemed to like it."

"They make a nice couple. Speaking of nice couples, who was that hunk Tanya was with? Someone new?"

"*That's it.* I won't have my wife talking about every other man at—"

"Why, Cole! Are you jealous?"

"Damn straight!"

Sucking on a fingertip, she tilted her head coquettishly. "Good. I wouldn't have wanted this expensive *silk* gown to go to waste."

"Come here, before I have to come get you."

Lifting her skirts scandalously high in the air, she fled.

He groaned. "I suppose the stockings are silk, too," he called after her, agony in his voice.

Pausing in her flight, she rounded a tree and peered at him coyly. "Why, yes, as a matter of fact." *Among a few other interesting bits and pieces he'd soon discover.*

The late summer sun had set awhile ago, leaving a magical twilight dimness in its wake. The stars overhead were just peeking out of the murky blanket of sky, the sliver of moon a pearly luminescence above the trees.

Breathing in a lungful of sultry, spice-scented air, she continued to stroll in the direction of the beautifully painted lodge in which they would spend their first night together after renewing their vows and affirming their love.

Cole sauntered toward her, obviously attempting to look casual in his pursuit.

She stooped to pick a wildflower, letting him come within a few yards before waltzing off. "Billy and Jeff were having a good time at the reception," she said.

"Yeah. They get along well. They've been really good for each other."

"He makes a terrific father," she said thoughtfully, temporarily forgetting about eluding Cole. "And your mother is in heaven."

"Don't I know it." He stuck his hands in his pockets and inched toward her. "Both mothers. They're turning out to be quite the buddies. Conspiring over who to fix Billy up with." He smirked. "What a pair."

She giggled. "Well, I think it's cute."

"You would."

He lunged and she squealed in delighted terror when he almost caught her. With a rustle of silk petticoats, she scurried off, skipping and sliding over the uneven ground in her formerly white slippers.

"You're going to pay for this, woman," he growled, a menacing expression on his face.

Her blood stirred heavily at the thought of what the price would be. "Why, for what, darling?" She turned and gave him a guileless look.

His eyes raked over her thoughtfully, systematically, artfully. Thoroughly. A frisson of anticipation shivered down her body. *Oh, yes.* She was getting nervous now. She took a step backward.

"You'll pay for making me chase you." He followed. "And for that gorgeous silk gown. And for each and every one of those lacy silk petticoats. But you'll especially pay for the stockings."

Another step back. "Oh, dear. I suppose I'll be wickedly punished for the rest, too." She peeked up from under fanned lashes.

He looked momentarily stricken. "The rest?"

She nodded solemnly. "You know. The *rest.*"

He pulled his chin up, unsticking his collar from his neck. His gaze fastened on the décolletage peeking tantalizingly through her gown's sheer upper bodice. "Like, for instance?"

"Oh, well, like, um, the other—" she gestured up and down her torso "—lacy, frilly, silky things. Underneath."

His lids drooped to half-mast and he actually licked his lips. He was hot. She could practically see the smoke rising from his broad, muscular shoulders. Pure electricity shot through her body, starting at the tips of her breasts and streaking directly to the junction of her thighs.

"Oh, yeah. You'll definitely pay for those." He took another step forward.

She was more than tempted to let him punish her right there and then.

"You bring your war paint, warrior?" she asked, a seductive curve to her lips.

He grinned lasciviously, pulling a small tube from his tux pocket. "Right here, wife. And I want you to put it on me."

She whirled on a toe and took off. His arm snaked out, his fingers grazing her wrist. She shrieked and ran for her life.

He was after her like a shot, his footfalls pounding in the dust right behind her. Five steps and he hauled her in. She screamed in excitement, thrilling to the feel of his strong hands capturing her.

Throwing his head back, he roared victoriously, lifting her, sweeping her into his strong arms. There was silk everywhere, petticoats flying, her gown floating and billowing on the breeze as he strode down the path with her flailing and wiggling and laughing.

He kicked the door flaps open and whisked her into his lodge. Wide-eyed, Katarina gasped at the sight that met her misty gaze, the laughter dying on her lips.

A huge mattress lay in the middle of the floor, draped luxuriously in white satin linens and pillows. Scattered everywhere were handfuls of sweet smelling gardenia petals. Soft music wafted from somewhere on the other side of the tepee. A low table held a feast of succulent delights—grapes, strawberries, aromatic cheeses, caviar and a magnum of Kristal champagne. Finally, her awe-filled gaze halted on the biggest flask of her favorite aromatic oil she'd ever seen.

"Oh, Cole." She sighed his name, turning in his arms, touching his cheek with her fingers. She wound her arms around his neck and gazed adoringly into the eyes of her husband, her soul filled to bursting for this man who had given her so much. His name, a home, her son. His heart.

The planes and angles of his handsome face softened in the murky light. His lips met hers in a tender promise of a kiss, and he whispered, "You've made me whole, Fire Eyes. Will you stay with me for a lifetime?"

She melted into his embrace. "I'll never leave you, my love, not for a million lifetimes and more."

"I love you," they whispered as one. "Forever and ever."

* * * * *